TWO LOST BOYS

L.F. ROBERTSON

TITAN BOOKS

Two Lost Boys
Print edition ISBN: 9781785652783
E-book edition ISBN: 9781785652813

Published by Titan Books
A division of Titan Publishing Group Ltd
144 Southwark Street, London SE1 0UP

First edition: May 2017
1 2 3 4 5 6 7 8 9 10

A CIP catalogue record for this title is available from the British Library.

Printed and bound in Great Britain by the CPI Group (UK) Ltd, Croydon CR0 4YY

/mm

TWO
LOST
BOYS

Also available from L.F. Robertson and Titan Books

Madman Walking (May 2018)

To Richard, who made my quixotic career possible,

and Michael, who helped me write about it.

1

California's death penalty long ago entered the realm of the surreal. The courts keep handing down death sentences at the rate of twenty-five or so a year, but almost no one gets executed. For the most part, condemned men live out their lives on death row, represented by a small army of underpaid but persistent lawyers, while their appeals make some sort of halting progress through the court system.

I have been a foot soldier in that army for more years than I care to count. A dozen or so of the men on the Row had been clients of mine at one time or another. We have moved from youth to middle age together, and I have watched as their children grew up, their parents died, and they themselves grew ill with the diseases that afflict old men. Now, against my better judgment, I was about to add one more client to my tally.

2

San Quentin State Prison sits on a spit of land overlooking San Francisco Bay, at the end of a potholed road lined with million-dollar fishermen's shacks. In Marin County, real estate with a water view costs a fortune, even at the gates of a prison.

I reached the visitors' parking lot with a couple minutes left to rummage in my wallet for dollar bills for the vending machines. Armed with the few items the prison allows visitors to bring—dollar bills and change, a couple of pens, a legal pad, my driver's license and bar card—I climbed the steep driveway to the long wooden building, something between a shed and a breezeway, where visitors wait to be checked in.

My new client was a man named, of all things, Andy Hardy. Andy was a nickname, an improvement, I suppose, on his real first name, Marion. Andy and his brother Emory had been convicted, about fifteen years ago, after kidnapping three prostitutes at different times over the course of a year or so. They had killed two, and the last one had escaped after two days of terror. Emory was serving life in prison without possibility of parole. Andy had gotten the death penalty. His conviction had been upheld on appeal, and he was beginning his next round of litigation, petitions for habeas corpus in the state Supreme Court and the federal district court.

Hardy's newly appointed post-conviction lawyer, Jim Christie, had called—directed to me by an old colleague who probably didn't know I'd sworn off death-penalty work—at a moment when I was feeling disenchanted with what I was doing instead. I'd just wasted a half-hour of my precious remaining years reading a Court of Appeal opinion affirming yet another conviction in a case I should have won—would have won, if my client had been a businessman getting sued, instead of a criminal serving life in prison for stealing a bottle of cheap brandy. I was feeling mired in futility and irritated with hack judges and assembly-line law. And I'd gotten a little bored with the lack of stress in my life. I was like a schizophrenic who goes off his meds out of disgust with the dullness of sanity. Listening to Jim tell me about the case, in his personable courtroom-lawyer baritone, I thought about working again where the stakes were high and felt a familiar little prickling of adrenalin. That in itself should have warned me. I asked Jim a few basic questions about time constraints, money arrangements, and whether the client was easy to get along with, and said yes before the end of the call.

Now, after a restless night and a three-hour drive to San Quentin, it didn't seem like such a great idea.

This was one of the visiting days reserved for attorneys and investigators. Jim, who would be flying from Los Angeles and driving from the airport, had made our appointment with Mr. Hardy at eleven o'clock; I had decided to come earlier so that I could visit another inmate, a former client. The door to the room where visitors are—in the argot of the Department of Corrections—"processed" was inside the shed. No one else was waiting, and I rang the bell. A buzzer sounded, and a second later I heard the door lock release. I pushed it open and edged inside.

There is a different guard at the desk every time I go there. This one, a chunky man with a round pinkish face, short steel-gray hair and silver-rimmed glasses, looked me over indifferently, checking for violations of the endlessly changing rules for what visitors can wear and bring with them. The list of what a lawyer can bring into the prison is short—legal papers, notebook, pens, some money for the vending machines—and I had left my purse and cellphone in my car. I gave him my ID, took off my jacket, glasses, watch and shoes, and walked through the metal detector, while my belongings went through the X-ray machine beside me. Nothing set off any alarms, and the guard stamped my wrist with a smudge of fluorescent ink, returned my ID and a visiting form, and waved me through, saying, "Have a good one."

"You too," I answered, with a sense that we had contracted some sort of truce.

On the long walk to the visiting building, I could see more of the bay, sparkling blue with a few whitecaps, the hills of Marin, dark green after the winter rains, beyond it. At a second open gate I turned left, past the high arched entrance of the old prison and down a service road.

The old prison is a nineteenth-century fantasy of a castle, like something conceived by N.C. Wyeth or Arthur Rackham. The entrance to the main building is a portcullis of stucco shaped and painted to look like sandstone blocks and gated with heavy iron bars. Beside it, a red-brick building resembling a Victorian factory holds two visiting rooms; one for mainline inmates and the other for death row.

I waited on the porch of the visiting building, peering through yet another iron gate, painted gray, with a thick sheet of scratched Plexiglas bolted to its face. Eventually the door slid open with a painful scraping and clanging, and I sidled into a small foyer with another barred gate at its far end. I gave my ID and visitor pass to a guard waiting behind a barred glass screen with a slot at the bottom for passing papers. He glanced at them and pushed a button on a board in front of him. The outer gate closed, and the inner gate screeched and clanged open.

The visiting area was a long, narrow room with a gray vinyl floor, institutional pale beige walls, a couple of vending machines, and two rows of cages to my right. The bars of the cages were coated in chipped white paint and, like the outer gate, sheathed with walls of scratched-up Plexiglas, in a less-than-successful attempt at preventing conversations inside the cages from being overheard. It was a typical prison fix, jerry-built and done on the cheap, and about the best that could be said for it was that you had to keep quiet and listen a bit to hear what your neighbors were saying.

On the opposite wall, straight ahead of me, was a gray metal door. As I watched, the door opened, and with a clamor of voices and clanking keys, two guards emerged with a slightly bewildered-looking prisoner between them. After a brief exchange with another guard, they headed, awkwardly but purposefully, to the aisle between the two rows of cages.

I walked down the aisle after the procession, looking for an old client of mine who I'd arranged to meet, Henry Fontaine. Henry was sitting in one of the cages, and a Latino guard, chunky in a bulletproof vest, his green uniform clanking with chains and keys, was chatting with him through the Plexiglas. So much for the soundproofing. I nodded to the guard, and Henry, catching my eye, called out, "Hey, Miss Janet."

"You want anything from the machines?" I asked.

"Sweet roll and a Dr. Pepper would be just fine."

Henry was a former client, but he still wrote me now and again, and I sent him stamps and occasionally put a little money on his books and visited him about once a year to see how he was doing. He was fifty years old when, at the end of a bender, he had stabbed his landlady to death in an argument over his overdue rent. When the police checked out the crime scene, they found her open wallet lying outside her purse on the floor. This was enough for the district attorney to up the charge from second-degree murder to robbery-murder and seek the death penalty—why, I don't know, since they have enough real capital crimes down in Riverside to keep them busy. Nevertheless, one thing led to another—Henry was black, he was on parole, he'd been in prison most of his adult life and he didn't have many family members who still knew him well enough to say much of anything good about him—so he ended up on the Row.

It took five years to find him a lawyer for his appeal, and that turned out to be the state defender's office I worked for at the time. It was another eight before his appeal was decided. Now, almost nineteen years down the line, he had yet another lawyer and his case was working its way through the federal courts. No one, including Henry, was inclined to hurry it along. Henry had a bathroom-sized cell on death row's equivalent of the honor block, some buddies to play checkers with, and enough money from me and his federal lawyer for little things like toothpaste and candy bars.

I spent five minutes or so coaxing dollar bills and coins into the vending machines and walked back to the cages with a tray—soda and sweet roll for Henry and a Diet Coke for me. The guard let me into the cage, and Henry and I waited in silence as he locked the gate. Henry backed over to the door, and the guard opened a metal slot in the door, unlocked Henry's handcuffs, and took them away.

"I always feel guilty getting this stuff for you," I said after he left, putting the cinnamon roll in its plastic package down on the table.

"No need. I ain't worried; when the Lord decides it's time for me to go, I go." He opened the soda can and took a long drink from it. "Cold soda, that's so nice. Stuff we get from canteen is room temperature. So, how you been? Working hard?"

"Just the usual. How've you been?"

"Just gettin' grayer and grayer. Doctor put me on some new heart medicine, but the nurse ain't giving it to me."

"Damn, not again!" I said. I promised to help his lawyer try to straighten it out, and we spent the rest of our hour and a half chatting about Henry's ailments, his sister's latest letter, and the joy he found in the Lord. When the guard came to take him back to his cell, Henry blessed me and said, "Come see me again soon. Maybe next time you can get me one of them ice-cream sandwiches from the machines."

"It's a deal," I said.

A wise criminal defense attorney once warned me, "Never seek validation from your clients." It's good advice, because how your clients feel about you has very little to do with how well you represent them. I once won a case on appeal for a man who tried to fire me because I didn't answer his letters as soon as he liked. It was a complete win—suppression of the drugs he was charged with possessing, and he walked out of prison a free man; I never heard a word from him after I mailed him the Court of Appeal opinion. Henry, on the other hand, liked me even though I hadn't accomplished a damned thing for him, unless you count an unsuccessful appeal to the California Supreme Court as putting a few bumps on the track of the death train.

While I waited for the guards to fetch Andy Hardy, I made a trip to the restroom down the hall. As I was walking back toward the cages, a tall, light-haired man in a suit caught my eye and flagged me down. "Are you Janet Moodie?"

"Yep," I said. "You're Jim, then?"

"I am. Nice to meet you." He stuck out a hand, and I managed to extricate mine from my notebook and coin purse for a handshake.

There were things I wanted to ask Jim about the case, but we were surrounded by guards moving prisoners in and out of the cages. So we made small talk, or tried to. He said something about baseball, and I said something apologetic about not really following it. Then the metal door to the back opened with a chinking of metal chains, and a sandy-haired man in blue denim limped out, flanked by two guards.

"Here's our man," Jim said. "Hey, Andy!"

Andy looked over and flashed a weak smile. "Mr. Christie? Hey, could you get me a coupla cokes and a cheeseburger?"

"Sure."

"Let me take care of that," I said. When I came back, my tray laden with a burger hot from the microwave, chips, drinks, ketchup packets and a fistful of the brown paper towels the prison puts out for napkins, the guard was waiting by the cubicle, and Jim and Hardy were already in conversation over some papers.

As the guard let me into the cell, locked it again, and left, Jim introduced me to Andy. Andy looked pleased, in a muted way. I knew he was around forty, but he looked younger. He was pale and clean-shaven, with a long, nondescript face and close-set pale blue eyes. His hair was combed straight back from his forehead. In his loose chambray shirt and prison jeans, he looked rangy, but it was hard to tell. He reached out to shake my hand, and I noticed he had no tattoos on his forearms.

"I've just started reading about your case," I said. "And I'm curious how you got your nickname."

"It was my mama's idea. The kids at school kept saying Marion was a girl's name. So she said I should say my name was Andy. She said it came from some old movie."

"So naming you Marion wasn't her idea?"

"Nah. It was my dad's. It was his grandfather's name. He was some kind of train robber; I guess they hung 'im back in Idaho. But my dad was real proud of 'im, named me after him. Then he used to say he should have given my name to Emory, 'cause Emory had more of the old man in him."

"How did you and your dad get along?" I asked.

"Not so good. But we didn't see too much of him. He was in prison up in Walla Walla for a long time, and then he left town."

"What's he do now?"

"Don't know."

"Do you ever hear from him?"

Andy looked at me and shifted a little in his chair. "Nope. Never have since he left."

"Oh," I said, "I'm sorry. That must have been hard on you and your mother."

"Not really. I didn't like him. And Mama—she said she never cried over no man—'specially not him."

Jim looked at the plastic-wrapped burger on the table. "Better eat your sandwich before it gets cold."

"Oh, yeah." Andy pulled open the wrapper, peeled back the top half of the bun and smeared ketchup from a plastic packet onto the half-melted cheese and wilted onion that topped the burger patty.

As he ate, Andy complained amiably about the congealed oatmeal and tough pancakes, the gristly stews and watery mashed potatoes that made up his diet between visits. When he had finished, he wiped his mouth with a paper towel and wrapped up the remains of his lunch with surprising tidiness, then tossed them into the scuffed plastic wastebasket next to the table. "Thank you," he said, leaning back for a moment and patting his stomach a couple of times as if for emphasis. He sat up again, took a drink from his can of soda and looked at Jim and me. "Don't you want to talk about my case?"

"Well, I do have some questions I'd like to ask," I said, "to help me get started on it."

"Okay." He folded his hands on the table in front of him and waited for the questioning to begin. There was something in the gesture and in the directness with which he answered that reminded me suddenly of my son at about five years old.

I turned to a clean page on my legal pad. "Let's see. The files say you were born in Washington and lived there until—what, about junior high?"

"No, high school," Andy said. "We moved down here after my dad left."

"Where did you live?"

"Lots of places. We moved around a lot till my dad went to prison. Then we lived in Leesville for a long time—till after my dad got out."

"Do you remember any of the schools you went to?"

Andy thought for a moment, squinting with the effort of remembering. "I remember a couple," he said. "McKinley was one. Gardner. Redbud—that was middle school—after we moved to California I was at Shasta City High. I went to some other schools, too, 'cause we were always moving. I don't remember all their names. Mama knows all that stuff."

"How did you like school?" I asked.

"Mostly not much."

"Why?"

"Oh, I never did too good. Never that interested in it."

"Ever get in trouble?"

"Little stuff—cutting classes, acting up. Got in a fight once during recess."

"What happened?"

"Couple kids jumped me. Teacher sent us all to the principal's office. They tried to suspend me, but Mama went and told them off, and they took me back."

"Anything else?"

"Nah, that's about it."

"Did you have any friends?"

He looked up. "Yeah, a couple."

"What were their names?"

"There was a kid named Eddy. Eddy Ford. But he moved away. In grade school he and I and Greg… Greg—I think my mom might remember his last name—we used to hang out together."

"What about junior high and high school?"

"A couple of the girls were okay to me. Althea Soames, Lisa Koslovsky."

"Do you remember any of your teachers?"

"Oh, boy, let me think." He stopped and looked down for a long moment, frowning with effort. "All's I can remember in high school, in Shasta City High, are Mr. Muller or maybe Mueller; he taught shop. Mr. Geleitner, or something like that, he was the principal."

"What about grade school and middle school?"

He thought for a moment. "I only remember one nice teacher and one mean one. Miss Brandon was the nice one. Mrs. Cooley, she didn't like me. She was fourth grade. I had to repeat it, 'cause she wouldn't pass me. Mama was mad. Went and talked to her about it, but it didn't do no good."

"Do you remember what school Miss Brandon was in?"

He frowned in concentration again and shook his head. "No, I sure can't."

"What about high school; did you graduate?"

"No. I got tired of school. I wanted to work, make some money."

"How old were you when you left?"

"Seventeen. Or maybe eighteen. I'm not sure."

"What year were you in then?"

"Tenth grade."

We went on like this for the rest of the visit. By the time the guard—a different one this time—came to take Andy back to his cell, I had a half-dozen pages of notes on schools, towns, doctors' and dentists' names, friends, relatives, hospitals, and so forth. Andy looked up at the guard and then back to us. "Well, guess I gotta go now. Would you send me some stamps and drawing paper?"

"Sure," Jim said. Andy stood up, and when the guard opened the metal port in the cage door, Andy turned and held his hands behind him for the cuffs.

We followed them out of the passageway and watched as they made their awkward progress toward the painted iron door that led to the cell blocks. Then we waited some more near the row of cages while, somewhere behind the door, Andy was searched to make sure we hadn't passed him anything illegal during our visit. When the guard behind the window told us we were cleared to leave and flipped the switch that opened the barred gates to the outside, I tried not to look too glad to be out of there.

3

The bay seemed even bluer and more sparkling under the noon sun, as Jim and I walked back to the parking lot. A white hydrofoil ferry, toylike in the distance, skimmed over the deep blue water toward the Larkspur Landing, a snowy plume of foam in its wake.

"Do you want to go somewhere for lunch?" Jim asked. "Talk about Andy and the case?"

"Sure."

The nearest restaurants were in a shopping center a mile or so away. I suggested one and gave Jim directions to it.

Gaia's Garden café was earnestly and fashionably green; more important, it was easy to find and quiet.

Jim had left his jacket and tie in the car; he looked more relaxed in shirtsleeves. He folded his long legs into one of the pale wooden booths, and I sat across from him, my toes just touching the floor. He had the look of a successful litigator—in his mid-forties, I guessed, but trim and athletic-looking, his short brown hair showing glints of gray above a still-handsome face. The lunch crowd of workers, shopping soccer moms, and business people meeting clients was thinning out, and we had enough privacy to talk comfortably.

Jim looked around. "Looks like west LA," he commented as he picked up the menu.

"You don't mind vegetarian, do you?"

"Nah. After that hamburger at the prison, meat's not looking so good right now." He ordered a garden burger, and I asked for a grilled veggie salad.

"So, what did you think of Andy?" Jim asked, as our server, a round-faced twenty-year-old with pink-streaked black hair and silver rings in her nostril and eyebrow, left with our orders and menus.

"Not your average rapist, is he? Assuming there is such a thing."

"No, he seems like a pretty likable guy. Mark Balestri—his appellate lawyer who handled his direct appeal—says he was a real easy client. Didn't ask for much, didn't try to control his case. His mother, though—she's another story."

"Uh-oh. What does she do?"

Our conversation stopped as the pink-haired girl returned with a tray and doled out our food and drinks.

I took a long, grateful pull at my iced tea. It was lightly flavored with some sort of tropical fruit. Jim gestured toward the mound of skinny French fries that had come with his burger. "Have some," he said. I took one and ate it slowly, trying to decide whether more of them would be worth exercising for.

"What about Andy's mother?" I asked.

Jim swallowed his bite of sandwich and said, "She's snoopy. Mark said she'd call every time he filed something in Andy's appeal, and sometimes in between, to ask what was going on. He said Andy's very dependent on his mother. Tells her everything, so you can't say anything to him unless you want her to hear it."

"So much for attorney-client privilege."

"Yeah. I haven't met her yet. She's called a couple of times, but I've been out. Corey, my paralegal, has talked to her. She knows I've associated you."

The conversation more or less died after that, and we ate in silence. After we had pushed aside our plates and ordered coffee, Jim pulled out his notes from the visit. "I'm representing one of the defendants in this huge prison gang case down in LA," he said. "Twenty-three named defendants, and maybe more to come. I took Hardy's case because it's looking like this other one won't go to trial in any of our lifetimes, but it's taking up more time than I thought. Discovery wars and a lot of motions work—it's never-ending. That's why I asked for money for a second counsel for Hardy. I hope you can help me out."

It seemed to me that he should have anticipated all that before taking on a capital case. "Well, I'm here," I said. "Let me know what I should start with."

"It's hard to say. The trial lawyer—Arnold Dobson—didn't do much. Balestri got his files while he was still alive, but there isn't much in them. Dobson didn't put on any defense at the guilt phase, and he's dead so we can't ask him why. At the penalty phase, he only put on two witnesses. So we're starting almost from square one, in terms of investigating the case. I think Dobson dropped the ball in not challenging the confession as involuntary—it seems pretty clear they got Hardy to confess by threatening to arrest his mother. I'm still looking for an investigator, but I think I'll be able to get Nancy Hollister on board to do the psychosocial history; we're working together on another case. Do you know her?"

"I haven't worked with her, but I've heard good things about her," I said. Most capital defense attorneys retain experts, usually psychologists, whose role is to identify the factors in a defendant's background that have contributed to making him what he is and explain to juries and judges how the lives that many of our clients have lived—growing up among alcoholics and drug addicts, beaten, molested, neglected or entirely abandoned—can create a mentally and emotionally damaged adult who can't make the sorts of intelligent decisions day to day that the jurors, and most of the people they know, do by second nature.

"She's not sure she can take this case—she's got a lot of other work. But I'm hoping I can talk her into it."

The waitress brought our coffee and the check. Jim paid it with a credit card, then looked at his watch. "I've got to get going. Got a meeting with Nancy at three about the other case. She's here in Marin; I was hoping she could meet us for lunch, but she wasn't free. I've got something Corey gave me for you, but I left it in the car."

In the parking lot, he unlocked his rental car, pulled his briefcase from the floor onto the back seat, opened it, and pulled out a small manila envelope. He turned and handed it to me. On it, someone had printed my name and below it MARION HARDY: CASE FILES. I could feel a small object through the thick paper. I opened the metal fastener and turned it over, and a silver flash drive fell into my palm.

"Dobson's files, Andy's prison file, and a few other things—school records, maybe. Happy reading." Jim closed his briefcase with a bright snap, shoved it back behind the seat and opened the driver's door. "Call me if you have any questions."

4

Heading north toward home, I stopped at the south end of Sonoma County, in Petaluma, the last real town between San Quentin and my place, and loaded up on groceries. Corbin's Landing, where I'd settled, is thirty miles from the nearest supermarket, and living there takes some planning.

The Safeway had BOGOF sales on beef pot roasts and cartons of eggs, so I bought two of each for me and Ed, my neighbor and sometime dogsitter, in addition to the other things on my list. Farther along the road I added asparagus, broccoli, spring onions, and a half-dozen baskets of strawberries from a stand on the Bodega Highway. Local berries were a welcome sign of spring, a treat after a winter of flavorless supermarket fruit.

The drive up the coast highway, dangerous and dazzling, cleared the sordid memory of the prison from my soul. The afternoon sun was shining blindingly over the ocean, and an almost transparent mist lay on the water's surface as I turned onto the road up the hillside, with its ragged scatter of houses that made up Corbin's Landing. The settlement, such as it is, was once a doghole port from which redwood, logged from the hills around, was shipped to San Francisco. It was named for a lumber baron who was forgotten as quickly as the village when the supply of old-growth timber ran out. Some of the logged-over hills were turned into cow pastures by dairy farmers, but in the sheltered valleys and canyons the redwoods grew back, second-growth trees not much more than a hundred years old, but still stately as cathedral spires.

During Prohibition the cove was a landing point for bootleg liquor from Canada, and later the village became something of an artists' colony. More recently, the area was discovered as vacation property by rich people from outside who liked its quirkiness and character and the fact that this part of the coast is protected by state law from further subdividing, so the old ranches and long stretches of undisturbed bluffs can't be covered with beachfront condos. They have built a few Sea Ranch-style houses and execrable stucco mini-mansions here and there, and some of the little board and batten cabins and old white farmhouses have been given Pottery Barn makeovers and turned into vacation rentals, but most are still occupied by old hippies, small ranchers, local workers, artists, and various types of end-of-the-roaders.

I turned up a side road and then down the long dirt driveway to my house. Bags of groceries in one hand, I unlatched the gate to the yard to let out Charlie, my dog, and backtracked to the door, Charlie prancing and barking ahead of me as I fumbled with the lock. My two cats materialized at the door and crowded into the kitchen with me and the dog. I stopped to feed all of them before heading out to the car for the rest of the groceries.

I changed out of my black slacks and white shirt—prison-visitor clothes—and into jeans, flannel shirt, and an old down vest and took Ed's groceries and two baskets of strawberries next door to his place. I could hear bluegrass music inside, and I called out, "Hey, Ed, are you decent?"

A hoarse voice inside called back, "Come in and find out, if you're interested."

I opened the door. "I don't know. Should I be?"

Ed appeared in the doorway of his kitchen, a dishtowel in his hand and another, stained with tomato juice, tucked like an apron into the belt of his jeans. He had grown out of his hard-living youth years ago, before I met him, but his face still had the spare, leathery look of a man who has spent too much time with cigarettes and booze. He wore his salt-and-pepper hair long and tied at the back of his head with an elastic band. "You're a hard-hearted woman," he said. "Whaddya have for me? Excuse me, I'm in the middle of putting together a tomato sauce."

"Guy food. Meat and potatoes. And eggs, and some strawberries." I followed him into his kitchen, into a comforting smell of sautéing green peppers and onion. "Shall I put them away?"

"Sure. No, give me the beef; I think I'll make a ragu. What do I owe you?"

"More dog-sitting?" I opened his refrigerator and found a spot for the eggs.

"No problem—I'm not going anywhere but work."

Ed is a carpenter, and his kitchen, like the rest of his small house, has been a work-in-progress ever since I've known him, cluttered with projects that he attacks between jobs. For the past week or so, pieces of a salvaged cabinet meant for the wall above the refrigerator had been propped against his kitchen table, and the table was littered with a jigsaw, drill, hammers and screwdrivers, and assorted small hardware. A thin film of sawdust coated everything but the counter where he was cutting vegetables.

"Cup of coffee?" Ed invited. "It's a fresh pot. Sorry about the mess. No time to finish putting those guys up yet. We're getting into the busy season."

Ed liked his coffee strong. I poured myself a cup, added milk from the fridge, and sat down at the table, pushing aside a couple of screwdrivers and a pair of wire cutters. I watched him work as I sipped my coffee.

"So how was your prison visit?" Ed asked. "Everyone still there?"

"Oh yes."

"Was this the day you were meeting that guy and his lawyer?"

"Yeah."

"So how'd it go? You taking his case?"

"I guess—I took the file home."

"Well, I don't know why you want to, but good luck. Want to come over for dinner later?"

"Thanks, but I'll probably be asleep by the time it's cooked. Long day, driving there and back." I stood up. "Thanks for the coffee. I need to get back home and start reading."

"Well, if you're still awake at seven or so, come on over."

Feeling a little livelier from the coffee, I picked my way back through Ed's front room, a clutter of books, CDs, boxes of paper recycling, and the detritus of more remodeling projects. It still smelled faintly of old dog, even though Panama, Ed's ancient labrador, had died last winter.

Back at my house, Charlie greeted me as though it were some sort of miracle that I had reappeared, and then bustled out past me and sat on the porch, to remind me that I owed him a walk. "A short one, Charlie; I'm really tired."

Braced against the stiff afternoon breeze, we walked up the hill to the end of the road. I stopped now and then to drink in views of the rocky coast and the sunset while Charlie lifted his leg against the fence of one or another of the Pottery Barn bungalows.

5

For the next couple of weeks I read what Corey had given me about Andy Hardy's case. A post-conviction case comes with a history ready-made, in the form of police and forensic lab reports, transcripts, pleadings, and court orders, from the first dispatch call to the crime scene through trial and sentencing. The theories and strategies of the police, prosecutor and defense counsel were laid out like the plot of an exceptionally bad play, with the witnesses as characters. My work was to read all of it and start asking questions. What are the holes in the stories? What was done by the police, the prosecutor, the defense attorney—and what wasn't? What documents, reports, evidence are missing?

From morning till night I read and organized facts. On my computer I typed summaries of testimony, notes, timelines, charts, lists of witnesses, potential issues, and things to be done. I let the answering machine pick up my phone calls and returned calls during breaks in my reading. When I needed to clear my head, I took walks with Charlie, cleaned house, or tied tomato, bean, and pea stems to trellises. I made strawberry jam and took a jar to Ed. I made salads and stir-fries, to use up the fresh produce I'd bought and the lettuce from my garden that needed to be eaten before it grew too bitter and tough. Ed stopped by once or twice, and my gardening mentor Harriet brought over some fava beans and wrote out a fertilizer formula for my tomato plants, but for the most part I was alone in the quiet house, working. I liked it that way.

Appellate law, which is most of what I do, is solitary work; a lot of research, analysis, and writing, and not much human contact except by email. Appeals are like a debate carried out in writing—opening brief, responsive brief, reply, rounded out with a fairly brief court hearing where the parties' attorneys present a summary of their arguments, and the panel of judges who will decide the case questions them to refine and clarify the issues involved. It suits me. I don't like being around people much; dealing with them takes too much time and attention for what you generally get out of the process, and it leaves me tired and on edge. Terry, my—I never know what to call him; "former husband" sounds as though we divorced, but "late husband" casts a pall over casual conversations—was pretty much the same way, really, though not many people figured this out because he was a great trial lawyer and seemed thoroughly at ease in a courtroom. But Terry kept a lot of secrets, even from me.

For the most part, the police reports and transcripts in

Andy's case expanded on the depressing story I'd heard from Jim. Andy and his brother Emory had been arrested after a runaway teenager from Sacramento, Nicole Shumate, was picked up by a rancher on a country highway twenty miles from Shasta City. Nicole said she'd been kidnapped while hitchhiking near Shasta City, taken to a ranch somewhere outside of town, and raped by two men, after which one of them had driven with her out onto the highway late at night in his pickup truck. She had jumped from the man's truck and hidden in the woods until after daybreak. The rancher drove her to the main police station in Shasta City, where she reported the crime. As the truck drove away, she said, she read and memorized its license-plate number. The plate came back to Emory Hardy.

The police put Emory's driver's license photo into a photo lineup and showed it to Nicole. She picked him out without hesitation as one of the kidnappers.

Emory's address, which appeared to be where Nicole had been taken, was outside the Shasta City limits, and the job of making arrests and investigating the crimes was assigned to the Pomo County Sheriff's Department. Several deputies were waiting at the house when Eva Hardy, Emory's mother, came home from work that night, but neither Emory nor his brother Marion showed up. Eva said she had no idea where they were.

It didn't take long to find them. They were arrested at a motel in the mountains near the Oregon state line, after the manager recognized the truck and license plate from the TV news and called 911.

After a night in jail and a long, mostly silent ride to the sheriff's station at Shasta City, Emory was ready to talk. He gave a statement saying Andy was the instigator of the whole sorry escapade, and he went along with it because Andy made him. They talked to Andy, too, and he said it was his brother's idea and he went along with it because, well, she was a hooker and she would have given it to them for money anyway. Reading their statements, I felt a little sick. It's hard to sympathize with someone like that, even if he's your client. But interrogating cops are trained not to show their real feelings when they're trying to get information, so the questions in the transcript were pure Joe Friday, neutral and bland, designed to get as much out of Andy as possible and keep him from lawyering up.

The sheriffs went out to the farm the next day with a search warrant. In the barn, they found the room where Nicole had been held, just as she described it. They also found a purse with a wallet belonging to a different woman. The ID in it turned out to be that of another young woman who had been reported missing the previous spring.

Two homicide deputies from the Pomo County Sheriff's Department, Ron Canevaro and Dave Hines, were assigned to the case, and they grilled Emory about the new information. They used a time-honored interrogation trick, telling him that Andy had confessed and fingered Emory as the killer of the missing girl. Emory took the bait, and in exchange for a promise that Canevaro and Hines would tell the district attorney how cooperative he'd been, he told them that Andy had killed not one, but two women, and where the bodies were buried.

As Emory told it, on both occasions, Andy and he had kidnapped a prostitute and hidden her in the barn on the ranch where they lived, where they took turns having sex with her. When they got tired of it, Andy decided the girl needed to be gotten rid of because she could lead the police back to the ranch. Both times, Andy had gone into the barn and killed the girl—Emory didn't know how. He and Andy carried the bodies out to the woods behind the ranch buildings and buried them. He had no idea why Andy decided to let the third one go. "Felt sorry for her, I guess," he said.

In the woods behind the ranch, the sheriffs found two grave-sized indentations in the ground pretty much where Emory had said they would be. Digging equipment and a crew of police officers and crime-scene investigators were brought out to the site. A couple of feet down, they found the decomposed bodies of two women.

Canevaro and Hines brought Andy out of his jail cell and questioned him again. This time, they turned up the heat.

When the police interrogate a suspect in custody, they're usually no longer trying to find out what happened and whether or not the guy was really involved. Police may interview witnesses to find out information, but an interrogation is something else entirely. By the time officers begin interrogating a suspect, they're convinced he's guilty; the point of the questioning isn't to find out what really happened, but to wear the man down psychologically until he confesses to what the police believe he did. Textbooks and manuals have been written on how to isolate and disorient a perpetrator and work a confession out of him, and cops go on training courses where instructors teach techniques for extolling, cajoling, frightening, and tricking confessions from reluctant suspects.

Hines and Canevaro knew their work. Andy told them a story—in fact, he told several. At first he denied knowing anything about the bodies. Then, when the detectives confronted him with what Emory had told them, he admitted to helping kidnap the women, but said he didn't know they'd been killed; they'd just disappeared during the night, and Emory had told him he'd driven them some distance down the highway and let them go. The detectives told him how incredible that sounded, and he admitted that maybe he'd suspected that they were dead. The detectives said they knew he was lying, that he knew the women had died and that he had killed them, and they wanted him to be straight with them and tell them how it had happened. Andy balked and kept insisting he didn't kill them and didn't know how they'd died. Then the officers told him that he was looking at the death penalty unless he came up with some explanation for killing those two girls. They lied, saying his fingerprints had been lifted from the skin of one of the women's necks. They suggested that Andy might have killed the women without meaning to, maybe during sex, or that he had grown angry because he'd had trouble performing and they had taunted him.

Andy, confused and tearful, continued to deny that he'd killed the women. He asked to see his mother, and the officers said they'd let her visit him when he'd told them the truth.

Andy stuck with his story for another hour or so, until the detectives threatened to arrest Eva for murder and conspiracy. Andy reacted with terrified indignation. "You can't arrest Mama—she didn't have nothin' to do with it!" The detectives, seeing a weakness they could exploit, took that as the opening they needed. They played Andy with it, telling him that if he knew his mother didn't have anything to do with the murders of the two women, then he must know who did and that the only way to keep her out of trouble was to tell them. From that, it was only a few minutes until Andy broke and let the officers tell him how the killings must have happened. Maybe he really didn't remember, they said. Maybe he'd done drugs on those nights or been drinking, or just blacked out. He had strangled them, perhaps, or stabbed them; it was up to Andy to tell them what he'd done.

Andy's confession, in its final form, was a lot like Emory's. He told the detectives that he and Emory had kidnapped the women; that the two of them had taken them to the ranch;

and that they had put them in a room in the barn behind the house, where they both subjected them to various sex acts. With a lot of prompting from the deputies, Andy said that each of the women might have said or done something that set him off, and, he guessed he could have strangled them. He and Emory buried their victims in the woods, far enough from the house that their mother wouldn't see the disturbed ground.

When the deputies asked him why he let Nicole go instead of killing her, he said, "I didn't want her to get hurt." He told how he had gone out to the barn while Emory was watching television and Eva was upstairs in the house, untied Nicole, told her to get into the truck, and started driving toward town. He told her he was going to let her go, but she didn't believe him and jumped out of the truck and ran into the woods. Andy drove back home. "But Em heard the truck, and when he found out, he was madder'n hell. He went out looking for her, but he couldn't find her in the dark. When he comes back he says we was both dead men and we had to take off. So we left that night in his truck."

Between the bodies, the confessions, and the testimony of Nicole, the district attorney had the issue of Andy and Emory's guilt pretty well sewn up. Arnold Dobson, Andy's court-appointed lawyer, apparently agreed with the prosecution's assessment of the case, because he put on no defense. His strategy, such as it was, was to rely on the mercy of the jurors at the second phase of the trial, when the jury decided whether to give Andy the death penalty or life in prison. In mitigation, Dobson leaned on the fact that Andy had no prior criminal record and no history of violence. There had been one referral to juvenile court for assault, but the charges had been dismissed when all the witnesses said Andy had been defending a girl against a couple of boys who were pushing her around. The prosecutor didn't even bother to introduce evidence of that incident.

But at the penalty trial, the relatives of the murdered victims get to come before the jury and testify—about the victim herself and about how her murder has shattered their lives and left them choked with helpless anger, grief, and guilt. The mother of one of the women, Lisa Greenman, said Lisa's murder had killed her stepfather. "He loved her like his own daughter. He died eight months after we learned what had happened to her. It was a heart attack; the doctor said it was the stress from all the grief. It just ate at us." As for herself, "I just can't keep from thinking about her last hours and wondering what she must have felt. I don't think I've had a day since when I felt really happy."

The grandmother of the other victim, Brandy Ontiveros, testified awkwardly, through an interpreter, about bringing up her granddaughter after her own daughter's early death in a car accident, and Brandy's struggle with crack cocaine addiction and her love for her own baby girl. Now she was raising her great-granddaughter and trying to find the right answer when the child asked where her mama was. The whole family felt the pain of Brandy's death; even though she was troubled, they loved her. "Her brother, he couldn't get over it. He got in with a gang, and he's in prison now."

Nicole Shumate testified about the aftermath of the kidnapping: her withdrawal into depression and heavy drug use, the months she had spent in counseling, the nights she still spent watching television until sunrise, afraid to go to sleep.

Even reading their words, unadorned by how they must have sounded, how their faces must have looked, I felt desolate. I could only imagine the impression they must have made on the jury.

To make the case for giving Andy a life sentence instead of death, Andy's lawyer had presented two witnesses: his great-aunt and a jail deputy. Both of them had said Andy was quiet, slow, and docile, and liked to be helpful.

The prosecutor argued indignantly that Andy deserved death if anyone did, for the horror and degradation he and his brother had inflicted on three helpless young women. "Look at him," he told the jury, "sitting with his lawyer here in this courtroom. He's getting a trial, with a jury of twelve honorable people to decide whether he lives or dies. Lisa Greenman and Brandy Ontiveros never had a trial before their lives were taken, and they never killed anyone. If you give this man life in prison, he will have three meals a day, a television to watch, time every day to go outdoors and hang out with his buddies in the sunshine. Lisa and Brandy won't have any of that. They will never see the sunlight, never have the chance they needed to turn their lives around and look for happiness. Brandy Ontiveros will never see her little girl, the baby she loved so much, grow up. Does this monster, this predator, deserve to keep his own life after taking theirs? Brandy's grandmother came here, all the way from Los Angeles, to tell you about her little girl. Who came here to speak for the defendant? No one who knows him. A great-aunt who hasn't seen him since he was a kid. A jail guard. Not even his mother stepped up to say anything for him."

In the end, it took the jury just over an hour to come back with a death verdict.

At the sentencing hearing, the judge made a speech about the horror of the women's deaths and Nicole's courage in surviving and coming to court to confront her tormentor. "Mr. Hardy," he had said—and even on the page I could hear the righteous satisfaction in his voice—"Mr. Hardy, if anyone deserves the death penalty for what they have done, it's you."

After Andy was sentenced, he sat on death row for four years, his case on hold, while he moved up the waiting list for the state Supreme Court to appoint an attorney for his automatic appeal. Mark Balestri was the lawyer they'd appointed. He'd written a good set of legal briefs, given how little there was to argue from the meager record of Andy's trial. The state Supreme Court had upheld Andy's conviction and death sentence, a little more than thirteen years after the jury's verdict.

Andy's case then went to the federal district court, where Jim was appointed and given a year to file simultaneous petitions for habeas corpus on Andy's behalf in the state and federal courts. The petitions would argue that Andy didn't get a fair trial and that the state Supreme Court had been wrong in upholding Andy's conviction and death sentence. All Jim needed was the evidence to prove it. The state and federal courts each gave him some money to investigate the case—not a lot, to begin with, but enough to hire an investigator and another lawyer as second chair. That's where I came in.

By this time, Andy's case was very, very cold.

We would have to turn the field again after nearly fifteen years, reading every piece of paper, looking for things not done, favorable evidence and witnesses that weren't found or, if found, were ignored—anything that might help convince some judge that Andy deserved a new trial. We were starting at square one, with nothing obvious to look for—hell, we were behind square one, because Andy had had a trial and an appeal. We'd have to convince a skeptical judge that enough evidence had been left out the first time that Andy deserved a chance to be tried again.

Along with the charts and timelines, I was keeping a running list of documents we needed to get, people we should find and talk to, possible legal issues, and questions. Which of the brothers had had the idea to kidnap women and kill them? Did Andy have any history of mental illness that might have foretold his being part of a scheme like this? Did their mother have any idea what was going on while it was happening? Was there anything in Andy's background, not mentioned at the trial, that might have persuaded the jury to show him some mercy?

The crime-scene photos and autopsy reports were worse than most, given the state of the bodies, though they lacked the Grand Guignol quality of images on television crime shows. There was no teasing suspense, no ominous music or disorienting camera angles—just dark earth and earth-colored bone and dried flesh and stained and crumpled shreds of clothing, made two-dimensional and nearly unintelligible by the camera flash. They weren't terrifying, just sickening and sobering—the human husk resolving itself back into earth, dust to dust, a crime scene as memento mori.

Sometimes, though, I ran across an unexpected detail, something in the background in a photograph or said in a report or transcript, that pierced my detachment. The reports and photos called up scenes: the policeman turning a shovelful of earth and smelling the musky, sour tang of decomposing animal flesh, saying softly, "Oh, hell," in the instant before collecting himself and calling out, "We've got one here." The faces of the mothers of the girls when they were told that their bodies had been found. The smiling baby in her pink sundress in a photo in Brandy's wallet, a child who would never see her mother again.

Working murder cases isn't easy for anyone. But prosecutors and policemen can at least fall back on a simple moral position. Their role is to bring punishment down on the killer, and they can feed their strength of purpose on the ugly facts and the pain and outrage of the victims' families. Prosecutors are easier for juries to understand than defense attorneys. Being the champion of the bad guy is the harder road. We have to embrace and explain something much more ambiguous, the Greek tragedy set in motion by capricious gods, in which everyone loses, hero and victim, and moral choice is a pretense, an illusory belief that only makes the downfall more complete.

It was a long couple of weeks. Toward the end, I started alternating my reading in the Hardy case with a lot of yoga and meditation. Sometimes I walked with Charlie down the rocky path to the beach and let him sniff among the tide pools and the slippery boulders while I sat on a rock in the salt-sprayed air, looking for calm in the rhythm of the breaking waves and the impersonal vastness of the ocean.

Working on a capital case again made me think more of Terry. It had been six years since that phone call from Dave Rothstein that had split my life in two. I'd half died, feeling myself pulled down the road he had gone, like Orpheus following Eurydice, but then come slowly back to life again, done therapy and antidepressants, and finally simply run away from the soul-crushing back-and-forth slam of grief, guilt, devastation, and overwhelming anger. I'd missed him, I'd hated him, I'd screamed in silence at the brass bell of the sky in disbelief that he was gone, I'd wondered what I hadn't seen and might have done to pull him back from whatever edge he'd fallen over. Our son Gavin, our only child, spun away from me, working out his own grief and guilt while I was too broken to help him. But nothing is as complete, as irrevocable as death. Nothing I could wish or hope would reverse the tape and bring him back—bring us back—to try again.

People who knew Terry—and there were a lot of them—seemed tacitly to blame me; and sometimes I blamed myself, wondering how I had missed his despair, the end of some exhausting trek through life that he had decided one day he couldn't endure any more. But unlike most of his friends and colleagues, I knew how well he could hide it.

There was always some inner space he kept out of sight, some part of himself he didn't confide. He was, on the surface, an unemotional man, quiet and even-tempered. He scarcely ever raised his voice in anger. People thought of him as unflappable, methodical. He was brilliant but not showy; he just seemed to know everything, to remember any fact he'd ever read, and to be able to slice effortlessly through obfuscation to the heart of an argument. I used to wonder what he saw in me; I'm not sure I ever really knew.

As a public defender, he was the legendary Terrence Moran, who tried twenty capital cases without a single death verdict. He spoke at conferences and wrote law review articles on forensics and capital litigation. He was a darling of the death-penalty defense community, though he stayed away from the cliques and hierarchies that sometimes made it seem more like a university department than a group of idealists laboring in a common cause. I lived and worked in his reflected glory, and after he died I understood how many of our colleagues had seen me only as an extension of him, and how many of them felt I was somehow responsible for his suicide.

But I didn't see it coming. I never really figured out what, if anything, tipped him into his final depression. He had just driven into Redwood Park on a gray February morning, pulled his car into the parking lot of a deserted trailhead, called his friend and investigator Dave Rothstein on his cellphone with a message where to find his body, and shot himself. He knew where to aim; the bullet severed his brain stem, and he died instantly.

And here I was.

After all the time that had passed, on the nights after I had spent the day reading about Andy's case I sometimes found it hard to get to sleep, and when I did, I had dreams filled with infinite and irresolvable sadness.

6

Finally, I finished digesting the materials on the flash drive. Besides my notes and outlines, I had a list of documents that I thought we should have but hadn't seen in the trial lawyer's files. I called Jim's office and got a secretary who told me he was in court and transferred me to their paralegal, Corey.

Corey's voice was a lilt that mixed Midwest and Deep South. "Honey, you've got everything we got from old Mr. Dobson," he said. "I went through those files myself."

This was bad news and good news—bad, because it meant Jim was going to have to get all this stuff himself, but good, because it meant that Dobson, the trial attorney, probably hadn't—more support for us to argue that he had been ineffective in representing Andy.

That afternoon, just before five, the phone in my home office rang. The voice on the other end was a woman's, unfamiliar. "Mrs. Moodie?" the caller said, a little tentatively.

"Speaking."

"I'm Eva Hardy." Her sentence ended on an up-note,

almost like a question. "I hope you don't mind me calling you."

"Oh, no, of course not," I said.

"I got your telephone number from Corey, Mr. Christie's paralegal? He's such a nice man. I told him I needed to talk to you."

Jim's warning started ringing in my ears. *What does she really want?* I asked myself.

"I have a lot of trouble getting hold of Mr. Christie," Eva said, almost apologetically. "He's always so busy. But he does find time to see Andy. I'm glad for that."

"That is good," I agreed.

"But I do worry," she said. "Andy doesn't always understand what his lawyers tell him, and he asks me. But I don't always know myself. Maybe you can help me."

"I hope I can."

"Oh, good. I saw Andy last Saturday, and he had some questions he was hoping I could ask someone."

"Okay."

"Well, we're wondering what's going to happen in this court. Is it like another appeal?"

"Not really. It's called habeas corpus, and it involves presenting evidence to the court that wasn't introduced by Mr. Dobson at Andy's trial, in the hope of getting him a new trial."

"Oh. What kind of evidence?"

"Well, right now I'm thinking that there might be a lot more mitigation evidence than Mr. Dobson presented."

"I'm not sure what you mean."

"Oh, evidence about Andy that might have made him more sympathetic to the jury, and maybe made them think he didn't deserve the death penalty after all."

"Mmm. What would that be?"

"I'm not really sure yet. Facts about his early life, influences that might have affected his development in childhood and made him less able to control his behavior as an adult. Maybe some mental illness."

"My Andy doesn't have any mental illness," Eva said flatly.

Uh-oh. "Of course, probably not," I answered, in what I hoped was a reassuring tone. "But we do have to investigate it. We're trying to save his life, and we have to investigate every possibility."

"I see."

"I'd like to get together with you and talk about Andy's childhood. Anything we can learn could be helpful."

"Okay. I used to have baby books for both the boys, but I gave them to Mr. Dobson, and he never gave them back."

Damn, I thought. "I'm really sorry to hear that."

"Yes. I had photographs, and I put in their weights and heights, and when they first walked. All those memories."

"Oh dear."

"I'll think about it and see what I can remember."

"That would be great. And if you have any photos of Andy, those would be helpful, too."

"I have some."

"That's great," I said. "I'd really like to see them. Maybe next time you visit Andy we can get together."

"That would be good. I visit him every month, on Saturday. I'll call you and let you know the next time, okay?"

"Yes, thank you."

Reading the transcript of Andy's trial, I'd been struck by the fact that she didn't testify. While I had her on the line, I thought I'd ask her if she knew why she hadn't been called.

"I wanted to, but I couldn't."

"Why?"

"The district attorney was threatening to have me arrested for helping the boys run from the police. Mr. Dobson said I'd have to plead the Fifth Amendment if I was called as a witness."

Nice move on the DA's part, I thought. He'd managed to keep the most sympathetic defense witness off the stand and leave the jury to draw its own conclusions about why the defendant's own mother wouldn't testify for him.

I called Jim again the next day, but he was out of the office for the day, so I told Corey about Eva's call. "She seems nice enough," I said.

"Oh, she always is to me, too," he said. "Just kind of pushy sometimes. And a little strange."

"Strange? How?"

He paused for a second. "I'm not sure how—just kind of peculiar. Maybe you'll see it when you talk with her a while."

7

The next morning I woke up to white mist swirling slowly outside my windows. The light in the house looked like winter light reflected from snow.

The thermometer outside my kitchen window read fifty degrees, and the previous night's fire was down to a few glowing coals. I nursed it to life with newspapers and more wood, shrugged into jeans and a sweatshirt, and went out for an early morning walk with Charlie, thinking I'd thin the cobwebs in my head by mixing them with the fog outside.

When we got back to the house, the sun was starting to burn through the mist, and the message light was blinking on my home office telephone. I made myself a cup of coffee before playing the voicemail.

"Janny, hi," it said. "It's Dave Rothstein—a voice from your past. Jim Christie's hired me to work on the Hardy case. I'd like to touch base, get together to talk about it. Give me a call, okay?" I could hardly wait for the machine to finish before punching in his phone number.

Dave answered on the second ring. "Janny! It's been a while. How are you doing?"

It was a question almost guaranteed to obliterate any memories I might have had about what was going on in my life. But Dave had a way of asking it that made me want to tell him everything—how I was afraid that the fog would mildew my tomato plants, how I worried that the phone would ring and it would be someone telling me that my son Gavin had been killed in a plane crash or mauled by a crocodile, how I couldn't shake the floating, homeless feeling I'd had since Terry died. It was a gift Dave had; I'd seen witnesses confess their darkest secrets to him as if he were their priest.

With an effort, I restrained the impulse to confess mine. "Okay—better. And you?"

He deflected the question. "Good, can't complain—really, how are you? Liking it up there on the coast?"

"Oh yes. I have a vegetable garden, and I make bread, and listen to the ocean. I'm good here."

"Back to the land, eh? Sounds like a good way to live. And you don't miss the big city and all your friends?"

"Not a bit—none of you. You all never come up here to visit me anyway."

He chuckled. "You ran away from us. What's Gavin up to these days?"

"Oh, God, in Australia, doing a post-doc. I think he went to the ends of the earth to get away from me."

"His loss. Australia—wow, I've always wanted to go there. Have you been to visit him?"

"Not yet."

"Shame on you. You should go before he moves back here." He changed the subject back to the task at hand. "So—I see you're still working on death cases."

"Only this one. Against my better judgment."

"Well, that may be both of us."

Dave had worked with Terry on many cases, and they had become close friends. On the morning Terry drove to a park in the Oakland hills and shot himself, it was Dave he rang to tell him where to find his body. Dave had gone with me to the coroner's office to identify Terry and had generally watched over me in the aftermath of his death, calling often and stopping by to take me to lunch or coffee every week or so. During all the guilt, blame, and weirdness that followed Terry's suicide, when colleagues I had thought of as friends were accusing me behind my back of negligence and worse in failing to see the warning signs and take some sort of action to save him, Dave had reassured me over and over again that I hadn't missed any signs, that there wasn't any way I could have seen Terry's slide into depression or change his course. "He was hiding it from all of us," Dave said, "and he did a hell of a job. He was one of my best friends, and I didn't see it coming, either."

He had talked me out of one or two of the crazier ideas that possessed me during that first year of grief, rage, and bewilderment, but not my determination to quit the state defender's office and go someplace far away from all of it—the grief and betrayal. Later, life and work had taken us in different directions, and we hadn't seen one another for a couple of years. It was a pleasure to hear his voice again.

"So you're working on Andy Hardy's case now, too?" I asked.

"Yep. Christie called me last week. Andy Hardy—I can't say the name without thinking of old Mickey Rooney movies."

"Believe it or not, that's how he got the nickname. His mother gave it to him. But I'm so pleased you're working on this case. I can never get hold of Jim. I'm starting to feel a little like I've been air-dropped onto a desert island with the case files."

"Yeah," Dave said, "I've heard that about Christie."

"Heard what?"

"He's the kind of lawyer who hires good people to do all his work for him. He doesn't like the dull preparation part—he prefers to shine in the courtroom and talk to the press."

"Oh, great," I said. "I wish someone had told me sooner. I'm really not ready for that."

"Too late to get out?"

"I'd feel stupid."

"Well, at least we can keep one another company."

I didn't want to think about what I'd gotten myself into, so I changed the subject. "How much do you know about the case?" I asked.

He told me, and I filled him in on the rest, as far as I had gotten with it. "So you think we're really going to be left on our own?" I asked again. "There's so much to do." I started listing witnesses who needed to be located.

Dave stopped me. "Why don't you email me the names, and let's make a time to get together."

"Your place or mine?" I asked.

"I can drive up there," Dave said. "There are great bike roads up where you are."

8

By the day of Dave's visit I'd found the answers to a few more of my questions in the transcripts of Emory's trial. Emory had been tried after Andy. His case had been tried in Fresno, because Emory's attorney had moved for a change of venue on the grounds that the Pomo County jury pool had been irreparably tainted by the publicity surrounding Andy's trial. And Emory's court-appointed lawyer, Mark Levenson, had done a better job than Dobson.

Like the prosecutor, Levenson had played on the fact that Andy was older to make a case that Andy was the instigator and leader in the crimes and the actual killer of the women. He portrayed Emory as the impressionable younger brother following his older brother's lead. He wasn't able to keep Emory from being convicted of the two murders, but at the penalty phase of the trial, he put on witnesses—teachers and friends of the family, a psychologist who specialized in investigating and explaining the effects of background on behavior—to talk about Emory's impoverished life, the abuse he, Eva, and Andy had suffered at the hands of a violent, alcoholic father, and why his behavior grew worse after his father abandoned the family.

The psychologist had gone over Emory's school records and the criminal history of his father, Len Hardy, and had interviewed Eva's aunt Margaret and her husband Ray, who were too old and infirm to come to court, and Eva herself. Her testimony synthesized the information she'd obtained into a portrait of Emory as a boy who got into trouble because of the traumatic effects of his early life and because he followed his older brother. She even said that Emory was afraid of Andy.

It was a doubly clever move: although the prosecutor had kept Eva herself off the witness stand by threatening to prosecute her, the psychologist, in the course of explaining the formative influences on Emory's life, was able to testify about Eva's love for her boys and her helplessness in the face of their father's drinking and his unpredictable rages.

Levenson had also committed one of those acts of civil disobedience that make lawyers on television glamorous and real-life defense attorneys unpopular. He asked the psychologist whether Eva had told her why she could not come to court to testify for her son. Before she could answer, the prosecutor objected, and the objection was sustained. But the question had been asked, and the jury knew who didn't want it answered and knew, also, that Eva had wanted to testify, and that the prosecutor had something to do with why she hadn't. Levenson's move ensured that the unspoken question Andy's jury must have had about why Eva didn't take the stand was answered, more or less, in Emory's trial.

The day before Dave's visit, I puttered fretfully around the house, washing windows and walls, running the vacuum cleaner behind the furniture and in corners where I seldom looked, tossing out old papers, and putting things away. I obsessed over menus for the next day's lunch, before settling on a potato frittata with sugar snap peas and a salad from my garden and an apricot tarte Tatin for dessert. Except for my son Gavin, none of the people I knew from outside had made the trip to Corbin's Landing to visit me in the five years since I'd moved here. Having someone from my past show up at my retreat filled me with performance anxiety.

Just before noon on Friday, Dave's little SUV rolled up the driveway. His bike, on its carrier, was just visible through his back window. Charlie ran ahead of me out the kitchen door, barking fiercely. I walked out to meet Dave, and he gave me a hug, and then bent down to pat Charlie, whose reserve lasted all of two seconds before his tail began to wag. "Good boy," Dave said, scratching behind his ears. "A corgi, right?" Dave stood up and took in the little house and the land around it, and the view down the hill to the distant ocean, and then turned to me. "*Nice* place. You're looking good, too. Life in the country seems to agree with you."

Dave didn't look much different from when I'd known him in the public defender's office. He was a bicyclist and had that spare, sinewy build that goes with it. His jeans were loose on his skinny legs, and the sleeves of his faded sweatshirt were pushed up, showing tanned forearms with thready muscles under freckled skin. He had always made me feel fat, but then just about everyone makes me feel fat.

I showed him around the place—the sprawling old fig tree and the old apples and pears, planted by some previous owner; the new trees I'd added; the garden inside the deer fence, the lemon and lime shrubs in their tubs on the wide deck Ed had put in for me. The sun on the deck was warm enough that we ate lunch outside. Dave duly admired my cooking and the home-grown peas, though I suspected he would have been almost as happy with a bowl of granola and a protein shake.

Over food, we caught up on each other's lives. Dave filled me in on what was happening among the little community of death-penalty lawyers—who was up now and who was down in the ongoing dominance struggles. "You know," I said, "for a bunch of outcast idealists, I could never figure out how they could be so competitive."

"It's the small club thing," Dave said, between bites of frittata. "The infighting is so bad because there's so little status to fight over."

"Well," I said, "they're not my problem any more." It brought up painful memories, and I changed the subject and asked Dave what was new with him.

Dave had broken up with the girlfriend he'd been with the last time we'd seen each other, but had met someone else. "Does she bike, too?" I asked.

"Now and then," he said. "She's not as into it as I am." A bad sign, I thought.

Dave's PI business had grown, and he'd hired an assistant. "Brad Irwin. Sharp kid, working toward his license. I'll probably have him do some work on this case."

After lunch, we moved inside to work. Dave gave a brief laugh as he looked into my office. "Just like at the state defender's," he said, shaking his head. "I guess some people work better in chaos."

"Sometimes I'd like to just throw a match in here and run," I admitted. "Most of what I have in Andy's case is on this thumb drive," I said, pointing to it, "courtesy of Jim's paralegal."

"Ah, the modern paperless office."

"If only."

We settled down to work at my dinner table.

"I keep thinking of these guys as the Hardy Boys," Dave said, with another, more rueful laugh. "Gallows humor. Jim sees this case as pretty hopeless, as far as guilt goes."

"Great," I said. "Just what we need, support from above."

"Come on, he's probably right about the guilt phase, what with the confession and all. But there's something strange about the release of the third girl, don't you think?"

"We'll have to try to find her and ask her about it— assuming she'll talk to us."

"And the brother—Emory."

"I should take you to meet Andy right away," I said. "And we should both meet Eva."

We talked about witnesses for the mitigation case. We'd definitely need to make trips up to Washington and Shasta City, probably more than once, but it was better to wait to interview people until we had some more paper history.

By the time we finished, it was close to six o'clock. I convinced Dave to stay for dinner, and threw together some linguine with a marinara sauce from the freezer and a salad. I had a glass of wine, but Dave stuck with water. He turned down my offer of the sofabed. "Change of plans. I have a reservation at a B&B in Mendocino, and Marisol is driving up tonight after work to meet me." I was disappointed, but relieved, too, because I had no idea what to do to entertain him. Go to Vlad's pub down the highway for a beer and then sit at home and watch DVDs—that was night life in Corbin's Landing.

As he left, Dave gave me another hug. "See you at the 'Q.' And you take care of yourself." I watched from the door as his car rolled down the driveway and turned onto the road. The sky was clear and still light, though the sun had set. A breeze sighed overhead in the redwood trees like the beat of a giant wing, and in the distance I could hear the rhythm of the surf. After the sound of the car engine faded, I stood outside for a while, unwilling to move inside and filled with sadness and confusion. Seeing Dave again had stirred the fragments of memories, and I felt a raw emptiness inside, an echo of how I had felt when my grief and anger about Terry still made a charred and hollow place inside my chest.

A couple of planets were hanging between the redwoods and the ocean by the time I finally walked back into the house.

9

"Bad day to visit, Monday," I apologized, as I put down the plastic tray, heavy with food, canned soda, bottled water, and coffee. "Visitors on the weekend just about emptied the machines. No hamburgers, so I got you a cheese steak."

Dave, Andy and I were huddled, elbow to elbow, around a tiny table in one of the smaller cages. As we sat, I could see a larger one, empty, across the narrow passageway.

Dave, armed with the information in my notes, did his usual magic. With quiet questions, he drew out the sordid and all-too-commonplace details of Andy's childhood: his father Len's intermittent rages, fueled by alcohol and probably meth; the fear Andy felt when he came home drunk and pissed off and looking for something to blow up about, someone to hurt; the late-night fights between him and Eva, as Andy and Emory lay tensely in their beds, listening to the shouting from their parents' room, the confused thuds and crashes of bodies and furniture, and Eva's crying. There was the Christmas when Len gave Andy and Emory bicycles and then wrecked them in an alcoholic rage when he felt the boys weren't grateful enough. The dog he shot to punish the kids for not cleaning the yard up after it. "I was glad when Dad went to prison," Andy said, "'cause we didn't have to be afraid all the time."

We talked about the murder charges and Andy's confession. I knew from Dobson's notes that Andy had told him the confession was a lie and that he'd confessed to the murders because the officers had played Emory's taped statement and told them they believed Emory's story and had threatened to arrest Eva if he didn't admit to killing the girls the way Emory said he had. "I didn't even know Em killed those girls," he told us earnestly, shaking his head, "and that's a fact. But no one believes me."

Dave asked him why he'd let Nicole, the last one, go. Andy hesitated for a moment. "I had a feeling something was going to happen to her."

"But why?" Dave asked, "If you didn't know what happened to the others?"

Andy looked confused, then downcast. "I don't know," he said. "It was just a feeling…" His voice trailed off.

Dave went back to the confession. "What did the officers say about arresting your mother?" he asked.

"That they didn't believe she didn't know about the girls," he answered. "That she helped us hide from the police. They said they could arrest her, too, and she was as guilty as we were."

"But they didn't arrest her."

"No."

"But you thought they could."

"If they said they could, I figured they could."

We were all a little surprised when the guard came by to tell us the visit was up. Andy had forgotten the ice-cream sandwich I'd bought for him. "Can I have a minute to finish this?" he asked. The guard nodded and went on to the next cell. Andy gave me a grateful smile. "I haven't had one of these in a long time," he said, pulling open the end of the plastic package.

"You think you can still eat it?" I asked, looking dubiously at the sagging plastic wrapper.

"Oh yeah." He leaned his head back, tipped the end of the package to his mouth, and half-drank the contents, stopping every now and then to chew a mouthful of cookie. When he had finished it, he tossed the package delicately into the wastebasket and cleaned his mouth and hands on a brown paper towel from the tray. "Sticky," he said, his mouth still half full.

The guard came back, and Andy backed to the door of the cell to be handcuffed. "I'd shake hands," he said, "but I got ice cream on mine."

"No problem," Dave and I said together.

"See you soon," I added.

"Yeah, see you soon," Andy echoed, as the guard unlocked the padlock and slid the cell gate open. Dave and I followed down the passageway as Andy and the guard, clanking with chains and keys like a pair of Marley's ghosts, walked toward the painted metal door to the cell blocks.

The first of the two gates to the outdoors opened with a metallic clatter. Dave stood back to let me go first into the sally port, then followed me. The first gate rattled shut and the second opened, freeing us into the late-morning sun.

"Well," Dave said, as we crossed the service road, "he seems like a pleasant enough guy."

"He is."

"Not the stereotype of a serial sex murderer," Dave said. "I think he'd be a big disappointment to a TV audience."

"So would we all."

"So," Dave asked, "when do we meet Eva?"

"She's coming down to see Andy a week from Saturday. Could we meet her here in the parking lot and go someplace to talk?"

Dave sighed. "Marisol made plans for us to go with a couple of her friends to Angel Island for a bike ride and picnic. I'll just have to tell her I've got to work."

Something in his tone hinted that Dave's work hours didn't always sit well with Marisol. "She won't be leaving the prison until after two," I said, trying to be helpful.

Dave looked a little less beleaguered. "Well, maybe I can go and just leave early."

10

On the Saturday, Dave's little SUV was at the far side of the visitors' parking lot when I drove in. Eva had told me she drove a blue minivan, and one was parked in the row nearest the door. As I pulled into a space near Dave, he jumped out and walked over to my car.

"How'd the bike ride go?" I asked.

He shrugged. "Didn't go on the ride. They started too late." He changed the subject. "Why didn't Eva testify at Andy's trial?"

"She told me the prosecutor was threatening to charge her as an accessory."

"On what grounds, do you think?"

"My guess is that she gave her boys money to get out of Dodge."

"If she did that, they must have told her something about Nicole."

The idea caught me by surprise. "Jeez," I said, "I hadn't really thought of that."

Dave shook his head. "Whoa—imagine how that must

have gone over. 'Mom, we kidnapped this girl, and she got away, and now we need to leave town fast.'"

I couldn't help coming to Eva's defense. "Maybe they didn't tell her what it was about. Maybe they made up some other reason why they needed to leave town. We don't really know."

"Maybe that's why they didn't prosecute her; they didn't really know, either."

Visitors were trickling into the parking lot, alone or in small groups, and getting into their cars. I saw a woman leave a small knot of people and walk toward the blue van. I motioned to Dave and walked toward her.

"Mrs. Hardy?"

She turned and looked at me.

"Oh, there you are. Ms. Moodie?"

"Call me Jan, please. And this is Dave Rothstein, the defense investigator."

"How do you do?" She stretched a thin, tanned arm out to shake my hand, then Dave's. Her hands were small, with freckles on their backs, the nails cut short. "You can call me Evie; everybody does."

I'm not tall, but Evie was an inch or two shorter than I am. The contrast between her and Andy was striking. She was small-boned, almost birdlike. Her face was without angles and smooth, except for some smile lines around her eyes as she narrowed them in the bright sun, and her complexion was fair, almost as pale as Andy's. Her mouth and nose were small, her eyes blue and a little widely set, like a doll's. Her wavy hair, brown going to silver, was cut in a practical bob. She looked, I thought, like the mother out of a childhood fantasy, waiting in the kitchen when you came home from school, with a glass of milk and a dish of oatmeal cookies.

"Well, it's been quite a day," she said. "I'm always sorry to say goodbye to Andy, but I'm glad to leave that prison."

"Believe me, I understand. How's Andy?" I asked.

"Oh, he's as good as always. He's always so pleased to get a visit. I wish I could get here more often, but it's a long way, and it's gotten so expensive, with gas prices and all. Two hundred and twenty miles. I started at seven this morning to get here by twelve. Then I stay in Sacramento tonight and go see Emory tomorrow and drive back, so's I can be at work on Monday morning."

"What kind of work do you do?" I asked.

"I keep the books at the Sunnyside Center. It's an old-age home. And most weekends I wait tables at Mary's, in Redbud. Helps make ends meet."

I got the feeling that she was waiting for a word of sympathy. "You work awfully hard," I said.

"I do what I can."

There wasn't much point in standing in the parking lot making conversation, so I suggested Gaia's Garden as a place where we could talk.

"You lead the way," Evie said.

At the restaurant, we settled ourselves in a booth far enough away from the nearest occupied table that we could talk without being overheard. A waitress—not the girl with the pink hair, but another, just as young, with huge hoop earrings and a Betty Boop face framed in a red-streaked bob—took our orders. I had iced tea and a Greek salad and Dave ordered black coffee and a vegie burrito. Evie gave the girl a bright smile and said she'd just have coffee, thank you. When I asked her if she wanted something to eat, she shook her head. "My doctor keeps telling me I should eat more, but I just don't have much of an appetite. Never have. Anyway, I had lunch with Andy. He made me eat one of those cheeseburgers with him."

"He does love those, doesn't he?"

"That's what he always wants. This time he really wanted me to have one, too. He said he didn't think I was eating enough."

"He really cares about you," I answered.

"I couldn't finish it," she said.

Betty Boop brought us our tea and coffee and disappeared again. Evie picked up her coffee mug and drank, holding it in both hands as if to steady it. "The place I work at— Mary's—looks a little like this. You should stop there if you come up. The girl who runs it, Carol Ann, her mother's a patient at Sunnyside. She says I should quit my job and come work for her full time. Said I'd make better money, and she's probably right. But I waitressed for a while when Len was in prison, and I wouldn't want to go back to it full-time. Two mornings a week is plenty." She took another sip of her coffee. "But you wanted me to tell you about Andy."

"Yes—and no," I answered. "We'd like to learn as much as we can about his family, too."

She gave me a questioning look from across the table. "That's what Mr. Christie said. But I don't understand why. You all said something about getting Andy a new trial, but I just couldn't follow it all. I don't know all this legal stuff." She shook her head. "You'd think I should, after all of it I've been through."

"What we're trying to do here," Dave said, "is show that Andy's trial lawyer, Mr. Dobson, didn't do a good enough job of representing him at trial. We have to find helpful evidence that Dobson could have put on and didn't, and show it to the state and federal judges. Information about Andy and his family can help show his human side, show that there were things about him and the influences on him in his life that might have made the jury sympathize with him and decide he didn't deserve the death penalty. The sort of thing Mr. Levenson did at Emory's trial."

"Oh," she said, more out of politeness than understanding, I thought.

"So we're looking for any information we can find that might help Andy," Dave went on. "I don't want to embarrass you or anything, but did you have any medical problems while you were pregnant with him?"

I wasn't sure about beginning with anything quite so intimate, but Evie seemed delighted to have someone interested in her travails. She bent confidingly toward Dave and me. "Morning sickness. I was so sick with both the boys. Couldn't keep anything down for months. I didn't gain much weight either time."

"How was Andy's birth?"

"Hard. I was in labor for thirty hours with him, and he was born with the cord wrapped around his neck. They had to give him oxygen because he wasn't breathing. He was a big baby, though, nine pounds."

So, I thought, *Andy could have suffered some kind of brain damage from lack of oxygen during his birth.* As far as I could tell, Dobson hadn't done anything to explore that possibility.

"What was he like as a child?" Dave asked.

"Good as gold. I remember he almost never cried as a baby. Emory was the opposite, fussy. He had colic. He cried day and night."

"Do you remember when he began to walk and talk?"

"Andy? I think he was a little late talking. But you know, I sometimes get him and Emory confused, because they were just two years apart."

"What about school?" I asked.

"Oh, lord, Emory was the class clown, always cutting up. Andy was the quiet one."

"And what about childhood illnesses?"

"Just chicken pox. They had shots for mumps and measles."

"Who was your doctor back then?"

"We moved around so much, we didn't really have a regular one. I took the kids to clinics, hospitals."

"Was Andy ever seriously ill?"

"He had pneumonia when he was three, and they put him in the hospital for two days. And he had his tonsils out when he was four. Emory had to have his appendix out when he was ten or eleven."

I asked her for the names of the hospitals and the clinics where the boys had been born and treated, and she told me the names of the ones she could remember. Then I asked her to sign authorization forms so that we could get medical records for her care during her pregnancy, if they still existed. She glanced at the forms, signed them rapidly, and handed them back to me.

Dave and I spent a while asking about the schools the boys had gone to and the towns where the family had lived. She gave us the names of some teachers and counselors but struggled to remember any children who had been friends of Andy's. "He didn't have a lot of friends," she said. "He mostly hung around Emory and them kids. But he always was a good boy. He was never any trouble." If the irony of her words crossed her mind, she gave no sign of it.

"How did he do in school?" Dave asked.

"Not as well as he should have. His teachers were always trying to put him into special ed, but I told them that was a lot of hooey, and they just needed to be more patient with him."

"There was evidence at Emory's trial that Mr. Hardy, your

husband, was pretty abusive," Dave said.

"He was that."

"How?"

"Well, Len drank a lot. And when he drank he got vicious. He'd hit the kids, just backhand them for nothing, really—if they made a noise while he was watching TV or didn't do their chores when he told them to."

"Did he hit you?"

"Oh yes."

"Hard?"

"Hard enough."

"How often?"

"Oh, it must have been at least once a week. He'd get drunk and pick a fight over some little thing. Come home from the bar and wake me up yelling because the boys had left toys in the living room or there wasn't any milk in the refrigerator."

"Were you ever afraid for your life with him?"

Evie thought about this before answering. "Yeah. I was afraid to leave him, 'cause I didn't know what he might do. It was a relief when he went to prison and I could go ahead and get a divorce."

"What was he convicted of?"

"Manslaughter. Killed a man outside a bar."

"When did that happen?"

She thought for a few seconds. "1982, maybe? Andy was seven, and Emory would have been five."

"But he came back to live with you after he got out."

Evie sighed. "Yes—he sweet-talked me into letting him stay with us for a few weeks till he got a job and could get back on his feet, and then I couldn't get rid of him. He just kind of settled in, started ordering me around like we were still married. I called his parole officer about him, and he called Len in, but Len just slick-talked his way out of it, and then he told me if I did anything like that again he'd have some of his friends take care of me. I thought he could, too. He knew some men—bikers—I guess he must have met them in prison. They'd come by the house sometimes to see him."

"So what happened with him?"

"He took off. Walked out one day while I was at work and the kids were in school. Took all his stuff, left his truck at the Greyhound stop."

"Did he ever get in touch after that?"

"No."

"Did you find out where he went?"

"No. And apparently his biker friends didn't know, either, because a couple of them came by looking for him once after he'd left. Said he owed them money."

Dave asked how she'd decided to move to Shasta City, and she said she had a friend who'd moved there and found work in the county hospital. She had called Evie to tell her about a job opening at the hospital for a bookkeeper. Evie drove down there with the boys. She got the job, signed a lease on an apartment and moved in in the space of two weeks.

Dave asked some more questions about how they had liked

Shasta City and how the boys had done in school. "Can you think of any people who might remember them?" he asked.

This seemed to stump her. "I have to think," she said, looking down and a little to one side. After a moment, she looked up and said, "There were a couple of teachers." She gave their names. "And there was a kid named Eddy that used to come over sometimes to see Andy. Emory had some friends, but I can't remember their names. They didn't come around much, 'cause Em knew I didn't like them. They were a bad crowd, and Emory got involved with them and got himself in trouble."

"What kind of trouble?"

She gave a small shrug. "Oh, breaking into cars, joyriding—that kind of stuff. Some of them were doing drugs. Emory wasn't much into that, though." She said the last sentence almost proudly.

"He went to jail, though, didn't he?"

Her mouth grew tense, and she picked up her cup, took a drink of coffee, and put the cup back down on the table before speaking. "Yes. But he was set up by the girl and that so-called friend of his."

"What happened?" Dave asked.

"They *said* Ron kidnapped the girl and he and Emory raped her. But she was Ron's ex-girlfriend, and it was all just he-said, she-said, you know? Em told me she stole money and drugs from one of Ron's friends, and they drove her to someone's house to get the money to pay him back, and she cried rape to get back at them. Emory pled guilty to false imprisonment, because he was looking at seven years in prison and having to register as a sex offender. He was railroaded, pure and simple."

"How long was he in jail?"

"About eight months. He was supposed to serve a year, but he got early release. After that, the police in Shasta City were always on his case, trying to catch him doing something they could arrest him for. That's why I moved out to Mr. Johansen's out in the country—to keep the boys out of trouble."

The incident she described had not been presented at Emory's trial, only the fact of the false imprisonment conviction. A prior rape would have been just the kind of evidence a prosecutor trying for the death penalty would want to put in front of the jury. I asked her. "The prosecution didn't put on anything about that at Emory's trial. That's kind of surprising, under the circumstances."

Evie nodded agreement, then stopped for a moment, as if she was trying to recall the trial. "I can't remember just why they didn't. Emory's lawyer told me—oh, yes, she'd died."

"Who?"

"The girl. A drug overdose, I think he said."

The tension ebbed from Evie's face, and she glanced from Dave to me with her usual cheery expression. She reminded me of a bird—bright, inquisitive, and unreadable behind the polished stones of her eyes. She straightened up in her seat, her hands resting on the edge of the table, and looked at Dave, then at me. "Is there anything more you need to know?" she asked.

"Well," I said, "it would be helpful to know something about your background, your family."

Evie's smile dropped away. "What do you need to know about me for?" she asked. *Damn*, I thought, baffled by her sudden suspicion. *Okay, Dave, do your magic.*

Dave did. "Well, when you're trying to understand how someone got where he did," he said, "it helps to know as much as possible about where he came from. Everybody is influenced by the adults who were around them when they were growing up, and those adults have their own stories that explain how they became who they were. So your upbringing—and Len's, if we can learn about it—may help us find mitigating evidence that might get Andy a new trial."

Evie seemed to relax a little when Dave mentioned getting Andy a retrial. "What do you need to know about me, though?"

Dave took that as an opening. "Let's start with when and where you were born."

"Arkansas," she said.

"Where in Arkansas?"

"Harrison."

"Are your family from there?"

"My mother's folks were. My father was from Iowa."

"Are they still alive?"

"No, they've both passed away."

"Did you grow up in Harrison?"

"No. My dad repaired farm equipment, and we lived in Missouri, Indiana, Nebraska, and then Iowa after he bought a farm there."

We picked our way through the details of her life. She was the second of three children. She had an older sister and a younger brother. Her parents and sister had died in an automobile accident, and she had been sent to live with an aunt and uncle, Margaret and Ray Rakowski, in Canfield, Washington. She didn't know where her brother was. "I haven't heard anything of him in years. I don't even know if he's still alive."

"Did you ever hear where he'd gone after your parents died?"

"To a mental hospital. That's all I know."

"Did you ever try to find him?"

"No, I never did."

"Do you have any other relatives that you know of?"

"None living, far as I know. I remember visiting my grandparents in Arkansas once or twice when I was young, but my parents and them weren't ever close. I don't think I ever met my Aunt Margaret till she came to take me to Washington."

"What about your father's family?"

She thought for a moment. "I don't remember ever hearing anything about them."

When she was sixteen, Evie, then Eva Bowden, had married a boy from Canfield, Jimmy Kitteridge. "We had to get married, because I was expecting. But we weren't suited, really, and we split up after a couple of years."

"Was Andy Jimmy's son, then?"

"Oh no. Andy and Emory were Len's kids. Jimmy's child was Carla."

"Carla?" I asked. The name was new to me; I hadn't seen anything in my reading about Evie having another child.

"Yeah. She didn't live with me growing up. After Jimmy and I split up, his parents took care of her. Jimmy got married again, and then him and his wife—Charlene—raised her after that. Then, when she was fifteen, she decided she wanted to live with me for a while. That was nothing but trouble."

"Why?"

"Lot of arguing and fighting between Len and me and Carla. Carla was Miss Priss, didn't want to do any work around the house. Then I found out that Len was trying to fool around with her. I caught him, one night, coming out of her bedroom. He tried to say nothing was wrong, but I could tell what was happening from the way he looked. He and I had a terrible row. I told him I was going to tell his parole officer, and he could send all the friends he wanted from prison; I didn't care. That's why he left."

"Did Carla go with you to Shasta City when you moved?" Dave asked.

"No—she went back to Jimmy and Charlene, and then she ran away."

"What happened to her after that?"

"She got into drugs. She came to see me a couple of times, and she used to call now and again—usually asking for money. But I haven't seen her in years. I don't know what she's doing now, or where she's living."

"Do you know who might know where she is?"

"You might ask Jimmy and Charlene. I have an address and phone number for Jimmy." She looked in her purse, brought out a small address book, leafed through it, and read the information to us.

I'd been thinking that one of the places we'd have to see was the ranch where the killings had happened. "Tell me," I asked, "is the place where you all were living when the crimes happened still like it was?"

Evie shook her head. "I don't think so. I haven't been out there since we moved away. Mr. Johansen—the man who lived in the trailer there—he died a long time ago. He owned the ranch. I saw in the paper a while ago that it was sold."

Johansen had been living in a house trailer on the property and renting out the house. The police had interviewed him; he was a very old man, hard of hearing and probably a little senile. He said he'd never noticed anything out of the ordinary while the Hardys were living there. I doubted that he'd have told us anything useful if he had lived.

"Did you stay on at the ranch after Andy and Emory were arrested?"

"No longer than I had to. I moved into town as soon as I could find a place."

"That must have been a rough time for you."

"Well, I had to hire a mover. Not that we had that much, but I couldn't handle it all by myself. It was expensive, too."

That was it—nothing about how she had felt about having her two sons arrested for murder and learning that the bodies of their victims were buried in her yard. "Did you have any problems with people over the fact that your boys were charged with this crime?"

She shook her head. "Not that much. The police came to my work a couple times, but I've been there a long time, and my boss didn't give me any trouble about it. Reporters, too, but after a while, the receptionist knew who they were and chased 'em away. Sometimes they called me at home, but I always said the lawyers didn't want me talking to them. Most of 'em let it go, but there was one or two came and knocked on my door. I told them if they wasn't out of my sight in five seconds I'd come after 'em with a shotgun. They got out, okay." Her face crinkled like an apple doll's as she laughed, relishing the memory. Then, as if she had turned off a faucet, the laugh stopped, and she shot me a look, checking my reaction.

I was a little surprised by her sudden shift. "Good for you," I answered, not knowing what else to say.

She looked down at her watch and back at us. "It's getting kind of late. Is there anything more you want to ask about?"

Dave and I looked at each other, and we both shook our heads. "We shouldn't keep you," I said. "You've got a long drive."

I paid the check, and we walked together out to the parking lot. I watched as she climbed into the high seat of the van, backed it out of its space, and drove off.

White clouds of fog were rolling across the Marin hills, and a chill sea breeze scoured the parking lot.

"So, now we've met Mama," I said to Dave, as we hurried, shoulders hunched against the wind, back to my car. "What did you think of her?"

"I don't know," Dave said. "She sure seems loyal to her sons. Won't hear a negative word about them."

"Yeah. She's probably the most devoted mother of a guy on the row I've ever seen. Most of them get a visit from their families once or twice a year, if they're lucky. But she's made that trip every month for fifteen years—for Andy and Emory both."

I paused. "By the way, I'm sorry about spoiling your day with Marisol."

Dave shrugged. "It's what it is. Did you know anything about that prior of Emory's?"

"Just the false imprisonment conviction, not the facts. And I didn't know anything about Carla. It never occurred to me to ask Andy if he had any sibs besides Emory."

"And he didn't bother to tell you," Dave said. "There's always something else out there, no matter how many questions you ask. People hold back the damnedest things."

11

It was true. Investigating an old case often feels like the cliché about peeling an onion; you find layer after layer of information, you cry a lot, and, at the end of it, there's no core of revealed truth. Okay, so it's not quite as bad as that; often you can arrive at an educated guess about the truth from different sources giving you overlapping versions of a story. But the interview with Evie had left me feeling that we were still a long way even from a good guess, and I had few ideas about what to try next.

At home, I let myself in through the kitchen door, greeted by a stiff and sleepy Charlie. It was dark outside; my little house felt chilly, and the missed-call lights on both my telephones were blinking. I cursed them silently and tried to forget them while I put away groceries, fed the animals, and got a fire going in the wood stove.

There was one voicemail on my home phone and two on my office phone. The home one was Ed, offering to lend me a DVD—a legal thriller I'd never heard of—before he returned it to the library. The other two were recorded messages from the San Quentin operator, saying that an inmate was trying to make a collect call.

I figured that Ed was really checking in to make sure I was okay, so I called him back to let him know I was home. Then I turned on my computer and checked my email and read the headlines of a couple of online newspapers. My obligations to the outside world fulfilled, I stoked the stove with several hours' worth of logs and curled up in bed with Charlie and both cats, a cup of hot chocolate with a shot of brandy in it, and an Andrea Camilleri novel, set in a hardboiled modern Sicily, from a small stack of mysteries I'd borrowed the last time the mobile library had stopped at the grade school up the hill.

On Monday morning, I called Corey to tell him I had releases from Evie and give him the names of the schools and hospitals I'd gotten from her. I scanned the releases and emailed them, then walked with Charlie to the mailbox next to the highway to send a set of originals to Jim's office. Back at the house, I read some more of the trial transcript and spent a half-hour in the garden, weeding and tying up wandering pea runners to trellises Harriet had helped me make from string and bamboo stakes. I had just come inside and washed my hands when the phone rang in my office. I picked it up and heard the recorded voice of the prison operator announcing a collect call, and then Andy's voice. I accepted the call.

"Andy, what's up?"

"Hello, Mrs. Moodie. I hope you don't mind my calling you."

"No, Andy, of course not."

He went on as if I hadn't spoken. "I tried a couple of days ago, but you weren't there. I should have known better. I figured after I called you were probably with Mama still."

"Yes, I was."

"Yeah, I figured that. After. Anyway, I just wanted to ask you—uh, did everything go okay?"

He was fishing for something, but I couldn't tell what. "Oh yes," I answered, working at bland cheeriness. "We found one another in the parking lot with no trouble, and we had a good conversation."

"Did you like Mama?"

I wondered what he expected me to say. "Yes. She seemed very nice. I can tell she cares about you a lot."

"I don't know how I'd make it here without her." He hesitated for a second before asking, with what I suspected was an attempt at studied casualness, "What did you talk about, anyway?"

It was time for the lecture on the ethics of investigation. "Oh, Andy, I really can't say. We have a rule when we're working on cases that when we interview someone we don't tell other people what they said, except the lawyers on the defense team."

"Why not?"

"When I talk to someone, I don't want them to think I'm going to tell other people what they said. Otherwise they might be afraid to be honest with me. You wouldn't want me telling other people what we talk about, would you?"

Another brief pause. "But Mama and me, we tell each other everything."

I wondered about that. "That may be true, Andy, but I can't just assume that. If you want to know what Evie said to me, you could ask her, you know."

"Yeah, I guess." He sounded disappointed. "But I have to wait till she visits. You all say I'm not supposed to talk about my case on the phone."

I wondered what he was so worried about. "Your mother wouldn't say anything to hurt you."

"I know." He was silent for a few seconds. "I guess I just wondered—did… did she talk about my dad?"

"C'mon, Andy, that's getting into what I can't talk about."

"Oh. Right. Sorry." He hesitated again, as if trying to remember whether there was something else he wanted to say. "I guess that was all. Thank you for talking to me. Is it okay— uh, can I call you again if I need to ask you something?"

"Sure, Andy. I can't guarantee I'll always have an answer, but yes, please feel free to call me."

"Okay. Thanks. I won't call too often, 'cause I know it costs you money."

"That's really thoughtful, Andy."

"I better go now. Thanks for taking my call. Bye, Mrs. Moodie."

"Bye, Andy. Take care." The line went silent, leaving me wondering what it was Andy wanted to know.

Later that day, Dave called. I told him about Andy's call.

"Sounds like dysfunctional family follies," Dave said. "Everyone wondering whether someone else is telling secrets. Speaking of which, should we go see old Emory now? He's in Folsom."

"Guess so."

"I'll set up a visit," he said. "Any day that's better for you?"

"No, they're all about the same." May as well get it over with, I thought; the prospect of another prison visit wasn't exactly a bright spot on my horizon.

12

And so it was that on a bright morning in June, Dave and I stood before a chipped Formica counter in the waiting room at Folsom Prison. I'd spent the night in a Travelodge in Sacramento, watching cable movies and rereading Emory's confession, and falling asleep, finally, to the city sounds of drunken voices, revving cars, sirens and the occasional odd thump from the rooms above and around me. That morning I'd gotten lost a couple of times in the town of Folsom, trying to find the road to the prison. Since the last time I'd been there, the turnoff had almost disappeared behind new subdivisions, and the town, perhaps in shame, marked it only with a small and carefully hidden sign. From there I drove a half-mile through what looked like pastureland until I reached the blacktop parking lot and saw the visitor intake building and behind it the buildings of the prison, surrounded by high chain-link fences topped with coils of barbed wire and overseen by guard towers.

Prosecutors in death-penalty trials always spend some

part of their closing arguments telling the jury about the good life the defendant will live in prison if they sentence him to life without parole instead of death. While his victims lie in their graves, they say, their killer will eat three meals a day; his laundry will be done for him; he'll be able to lie in bed all day watching television, hang out with his homies, masturbate to skin magazines; and, if he's inclined to improve himself, get a paying job in some prison industry, take classes, sketch and paint.

Emory Hardy was living that idyll.

The cool air of the prison waiting room smelt faintly of dust, old cleaning rags, disinfectant, and children. Outside the scratched glass of the front windows, though, the space above the parking lot seemed to ripple with the heat of the midsummer morning. The heat of summer in the Sacramento Valley was something I could never get used to.

A few families, mostly women and children, mostly black or Mexican, were waiting in line at the counter or seated in the rows of plastic seats. The children's voices reverberated from the pale tan walls and the chipped vinyl floor. The older women's faces were leathery and resigned; the younger women looked hard under the fluorescent lights. Many of them carried the kind of fat people get from too much fast food and not enough exercise. They wore too much makeup or none at all on their tired, heavy faces, and their clothes were cheap: capris or cotton skirts as tight and short as the prison regulations would allow; print blouses; bright-colored flats or running shoes. Several were weighted down with babies and diaper bags.

The portion of the counter where we were standing was marked with a sign saying LEGAL VISITORS—reserved, in other words, for cops, lawyers and investigators—and we were the only people there. On the other side of it a round-faced young woman in uniform, with a blond ponytail and dark roots, took our ID and looked at it and at the handful of change and car keys and other paraphernalia Dave and I had set on the counter in front of her. "You can't bring these pens in," she said, with the finality of someone who knows her word is the last one.

"Oh no—what's wrong with them?" I asked, in my most naive tone of voice.

"We only allow pens with transparent barrels. It's a change in the rules," she explained. Relenting, she reached into a drawer. "A lot of people don't know about it yet. We've got some pencils here." She pulled out a couple and handed them to me. Their points were blunt, but I didn't feel like spoiling the moment by asking her for a sharpener. "Bring them back here when you leave, so I'll have them for the next person."

We were humble and grateful. "Thanks," we both said. "We sure will."

We took off our shoes and walked through the metal detector next to the counter, while she ran our file folders and shoes through the X-ray machine. Then she pushed the rest of our belongings, except for the offending pens, along the counter to us and handed us a pair of laminated tags with something printed on them. "Clip these to your shirts," she said. "Bus stops outside that door." She turned and pointed toward a door straight ahead of us. "You'll be in Section Three."

The lock in the gray metal door clicked open as we approached. We waited in a vestibule while that door closed and a door ahead of us opened. When we emerged, we were outdoors, under a concrete awning. Five or six women were waiting there, day visitors like us. In the shade, the air felt warm and sleepy and smelled like watered soil and roses. Across a service road, in neat, weedless beds, were the inevitable prison rose bushes, pruned by inmate gardeners into tight little spheres and spangled with old-fashioned, heavily scented flowers.

A woman next to me looked at us and asked, "Legal visitors?" She was middle-aged, heavy-set and bottle blond. She had tattoos on her upper arms, and in the V-neck of her red shirt I could see the top of another one in the leathery skin of her chest. Her voice was a whiskey-and-tobacco scarred baritone.

I nodded. "Yep."

"You just missed the last bus," she growled. "So'd I. 'Nother one should be along any minute. Goin' to see my ol' man; he's gonna be pissed that I'm late." She rolled her eyes heavenward and sighed. "God, I could use a cigarette. They don't let anyone smoke now. It's gonna be a long morning."

Dave and I murmured in sympathy, and we all stood in a sort of awkward, companionable silence for a minute, until the next bus pulled up. We climbed into it in an orderly line. The bus was small, old and battered, with gray, unpadded seats. We all sat silent as it threaded its way through a maze of service roads, past low gray barracks and more metal mesh fences topped with concertina wire. The area was empty of people, and despite the sun and cloudless sky above, it seemed dim, almost dark. Anxiety closed around my stomach like an invisible small hand. If anything were to happen here, I was far from the outside world, with no idea how to get out. Dave caught my eye and raised his eyebrows in sympathy. "Kafka, anyone?" he whispered. I nodded, mute.

The bus slowed down. "Section One," the driver said, as he stopped in front of a concrete portico with a double door at the back of it. "Anyone for Section One." Two of the women got up from their seats and sidled down the aisle and out into the shaded porch. The bus started again and meandered for another few minutes until it reached Section Two and let off the tattooed woman.

The bus stop at Section Three looked just like the ones at Sections One and Two. Dave left the bus, with a nod and a "Thank you, sir" to the driver, and I followed behind him, with a wan smile. I found myself thinking that there were times—and this was definitely one of them—when it felt awfully good to have a man around. It didn't even matter that it was Dave—stringy, bike-riding, nerdy, middle-aged Dave. What mattered was that this was a sinister metallic place full of armed men guarding other men, and Dave, whatever his physical appearance, was clearly one of *them*, while I just as clearly wasn't. He was more at ease here than I could ever be, and his relative comfort reassured me in some primitive way.

Someone inside was watching the gray-painted metal door; as soon as we reached it, the lock clicked open with an electric buzz. Dave pulled it wide, and we slipped through and found ourselves in another vestibule, facing another gate. The door closed behind us, and, a second later, the gate unlocked with a loud metallic click, and slid, or rather lurched aside, screeching and clanking. The bare gray foyer on the other side felt anticlimactic. A guard behind a window checked our IDs and buzzed us through yet another metal door into the visiting room.

The room looked like a school cafeteria, only darker, with pale gray walls, a floor of dark green vinyl tiles, and a scattering of plastic tables and chairs. Only two of the tables were occupied. As we stood just inside the door, looking around, a guard in green prison uniform walked out of a door and toward us, a fist-sized knot of keys chinking on his thick leather belt.

"You're here to see Hardy?"

"Yes," we both answered.

"Legal visit, right?"

We nodded.

"Attorney rooms are over here." He gestured to two doors to our left.

We followed him meekly and waited while he unlocked one of the doors and flipped the light switch. The room was fairly small, windowless, and bare, except for a worn and scratched wooden table and three scuffed chairs, and a cheap veneer bookcase holding several Bibles and a couple of Scrabble games.

"Prison furniture," I said to Dave, when the guard had left us. "Where do they find this stuff?"

"I'd like to know who plays Scrabble during legal visits," Dave said.

We'd talked ahead of time about the interview with Emory. Dave was going to do most of the talking. Our major goals for this visit were to put Emory at ease by asking for some of the same information we'd gotten from Evie and Andy, and to get him to sign an authorization for us to get his records—school, medical, prison, jail, whatever. It wasn't likely that he would tell us everything we wanted to know this time—no one ever does—so we hoped to leave him willing to see us again.

A lanky, dark-haired man in the prison uniform of blue jeans and blue chambray shirt appeared at the door, followed by a stocky uniformed guard. Dave and I stood up, and Dave extended a hand. I realized, a little surprised, that Emory was not handcuffed. "Mr. Hardy?" Dave asked.

Emory Hardy lifted his right hand to shake Dave's.

The motion was a little awkward, that of a man no longer accustomed to handshakes. "Yes, sir."

Somehow, without touching him, the guard moved Emory farther into the room and over to a chair. Before leaving, he said from the doorway, "When the door is closed, it locks from the outside. When you're ready to go, or if you need anything, push that button there." He nodded toward a red plastic button on a switch plate on the wall near the door.

"Hey, can I get something to drink?" Emory asked.

"May I?" I said, with an inquiring look toward the guard, who stepped aside obligingly.

"Couple of sodas, Coke or Pepsi, if you can. And maybe a bag of chips?"

I'd spotted the food and drink machines on one wall of the big visiting room. I walked across the echoing space, my footsteps tapping on the hard floor, feeling every second, every foot of distance as if it were doubled. As quickly as I could, I shoved dollar bills and coins into one machine after another, until I had drinks for all of us and a bag of potato chips for Emory. Back in the legal visiting room, I dumped them on the table as the guard pulled the door shut behind me.

Emory opened one of the sodas, took a long swig from it, and set it down with a grunt of satisfaction. "Hot day," he said. "I guess you're Mrs. Moodie. Mama said you'd be coming to see me." He looked around at Dave and me. "So—what can I do for you?"

Emory was darker than Andy and better looking, almost

handsome. His face was thin, with high cheekbones and a light tan. He had dark brown hair, combed, like Andy's, straight back from his forehead, blue eyes almost the color of Evie's, and a neatly trimmed mustache starting to show a bit of gray. He was a bit over forty, but he looked younger, his face still smooth except for tiny lines at the edges of his eyes and mouth. I could still see the boyish young man who had moved the hearts of a jury fourteen years ago. Now, though, he had the watchful, not-quite-direct look and the carefully casual movements of someone who'd been in prison a while, who had learned to get along by not standing out, making no moves that could be misinterpreted, inviting no one to move into his space. His arms, in his short-sleeved blue shirt, were a frieze of blue prison tattoos. I saw the word "Mom," but couldn't make out any of the other patterns.

"I guess you know I'm one of the lawyers for your brother Andy," I said, "and Dave Rothstein here is our investigator."

He looked from Dave to me and nodded once, his face unreadable. "Yeah, I know. Mama told me."

Dave picked up the ball. "Being Andy's brother, you could be an important witness about a lot of things."

Emory leaned back a little in his chair and looked from me to Dave. "I told the police everything I knew at the time. I told Mama, I got nothin' more to say about the case."

Dave shrugged. "Actually, that's okay. We're really looking more for background at this point."

"Like what?" With careful casualness, Emory hinged

himself forward and picked up his soda without looking away from Dave.

"His life. Your life. What Andy was like as a kid, what things were like for both of you growing up. You know, the sort of things your lawyer put on in your penalty phase."

Emory's shoulders relaxed a little. He made an expression of distaste. "Okay. I don't see why I should do him any favors. But sure. I promised Mama I'd try and help. Didn't his lawyer put on all that stuff at his trial?"

Dave glanced at me, passing the conversational ball. "Not like your lawyer," I said. "He didn't put on much at all, just your great-aunt and a jail guard."

"Shit." Emory shook his head in disbelief. "That's Andy. Weren't for bad luck, like they say, he wouldn't have no luck at all. So he didn't even get a decent lawyer."

"Your mom said you'd be okay with signing some authorizations so we could get records," Dave said. Somehow, without my seeing, the records releases and a pencil had materialized in front of him.

"Oh, right. Lemme see 'em." Dave pushed the papers and pencil across the table. Emory made a show of running his eyes over the top sheet and then signed each one slowly, pressing the pencil hard on the page. Then he sat back again in his chair.

"So. What do you want to know about my asshole brother?"

"Don't like him much, eh?" Dave asked.

"Shit, no. He's the reason why I'm here. If it wasn't that Mama asked me, I wouldn't do shit for him."

Dave saw the opening and went for it. Almost offhandedly, he asked, "Don't you think you'd have ended up in prison anyway? I mean you were both involved in kidnapping those girls."

Emory pushed himself back from the table, a look of irritation on his face. "Well, that's what she said, didn't she. The one ol' Andy let go."

"Yeah, I know. I wondered why he did that."

Emory shook his head. "Shit, I don't know. He's just fucking feebleminded."

Dave hesitated slightly, then said, as if bemused, "Maybe. That's what's so crazy about this case. He kills the other two girls, but then just decides to let this one go."

Emory shook his head in a gesture of disgust. "I really don't know why he did it." He opened the bag of chips and poured a small pile onto a paper towel, then looked back at Dave. "Shit, I don't know why I'm telling you any of this. I told you I wasn't gonna talk about the case."

"Sorry," Dave said.

"Okay." Emory gestured toward the chips. "Have some if you want 'em."

Dave let Emory eat a couple of chips and take a drink of his soda before asking his next questions. He started with easy ones like where Emory was born, where he grew up, what schools he went to, that sort of thing. By the time he got to the more personal stuff, Emory was in the rhythm of being interviewed, relaxed, even smiling and occasionally volunteering information.

"So what was Andy like when you were kids?" Dave asked.

"Stupid," Emory said. "Dumb."

"In what way?"

"He just never got it, whatever it was. I mean, I had friends who had big brothers and they looked up to them. Andy was my big brother, but he was more like a little brother. He was an embarrassment. Mama would slap me when I said it, but she knew, too."

"Knew what?"

Emory sat back, with a scornful chuckle. "That he was kind of a retard." He seemed surprised that anyone could have missed it.

"She wouldn't admit it?"

"Yeah. She was always fighting with the school people and moving Andy from this school to that one because they'd want to put him in special ed and stuff. It was like everybody knew but her."

"So what was Andy like?"

Slowly, a story at a time, Dave pulled from Emory a description of Andy from his point of view. Andy losing Emory's bike because he borrowed it and then left it in a park. Forgetting to change his clothes unless someone laid new ones out for him. Getting in trouble when he was with a group of kids shoplifting at a department store—everyone but Andy managed to ditch their stuff when they saw the mall guard looking at them. "God, he was so dumb," Emory said, shaking his head and chuckling. "We could get him to do just about anything. We used to break into places at night—stores, the high school, vacant houses. Andy always wanted to come along on anything I did. So we'd send him in first. We'd tell him, 'You're the advance guard, Andy; you get to tell us if it's safe.' And then when Carla came to live with us, and he wanted to be her boyfriend—God, that was funny! Carla explaining to him that they can't be boyfriend and girlfriend because she's his sister, and he got so embarrassed, he didn't say nothing, just turned bright red and hung his head like a dog." Emory laughed. "I can't believe you got me remembering all this stuff. Just don't tell Mama. She'd be real upset."

Dave and I promised that we wouldn't.

"What do you remember about your father?" Dave asked.

"That he was a sonofabitch." Emory looked hard at Dave, and something like a shiver hunched his shoulders under his loose shirt. "But you know, he was in prison most of the time. And he run out on us after he got out. Mama probably told you that."

"What was he like? Did he drink? Do drugs?"

"He drank, mostly. Did meth, too, after he got out of prison—that's what Mama and Carla said."

"Did he hit you?"

"Yeah, when we were little. After he got out of prison, we were too big and fast for him. Mostly he just sat around all day and drank."

"What about your mom? Did he hit her?"

"Yeah."

"How bad?"

He shifted in his chair and looked down at his hands and then at the table in front of him. I could see his jaw tighten. "Look, I hated him, okay?" he said in a low voice. "He was always pissed off about something. If we got too close, we'd get backhanded or kicked—like a couple of dogs. He'd get into it with Mama—he'd come home drunk in the middle of the night, and if she said anything he'd start yelling and throwing her around. Just stupid stuff."

"Why did your mom stay with him?"

"I don't know—maybe she was afraid to leave him. We were all afraid of him. He was a pretty big guy, and real strong, at least when he was younger. I thought she divorced him after they put him in prison. But for some reason, when he got out, he was just there. Showed up one day and then just sat around the living room, drinking and ordering us all around."

"Did he work?"

"Before prison he worked in construction, building houses. And I think he worked as a bouncer in a bar sometimes, too. That's where he killed a guy—in some cowboy bar."

"What about after he got out? Did he work then?"

"Not if he could help it. I think he did odd jobs sometimes, maybe delivered newspapers now and then, stuff like that. Mostly he just drank his cheap bourbon and coke and felt sorry for himself."

"But then he left."

"Yeah."

"Any idea where he went?"

"No, none at all."

"Have you ever heard from him?"

"Not a word."

"How did you feel about that?"

Emory looked sharply at Dave. "About what?"

"About your father leaving you like that, and never getting back in touch."

Emory's hands clenched into fists on the table in front of him, and I could see his right knee shaking up and down in a nervous rhythm. He opened his mouth as if to say something, stopped, and then started again. "How was I supposed to feel?" he asked angrily. "How—" He backed his chair away from the table. "This is bullshit. I don't know why you're asking me this stuff. I don't want to talk about it. I want to go back to my house." He stood up and pressed the red button near the light switch.

I sat, frozen and unnerved. Dave stood up.

Emory turned back around, and something in our expressions must have impressed him, because he calmed down—not completely, but enough that he looked a little embarrassed about his reaction. "Look, this isn't a good time," he said, shaking his head. "I just need to go back."

"It's okay, man," Dave said. "We can talk another time if you'd like."

"Yeah—yeah. Whatever."

Emory sat down sideways in his chair, not looking at us, and we waited in awkward silence until, with a distant clink of keys, the guard finally showed up at the door. "Thanks for the chips and soda," Emory said flatly, with a quick look back at us as he walked out of the room.

Dave and I cleaned up the table, picked up our papers, and headed for the guard's booth near the exit.

"Sorry," Dave said.

"What for?" I asked. "Who could have known he'd go off like that?"

We were both quiet on the bus and while we signed out and returned our laminated badges to the guard in the reception area. Outside, as we walked to our cars, the air felt like a hot washcloth. Dave said, "Let's get lunch. I saw a Mexican place on the way in that looked okay."

Over plates of soft tacos and glasses of iced tea, we talked about the visit and gradually began feeling a little better about it. Emory had signed releases and given us some helpful information and had, at the end, at least left the door open for us to come back. Neither Dave nor I felt very chatty, though. I was feeling the way I often do at the end of a witness interview: as though a truckload of words, gestures, facial expressions and body movements had just been dumped in a heap into my brain. I needed time to sift through what I remembered and to try to figure out how any of it might connect to anything else I knew about the case.

"Cheer up, kid," Dave said, reaching across to give my forearm a squeeze. Dave's hand was warm and tanned, with thick fingernails and a sprinkling of rough black and gray hairs on its back—reassuringly male, I thought, a little surprised at how comforting it felt.

"Thanks," I said. "I'm okay—just kind of tired."

He squeezed my arm again and pulled his hand back. "Good food," he said, picking up a forkful of rice and black beans.

We made some small talk about news and politics—things that were seeming more abstract to me, the longer I lived in Corbin's Landing. And Dave commented that I looked calmer than I had when I lived in Berkeley. "I feel better," I agreed.

"You should try cycling," he said. "Works the mental stress right out of you. Are you going to eat that last taco?"

"No," I said, pushing my plate toward him. "Maybe I could if I took up biking." I watched wistfully as he ate it in three or four bites.

When I reached home that night, thoroughly road-weary, the smack of cold sea fog on my face was like heaven.

Charlie was beside himself with joy, bouncing and barking as he rushed out the gate of Ed's yard. "Did you miss me?" I cooed in my dumbest "good-dog" voice, and he ran back and forth between me and the car until I opened it and hefted him into the back. I marveled again at the goodness of dogs; if my significant other was always running off and leaving me with neighbors for days at a time, I'd be barking a much different tune.

13

Somehow Jim found the time, between court appearances, to call and tell me he'd retained Nancy Hollister, the psychologist he had mentioned at our first meeting, to prepare a psychosocial history on Andy and his family. He suggested that since she lived in Marin County, "up your way," I should meet with her to brief her about the case. I didn't bother to tell him it was a good three-hour drive from my place.

After a round or two of phone tag, Dr. Hollister and I agreed to meet at her home in the early afternoon the following Wednesday. To make the trip worthwhile, I set up a visit at San Quentin that morning with Andy.

Andy seemed mildly pleased when I told him about the new person who would be working on his case, but what he really wanted to talk about was a new prison program that let inmates special-order pizza from Costco every few months. "It's next week. Mama put money on my books to buy one. I ordered Italian sausage and pepperoni. Man, it's been a long time since I've had pizza." He sighed in happy anticipation.

After a lunch of vending-machine burritos and a Diet Pepsi, I left Andy to his pizza dreams and set out to find Nancy Hollister's house in a woodsy neighborhood of older houses and winding streets that looked as if it was being slowly absorbed into the oak forest around it. The roads twisted and turned back on themselves among gnarled trunks and grasping branches until I began to wonder whether I should have brought a ball of twine to mark my path. Even with my GPS tracker, I made a couple of wrong turns before finding the house, almost invisible behind an overgrown hedge.

In the hills, away from the bay, the afternoon was warm. Dr. Hollister, slender and elegantly casual in a long linen dress, offered me iced tea and put a plate of madeleines and a bowl of hulled strawberries on the dining-room table. The room was quiet and uncluttered, and French doors looked out onto a wide deck shaded by an oak tree, and a lawn fringed with beds of flowers, rosebushes, and flowering vines.

"This is lovely," I said, lamely.

"Thank you," she answered. "I like working here. I only go to my office to see patients these days."

I handed her the binders of case materials I'd made, and she thanked me. "I know Corey likes the high-tech stuff," she said, a little apologetically, "but I'm still a paper person. I like to mark things up and put sticky notes on them."

When I called her "Dr. Hollister," she said, "Please, call me Nancy." We sat at the table and drank our iced tea and ate strawberries and a madeleine apiece. She said Jim had talked with her and given her some basic information about the case. I filled that in with more detail and told her what Dave and I had learned from our interviews with Andy, Emory, and Evie.

"That's about as far as we've gotten at this point," I said, "and Jim—well, I guess he's been too busy to really give us much in the way of direction."

Nancy nodded. "I know Jim. I've been working with him on another case, and I almost didn't take this one because of it. It hasn't always been a comfortable working relationship; it's so hard to get him to engage. He's a nice guy, though, and a good courtroom lawyer, I'm told."

"Good to hear that," I said.

"I think he's overextended," she went on. "Just one of those people who can't say no to a case. One of the things he said to talk me into taking this one was that this time he had second counsel who'd be available to work with me. He was very complimentary about you."

She smiled, I thought hopefully, and I tried not to look as uncomfortable as I felt. *I could use another madeleine*, I thought, and then decided it would just make me feel worse.

We talked a little more about the case and agreed to meet again in a couple of weeks, after Nancy had had a chance to digest the material I'd given her and to present Jim and me (or, as it was starting to seem, me) with some observations and impressions about Andy's psychological makeup and possible risk factors and stressors in his background. As we said our goodbyes at her front door, I silently damned Jim and kicked myself for being so easily manipulated.

A week later, Corey called me, as I was reading transcripts from a murder appeal I'd agreed to take on before taking Andy's case. "How are you?" he asked.

"So-so," I said.

"Just that? Well, if it will make you feel better, I have actual progress to report. Jim asked me to call you. He's been talking with the district attorney in Shasta City about discovery. The DA has scanned a lot of files, and Jim wants to go up there next week to meet him and look at the trial exhibits and drive out to the ranch where the crimes happened while he's there. He wants to know if you can go next Tuesday or Wednesday."

I looked at my calendar; both days were blank. "Either day is fine," I said.

"Great. I'll let him know. I think he wants Dave Rothstein, too, so I'll have to call him and get back to you. Oh, and we got Mr. Hardy's high-school transcript and the court file of his father's manslaughter case."

"Great!" I said.

"All in a day's work," Corey said modestly. "Mr. Hardy is, shall we say, not a candidate for the academic decathlon."

"Really! I can't say I'm surprised after what Emory said about him."

"I guess. I'll scan and email them." He rang off and called me again an hour later to confirm that Dave was available and that the meeting was set for the following Tuesday.

I called Ed and left him a voicemail about dog-sitting again. "I'm going to owe you more dinners than I will ever be able to afford," I said. "You've got to get another dog, so I can start paying you in kind."

14

I'd been to Shasta City before, but not in a long while. The last time was to talk to the family and friends of Clay Van Arsdale, a Vietnam veteran who'd killed his ex-wife and her boyfriend in a meth-fueled rage. Neither a psychologist's testimony that Clay was suffering from severe PTSD nor wrenching descriptions from army buddies about the bloody jungle warfare he'd lived through managed to move a Pomo County jury to give him life without parole, and it didn't seem to matter much to the people he'd grown up with, either.

One of Clay's uncles had informed me, from the porch of his bungalow, that Vietnam PTSD was just a bunch of bull. "Boy was just weak," he said, "wanted to live that life, do drugs, and now he's trying to make excuses for what he did." His wife, a mousy woman with frizz-permed hair and an American Gothic face, had stood behind him and added, "It just killed his poor mother, what he did."

"Go back inside, Etta," her husband had ordered without

turning to look at her, and she had disappeared in silence from the doorway.

That was pretty much how everyone we talked to had been, including the jurors. Pomo County was a place where the myth of the frontier endured, where men hunted and women home-schooled, where messing up your life was your own damned fault, and where the current district attorney had sought the death penalty in eleven cases in the past eight years and had gotten it in all eleven. Given this background, I was surprised that Jim had gotten any cooperation from the district attorney's office. But they had agreed to give him discovery of their files of both Andy and Emory's cases.

Shasta City was nearly a day's drive from my place, so I drove up there the afternoon before. Corey had reserved rooms for all of us at the same motel, and we met for breakfast the next morning at a Denny's, to plan the day's activities. We had an appointment in the morning to look at the exhibits from the trial and another after lunch with the deputy district attorney. While Jim and I were at the DA's office, Dave would stop at the jail, police station, and medical examiner's office in a search for records and reports. Time permitting, we would also drive out to the old ranch where the murders had happened.

The Pomo County courthouse was a handsome old stone building in what had once been Shasta City's business district, before it had been abandoned for the outlying rings of newer suburbs and shopping malls. At some point the courthouse had been expanded with an ugly institutional annex, and several blocks around it had been turned into a civic center of four-square buildings of gray concrete, some topped with bristling fields of antennae, and all landscaped with durable, rubbery hedges, spongy green lawns, and spindly shade trees.

Around the civic center, rehabbed Victorian buildings with antiques stores and restaurants on their retail floors and law offices upstairs shared city blocks with mid-twentieth-century cinderblock bunkers housing bail bondsmen, taquerias, thrift stores, and storefront churches.

The sun was already hot on our shoulders and pulling humid, earthy air from the overwatered lawns as we walked from the visitors' parking lot to the courthouse. At the main door, a sheriff's deputy at the metal detector looked out at us and asked, "Attorneys?" When we nodded, he motioned us into a separate lane, letting us bypass the line of tattooed bikers, massive women in flip-flops and spandex tank tops, and sallow-faced tweakers filing through the general public metal detector.

Mr. Ferris, the clerk in charge of storing trial exhibits, had his own office on a side hallway in the old part of the courthouse, behind a varnished oak door with a frosted glass panel. He had pulled the boxes of exhibits from Andy's trial, seven of them, and he pointed to them where they stood in two stacks pushed against one wall of the L-shaped office he shared with another clerk, a spare desk, and a copy machine. Apparently the county's budget didn't allow for enough storage boxes; these were a random collection of cheap banker's boxes and copy-paper boxes. After almost fifteen years, they looked frayed and softened.

Mr. Ferris greeted Jim, Dave and me like the curator of an obscure and neglected museum, showing the collections he had painstakingly stored for those rare occasions when someone actually wanted to see them. He and his deputy, a plump young woman who had decorated the wall beside her desk with a collage of snapshots of children and cats, occasionally looked over with mild curiosity at the objects we pulled from the crumbling boxes: folded paper diagrams, 8 by 10 enlargements of crime-scene photos, fingerprint cards, evidence envelopes, papers, and a few seemingly random objects in frayed brown paper bags—a black fake leather purse with rusting chrome grommets; a woman's red high-heeled sandal, its straps brittle with age; a thin wallet of shiny blue plastic.

We went through one box at a time, setting it on the empty desk, unfolding drawings on butcher paper, peering at clear plastic bags and vials, and handing each other photos. Dave photographed exhibits with his phone, and Jim and I checked each one off against the list of trial exhibits from the court file. There were two numbers on most of them, one from Andy's trial and another from Emory's. The manila envelopes containing photographs and small objects were fragile and beginning to tear along the seams, and everything smelled a little musty. After about an hour, my fingers were gray with old dust, and I felt as if a thin coating of it was lining my throat and sinuses and stiffening my hair.

Some of the exhibits made my heart sink: a portrait photo of a smiling round-faced, dark-haired girl in a V-neck sweater, the sort of picture that high-school yearbook photographers take, but fading with age and dog-eared on its edges; a green plastic barrette; a Disneyland keychain; a worn and faded color snapshot of a smiling baby girl. I remembered from the transcript of Andy's trial that one of the victims, Brandy Ontiveros, had a daughter and that Brandy's grandmother had brought a photo with her to the trial. The toddler in the picture would be about seventeen by now. I wondered what her life had been like and whether she looked like the girl in the yearbook photo.

Given the nature of the crimes, the crime-scene and autopsy photos were pretty bland: the judges in both trials had sustained defense objections against showing the jurors full views of the women's decomposing bodies in the ground or on the autopsy table. There were photos showing the ranch where the bodies were found and the graves themselves, and lab photos showing the victims' clothing and other things—a bracelet, an artificial fingernail—recovered from around the bodies. The pathologist hadn't found any obvious injuries to either of the victims; Andy and Emory's confessions were the only evidence of how the women had died.

* * *

We were finished with the exhibits by lunchtime. Jim called the district attorney's office to make sure our appointment was still on, while I arranged with Mr. Ferris to have photocopies made of some of the papers and photos.

Jim treated Dave and me to lunch at a restaurant a block or so from the courthouse—one of those old-fashioned places lawyers and businessmen seem to like, with a full bar and cushioned banquettes. As we walked there, the air above the sidewalk felt like the inside of a clothes drier. *No wonder the people up here think they're tough*, I thought. The combination of blast-furnace summers and mountain winters would have culled the weak from among the early settlers.

A little after one, Jim and I said goodbye to Dave as he left on his search for police and property records, and walked over to the district attorney's office, in the courthouse annex. It seemed the county was trying to economize with air conditioning, and the tiny waiting room, bland as a doctor's office, was cooled just enough to feel vaguely uncomfortable. A cheap table fan on the floor behind one of the chairs made a barely discernible movement of air in the room.

The young woman who greeted us at the receptionist's window was blond and thin, with a face a little too long to be generically pretty. We told her we had an appointment with Deputy District Attorney Ibarra, and she made a phone call and told us he'd be right out.

Roberto Ibarra came out the door within a minute. He was fairly short—about five foot seven—and looked to be in his mid-thirties. He shook hands with each of us, and held the door as we walked into the suite. "Everything is in the library," he said, "this way."

We followed him in single file. Offices lined the window walls, and secretaries and paralegals worked in cubicles in the central area, among rows of file cabinets and bookshelves.

As we walked, Ibarra explained, "We made copies of the tapes and scanned all the paper files we have except the work product material. I hope it's all here, but the case is really old. Ross Dannemeier retired before I started here."

"How did you get assigned to pull the files?" Jim asked.

"Murder case I was working on settled just before you called, so I was the one with some free time. Lucky me." He shrugged. "Actually, my secretary did all the work of getting them from storage and having them scanned. All I had to do was go through and pull out Dannemeier's notes."

He showed us into the library, which seemed to double as a conference room, judging from the long table down its center. Tall bookshelves of dark wood, filled with law books, lined three walls. Most of the fourth wall was a floor-to-ceiling window shaded with vertical blinds.

On the table sat eight banker's boxes labeled with the names HARDY, M. AND E. and the Supreme Court number of the case; a little apart from them was another box holding a dozen cassette tapes and a couple of CDs in paper envelopes.

Ibarra picked up a thin file folder and turned to Jim. "This is what I pulled out," he said. "I can't copy it for you, but I thought you might want to see that it's all just notes, nothing else."

Jim leaned over while Ibarra opened the folder and riffled through the sheets of yellow legal paper inside it. He nodded, and Ibarra closed the folder. Work product—an attorney's private notes and memos reflecting his thinking about the case—was something neither side had to give to the other in discovery proceedings. True, we had only Ibarra's word that that's what was in the folder, unless Jim wanted to insist that Ibarra itemize it in a privilege log and ask a judge to read it and see whether he was telling the truth. All that would come later, if Jim filed a formal motion. For now, it seemed we had plenty to keep us busy, and it was unlikely that the thin folder of notes had anything in it we needed right away.

We spent the next half-hour or so looking through the boxes and comparing what was in them to an inventory Corey had made of Dobson's case files. Dobson's files, when he gave them to Mark Balestri, had been a mess. Between alcoholic disorganization and moving his office a year or so after the trial, he had lost a lot of his papers from Andy's case. When Mark Balestri had driven to Shasta City to meet him and pick up his files, what Dobson had found to give him was piled, in no particular order, in three boxes. When Corey had described them to me over the phone, I could almost see him rolling his eyes: two boxes of transcripts and another one of draft motions, parts of police reports, notes on yellow legal pads, loose papers, and file folders whose labels didn't relate half the time to what was in them.

When we'd finished, Jim took our box of tapes, and Ibarra led us back to the elevators.

As we emerged into the sun and the baking sidewalk in front of the building, Jim said, "Do you still feel up to driving out to the ranch?"

"Sure."

"I'll call Dave." He pulled out his cellphone, while I went to fetch my car. He seemed more into the case than I'd expected, and I began to figure him for one of those trial lawyers who are at their best when they can see the physical evidence and meet witnesses face to face. A lot of them, it seems to me, are like that: impatient with reading and organizing information, and much more at home in court and in the field. I'm not that kind of lawyer, never have been, which is why I ended up doing appellate work and being the backup on legal teams.

My husband Terry had been one of the rare trial lawyers who did both types of work well, who spent evenings and weekends poring over the minutiae in police and lab reports and reading technical articles on forensic evidence, but who also shone in negotiations and in court. He wasn't flashy: in court, he came across as low-key and controlled; his brilliance came through in the way he seemed to have prepared for every contingency and to be a step ahead of the prosecutor at every turn of the trial. Judges were impressed by his encyclopedic knowledge of the law and the facts of his case. Jurors came to believe his evidence and arguments after seeing that whenever the prosecutor or a witness disagreed with him he was always right. On the other hand, judges and jurors also like lawyers with the type of high energy and charm that Jim possessed. I imagined he did well in trial.

15

The ranch where the Hardys had lived was about twenty miles from Shasta City. The road out of town tracked the growth of the city, passing old, tree-lined neighborhoods, strip malls, newer subdivisions behind sound walls, country markets, junk yards, dive bars with dirt parking lots, tired motels, Assembly of God and Jehovah's Witness churches, and farms, until it became a two-lane highway winding through the Sierra foothills. Cattle or sheep grazed on straw-colored hills dotted with dark green oak trees and outcroppings of gray rock, and once in a while a rutted dirt road made a pale gray line from the highway to a distant compound of ranch buildings—usually a long, low barn, sheds, an original white Victorian farmhouse, and a mid-twentieth-century house where the family now lived. Here and there, dense stands of green brush marked the channels of invisible creeks. The glare of the afternoon sun leached the colors from the landscape.

We crossed another highway with a sign for Redbud, where

Evie lived now, and then passed a place marked on the map as Johnston, which consisted of a bar, a market, a hardware store, and a few houses hidden behind peeling picket fences and overgrown trees. At the far end, opposite a deserted gas station, we made a right turn down a smaller road.

The area had been mostly ranch land when the Hardys lived here, but that had changed. Now there were fences along the road and a new driveway every few hundred feet, and new houses, barely visible, set well back from the road among tall oak and pine trees. There were white fences, prefab barns, and paddocks, some with horses, and some of the driveways had barred gates. A couple of miles down, the road crossed a culvert, and a graveled track led off to the left. The house number, on a sign below the mailbox at the entrance, told us that this was the place we were looking for.

"11734," Jim read. "What did they call this—the Cantwell ranch?"

"Yeah," Dave said. "But I don't think the Cantwells had owned it for a long time. The old man who rented the house to Evie was named Peter Johansen."

"He's not still here, is he?" Jim asked.

"No," Dave answered. "He died a couple of years after the trials. I looked up the property records today; the ranch was sold in a probate sale and then sold again, to a Carl and Emily Bolton. Husband and wife."

The gravel road had a gate, but it was open. Manzanita and coyote bushes lined both sides of the track, but a strip of shoulder on each side was cleared of brush and seemed to have been mowed fairly recently. The road curved to the left, and we emerged from the bushes into a large clearing, where the road ended, making a circle around a huge old walnut tree. To its right was a stretch of mowed grass, with a row of young evergreen trees along it and a new prefabricated shed behind them; past that and ahead of us stood an old apple orchard. Behind that, the ground rose into a low hill, planted with young grapevines.

The house and a two-car garage, both newly painted pale yellow with white trim, were on the left. The house was a nineteenth-century farmhouse, two stories high, with a peaked roof with two gables and a bit of gingerbread woodwork along the eaves. The garage—a Lexus SUV parked in front of one of the doors—looked as though it had once been a carriage house.

A golden retriever ran to the edge of the driveway and stood twenty feet away from us, barking. Behind it, a man and woman walked toward us around the side of the house.

"Can I help you?" the man said, as he came within earshot. He was gray-haired, but trim and fit-looking, in jeans and a pale green polo shirt. The woman, ash-blond hair under a straw gardening hat and white shirt tucked into faded jeans, hung back a dozen or so feet behind him.

Jim was the first out of the car. He walked over to the man and said a few words, then they shook hands, and all three of them looked over at us. Dave and I took that as a signal to join them, shaking hands with the couple. The man introduced himself. "I'm Carl Bolton; this is my wife Emily."

After we exchanged names, he continued his conversation with Jim. "Yes, I knew about it. The realtor told us, and people in town mention it sometimes. Terrible, really. But to get to your question, I'm not sure where the bodies were buried; Carol, our realtor, wasn't sure herself. She thought a clearing in the woods beyond the orchard. We walked out there with her once—I guess morbid curiosity got the better of us. But there isn't anything to see any more. It's all grown over."

"We have some photographs of the site and a map from an old police report," Jim said, "but it looks like this area has changed quite a bit since then." He looked around, approving. "This is a nice-looking place; you must have really fixed it up."

"Thanks," the man said. "We bought it a few years ago, with the idea of retiring here someday. Did a lot of work on it. We live in Sacramento, and we're usually only here on weekends. You're lucky you caught us."

Jim was leafing through a stack of crime-scene photos as he listened. He pulled one out and showed it to Carl. "Here's a shot from a distance, shows the barn in the background. Do you know where that might be?"

Carl bent down to look at it, looked up again, and pointed. "It was over there, behind where the storage shed is. We had the barn torn down, I'm afraid. It was in bad shape, and Emily said it gave her the willies." He looked at his wife solicitously.

Emily caught his eye and took her cue to speak, looking at each of us with a practiced social gaze. "I feel silly saying it," she said, with an apologetic half-smile, "but I really did feel like there were ghosts in that barn."

"It looked that way, for sure. The whole place was pretty rundown," Carl said, with a proprietary sweep of his arm. "If you want to look around, I'll walk with you out back, where Carol thought the bodies were found."

We crossed the oval made by the driveway, then walked along the orchard's edge. Carl pointed toward the grapevines. "That all used to be pasture land," he said. "There's a creek over there, and a lot of brush grows around it." He turned and followed a dusty, rutted tractor path along the edge of the vineyard. To our left was a verge of mowed grass, yellow and dry, and beyond that a leaning old fence of narrow wooden slats.

A couple hundred feet down the track Carl stopped at a break in the fence. Beyond it I could see a few oak trees, and beyond them the creekside brush. Carl stopped and turned toward the grove of trees. "This is where she said they were. Careful—there's some poison oak in there."

There wasn't much to see, just a sun-dappled clearing surrounded by oak trees. Dead leaves and years of winter rains had smoothed over any disturbance in the contour of the earth that might have shown where a grave had been dug out. The shadows of the trees around the clearing were lengthening into it, but the air was hot and still except for an occasional puff of wind—hardly a breeze—that lifted more than moved it.

Thinking of the history of the place and the crime-scene photos, perhaps I ought to have felt something—a chill, a catch in the throat. But I didn't. It was just a clearing. Cows in the old pasture had probably gathered in its shade on hot afternoons. Children might have played in it, high-school kids might have sat there, none the wiser, smoking pot and drinking beer. When you thought about it, human history was full of such places. People have killed and buried each other in the woods for millennia, and the forest, after a few years, covers all the evidence, taking it back to itself.

Dave pulled out his phone and began shooting pictures. Emily spoke, her voice lowered. "It's funny, but I've never felt odd out here. Not like the barn."

"Do you need to see any more?" Carl asked politely. I sensed that he, at least, was impatient to leave the spot.

We followed him and Emily back out of the clearing. Carl said, "I understand that these men on death row need lawyers, but to be honest, I don't know how you defend those people."

Jim gave him the thirty-second answer. "Someone has to stand up for the underdog," he said. "And I've never believed in the death penalty—at least, not as long as I've been a lawyer."

"Seems to me they gave it to the right people this time," Carl said.

We walked through the orchard, picking our way over the ploughed, uneven ground between the trees. Back at our car, we thanked the Boltons. "No problem," Carl said. As we drove around the circle and headed out toward the highway, he and Emily turned and walked together, heads bent in conversation, back around the house. Growing old together. I felt a twinge of resentment.

"Nice place," Dave said, as we drove back down the road toward Johnston.

"Too remote for me," Jim answered. "I can't imagine living someplace so isolated. As a crime-scene view, that was kind of a waste of time, don't you think?"

"We had to do it, though," Dave said. "You never can tell. Pity they pulled the barn down."

"Well, what now, kids?" Jim asked. "Anything else we can do here before heading back to town?"

"I figured I'd stay another day or two," Dave said. "I have addresses for the bailiff and a couple of other people, and I may be able to track down some teachers."

"Unless you need me to stay," I said to him, "I think I'll drive home tomorrow morning. Maybe do some research at the library tonight, if it's open."

"It is," Dave said. "I'm headed there myself."

"I have a ticket on an eight o'clock flight tonight," Jim said. "Gotta be in court tomorrow at nine."

The conversation turned back to the couple at the ranch. "Nice to have that kind of money," Jim said.

"What do you suppose he does?" Dave asked.

"He's a doctor," Jim said. "Sports medicine. He told me he's the doctor for the—" Jim recited the name of some team I didn't recognize, and he and Dave launched into a conversation about sports.

I played solitaire on my phone.

16

The Shasta City main library had been a classic Carnegie library, but the original building was now a children's wing, enfolded and dwarfed by a larger modern annex. The familiar smell of books and copy-machine toner permeated the cool air inside, and the carpeted floors and rows of bookcases absorbed the small sounds of people working at the counters and tables. At the reference desk, Dave got directions to the newspaper archives on microfilm, and I asked for high-school yearbooks. The librarian, a pretty dark-haired woman, led me to a locked case. "We have most of the yearbooks from Shasta City High, back to 1940, I think. Do you know which years you want?"

I'd been doing rapid arithmetic in my head, trying to calculate the years when Andy and Emory would have been in high school. "Let's see—1989 through 1996 I think." She bent down and ran her finger along the shelf of tall, narrow books, in various shades of fake-leather binding. From them she pulled out eight and handed them to me.

I sat down at a table nearby, stacked the yearbooks to my right and pulled a steno pad and pen from my shoulder bag. I took the top one from the stack and opened it. It was called *The Mountaineer*, the title sketched on the cover in gold leaf script above a few lines that suggested, in a minimalist way, the contours of an alp and a hiker with a Swiss-style hat and a staff.

Inside, I looked for photos of Andy and Emory and the people Andy had named as his friends, among class pictures, group shots of athletic teams and clubs, and the little individual portraits of seniors. It was sobering to look at them, so young, smooth-skinned, and pretty or gangly, with their nervous smiles or tense stares into the camera, their outdated clothing and hairstyles. I wondered what life had brought to Billy Hofscheier, looking stolidly out from the page from under a blond crew cut, or Cecilia Cuevas, with her sharp, small face and forward-swept hair. They'd be heading into middle age now, having, most of them, set the course for their lives. Working at the job they'd retire in, maybe, or taking over their parents' business or ranch, raising kids as old now as they were in these pictures. Or drinking too much and watching their lives turn into a bitter parody of whatever they had dreamed of at seventeen; or falling into the lowest circle of drugs and jail. *Oh, come on*, I told myself; most of them would be pretty content with how things were turning out for them. They'd be getting a bit broad in the face and thicker in the waist, living in clean, well-kept houses with comfortable furniture, doing household projects or going fishing or camping on the weekends, volunteering for their churches, helping out their parents, worrying about their kids. Solid people. Baffled— if they thought about it—that anyone like Andy or Emory could have walked among them.

I turned pages, jotting down the names of teachers as I found them. I found both Andy and Emory in the freshman class photo for 1992 and the sophomore class of 1993, but not in any club or team pictures. In 1994, Emory was a junior, but Andy was still in the sophomore picture. Emory's individual photo appeared in the graduating class of 1995, but Andy's wasn't there. That fit with what we had in his school records, that Andy had dropped out of high school in what amounted to his second sophomore year.

I made copies of several pages, brought the book back, and headed over to the local history section. There, I leafed through a different set of annuals, city directories with glazed paper covers and cheap, fibrous pages, looking for neighbors of Evie Hardy twenty-five years ago, people we might interview, if we could find them again, about what they remembered of Evie and the boys.

I took more notes and made more photocopies; and when I was finished, I joined Dave, who was patiently working the finicky dials of the microfilm copier. When he had copied the last of the newspaper articles he'd found about the case, he stood up slowly, blinked his eyes, shrugged and rolled his head back and forth a couple of times to loosen his neck muscles.

"Nothing like obsolete technology," he said. "I could use some dinner."

We ate at a place downtown that served barbecue on wooden trestle tables with paper placemats. Three or four big-screen TVs showed baseball games and car races, and the restaurant was crowded with families looking wilted from the heat of the day.

After we paid the check, Dave said, "Let's go somewhere where we can talk."

We went back to the restaurant where Jim had taken us to lunch, but this time we sat at a table in the bar. Dave had a draft ale, and I had a mojito from the bar's menu of "specialty cocktails." Smooth jazz from a speaker system pervaded the air like a faint scent. Beyond the low partition between the bar and the restaurant, I could hear the murmured conversations of a few late diners and the occasional clink of glassware.

"Jim seemed pretty engaged," I said.

"Yeah, this appeared to keep his attention," Dave said. "But I'm going to have to come back here or send Brad."

"Lots of witnesses here," I said.

Dave was looking at my mojito with some amusement. I gave him a "so what" look in return, and he said, "Pretty festive drink there."

"Yeah, well. Makes Shasta City seem almost fun."

"You don't like this place, do you?"

"No, it makes my spine creep."

"As bad as the Central Valley or San Bernardino?"

"I don't know," I said. "Worse, in some ways. More isolated, or something. Lots of cowboys, crazy right-wing politics, meth labs in the hills."

"Well that's true in every rural area now. That or marijuana grows run by drug cartels."

"Yeah." I decided to change the subject. "So do you have any plans this summer?"

"Bike rides. Couple of bluegrass and old-time music festivals. Maybe a backpacking trip in the Sierras. And you?"

"Nothing much. I've become a real stick-in-the-mud. Probably a trip to Alaska in the fall to see my sisters."

"And what about Australia? That's where Gavin is, right?"

"Oh, God, I just can't seem to get up the courage to make that flight. Damn—Gavin will probably be back living in the States again before I make up my mind to go."

"Well that won't be good. You really should go."

The mojito was warming and loosening my tired brain, filling me with some urge to empty out its emotional baggage in a cobwebby heap on the table. "I'm still pretty close to the edge sometimes," I said. "I need a lot of quiet and routine."

"So you took another death case."

"God knows why," I said, raising my eyes in the general direction of where God was supposed to be.

"I know the feeling," Dave said. "It's some sort of weird addiction. I can't stay away from it. None of us can."

It was true. Most of the capital attorneys I knew—friends of Terry's, friends of mine in private practice—had sworn at one time or another they would never take another capital case, only to be drawn in again for reasons none of us could fathom.

"What's the pull?" I asked.

"The big money, obviously," Dave said, drily. "And you get to meet celebrities. Famous mass murderers, serial killers."

"And travel to exotic places," I added, with an all-encompassing wave that almost toppled my drink.

We went on for a while, getting sillier, until I'd finished my mojito. "It's getting late," I said, feeling suddenly tired. "I think they'd like to close the restaurant and get us out of here."

We got up. I felt a little lightheaded, and I was glad Dave was driving.

Back at the motel, as we said goodbye and moved apart to our rooms, it occurred to me that twenty-five or thirty years ago we might have ended up in bed together. So much was different now. The urge, the need wasn't there; it was better—clearer, at least—just being good friends. In a way it was a relief, but I also felt an ache of regret for the time when I was young, attractive, and impulsive instead of old, heavy, and cautious.

The bed in my room felt cold. I turned down the air

conditioning, put on a pair of socks to warm my feet, and draped my light jacket over my shoulders above my nightshirt. I read half a Nero Wolfe novel before I fell asleep and dreamed of wandering lost in an endless oak forest, trying to find my house.

17

After the Shasta City trip, Jim seemed to lose interest again in Andy's case. I heard nothing from him as I read through the new discovery. There were a lot of police and laboratory reports, but they didn't add much to what I already knew.

For all its apparent magnitude—three separate sets of crimes, two bodies—the case really wasn't that complex. The forensic evidence was unusual, because the bodies had been in the ground so long. But it had all been presented at trial. The identities of the two victims were established by dental records, comparing their DNA to that of living relatives, and the identification of other physical evidence: Brandy Ontiveros's purse, with her driver's license and the photo of her baby, found in the barn; the red sandal, like the pair which another hooker recalled Lisa Greenman wearing around the time she was last seen in Shasta City. The condition of the remains was consistent with the time when each of the victims had last been seen alive.

The additional police reports contained more about the

investigation into their disappearance. Both women were drug addicts and prostitutes, and no one on the street, it seemed, paid much attention to where they went. Brandy Ontiveros's real first name was Socorro. Her parents had died when she was a child, and she had been raised by her grandmother, who was also taking care of the baby Brandy had given birth to when she was sixteen. Her grandmother had gone to the police after Brandy failed to show up for a couple of months to visit her baby girl. She spoke little English, and from the police report, it seemed that she had assumed Brandy had died of something drug-related and was just trying to find out if she was right.

Lisa Greenman had simply stopped being seen on the streets of Shasta City, and no one, not even her family, missed her. Her father lived in Indiana and hadn't had any contact with her for five or six years. Her mother, who lived in a trailer park in Reno, didn't see her much, either. Lisa wasn't particularly welcome because she and a boyfriend had stolen her mother's TV and some of her jewelry and sold them to buy drugs. Lisa's mother had testified at the two trials about her grief over her daughter's murder, but even there she had admitted that she hadn't heard from Lisa for over a year before the police called her. "She was going to come see me for my birthday, but she didn't show up. She called a couple of days later, with some excuse. I don't even remember what it was." Even on the page, her words sighed hollowly with echoes of lost patience and resigned irritation—the too-typical words of a mother of a down-and-out drug addict, exhausted by her daughter's problems and her own. She had said almost the same thing to the policeman who called her; the report said nothing about her reaction to hearing that her daughter had been murdered.

People on the street had remembered the women only vaguely through the drugged haze of their own lives. They were just two more of the dozens of girls who claimed small territories on the sidewalks in front of the bars and liquor stores around First and Elm, Shasta City's red-light district, waiting to be picked up by the men who cruised slowly down the yellow-lit street, and having sex in the back of parking lots in their customers' cars. When they stopped showing up, no one paid much attention. If people thought about it at all, they assumed the girls were in jail or had left town.

Weeks went by, and I was starting to feel pressured by how slowly the investigation was going. It was nearly August; the year we had to file the habeas petition was almost half gone. Dave had made another trip to Shasta City, where he'd looked for court records on Evie, the judge, the district attorney who'd tried the case, and the jurors, and talked to more of Andy's teachers and the few former neighbors who could still be found.

For several years, before they moved to the ranch, Evie and the boys had lived in a bungalow on a leafy street in the older part of town, not far from the old courthouse. Before driving home from Shasta City, I'd driven out to take a look at it. The neighborhood had been—was still—working class, a grid of flat streets and back alleys, big shady trees, and rows of little houses set back from the street behind grassy front lawns. It had grown rundown as the people who owned the little houses grew old and died, and younger people preferred bigger homes in new subdivisions or Craftsman houses in gentrifying neighborhoods with more character. Many of the little houses were rentals now, cheaply painted and minimally landscaped, their lawns dried out and mottled with patches of bare ground and a shrub or two straggling next to the house.

On his other trips to Shasta City that summer, Dave had found that Evie's landlord was dead, and the house had been sold long ago. Dave had interviewed the former landlord's son, who lived in one of the new subdivisions outside Shasta City, but he had no recollection of the tenants twenty-five years ago, except that his father had once said one of them had turned out to be some sort of serial killer. Most of Evie's neighbors, themselves renters, had died or moved away long since. The ones Dave could locate remembered Evie, but not too well. "Nice lady," one couple said; "a little strange," said another woman, but couldn't articulate why she thought so. The boys didn't leave much of an impression on them, either. "She kept them on a pretty tight leash," one former neighbor said. "My boys didn't like them much," another recalled. She remembered that "they moved away after some trouble with the younger one, I think."

Several of the teachers were away on vacation, but the two Dave found at home both remembered Andy, or rather, Evie. "He was failing everything," one of his English teachers said. "We offered to test him for special ed, but she wouldn't even consider it." The school psychologist, retired now, said the same thing, and added, "I never saw a woman in such denial. You'd try to tell her he was intellectually disabled, and she just wouldn't go there. I can still remember her telling me, 'There is nothing wrong with Andy. He just needs someone to pay more attention to him.' Pity the law in this state doesn't allow us to do IQ testing on kids. I'm sure he'd have scored pretty low. But then Mrs. Hardy would probably have found some reason not to believe it."

The psychologist was, in his words, "astounded" about the murders. "He's just about the last kid I'd think would do such a thing. His brother was a bit of a troublemaker, but Andy—no. He was slow, but not like that." None of which left us with much that we didn't already know.

Learning problems in a child can be the result of brain damage. The birth complication Evie had described, when Andy had been born with the umbilical cord around his neck, could have accounted for Andy's difficulties. Or they could have resulted from heredity, some toxin or virus Evie was exposed to when she was pregnant, or maybe a beating by Len. Brain damage can cause a lot of bad behavior, from lousy choices to explosive rages to hallucinations and full-on psychosis. I'd been calling Jim for weeks about retaining a neuropsychologist to test Andy's brain function. I even got a few recommendations from Dr. Nancy Hollister and a colleague or two from my past. But Jim was always somewhere else and didn't return my calls and emails. "He's in a *big* trial," Corey told me in his wry, so-here-we-are-again voice. "He's just not thinking about anything else right now."

Without Jim's go-ahead, I couldn't commit to anything that required spending serious money, like retaining an expert; and Dave and I were running out of things we could do ourselves. Then the Washington school records came.

I read through them, jumped up with a whoop, ran to my phone, and called Dave's cell, and was a little deflated to get his voicemail. Then it occurred to me to call Corey and ask him whether Jim knew about the IQ score. "I don't think he's looked at the records yet," Corey said. "What was it?"

"Sixty-five," I said. "In fourth grade. Mentally retarded."

"Doesn't that mean they can't execute him?"

"Hopefully," I said. I was backtracking, after my initial enthusiasm, considering the reality of litigating mental retardation in a death-penalty case. The Supreme Court has said it's unconstitutional to execute a mentally retarded defendant—that it's inhumane to hold them as responsible for their crimes as fully functioning adults. But instead of emptying death row of the mentally retarded, the decision created an angry and determined backlash from prosecutors who just couldn't stand the idea that a murderer might escape lethal injection—might, God forbid, merely spend the rest of his life in a maximum-security prison—just because the Supreme Court has said he was too stupid. Prosecutors, abetted by psychologists with old-fashioned beliefs in the workings of the criminal mind, fight to convince the courts that the defendant is more capable than his IQ scores reflect, or just faking retardation. And all too often, standing before a judge looking ahead to the next election, they'll win.

When Dave called back an hour later, I was out in my garden picking some lettuce and cherry tomatoes for a salad. I dropped my scissors and dove for the cordless phone I'd left on the deck.

"So, what's up?" he asked. "Your message sounded like it was something pretty big."

"It is. We got some of Andy's grade-school transcripts. His IQ in fourth grade was sixty-five."

"No way—that's great!" He gave a short laugh. "What a profession we're in. Where else would hearing that your client is retarded be good news?"

Now that I had Dave's ear to bend, I couldn't help burbling on about Andy's grade-school records. "He was kept back— we already knew that. But there are also achievement tests that show him reading and doing math at second-grade level in the sixth grade. He was thirteen—*thirteen*—at that point. Dobson never got these records. I'll bet he never knew."

Dave was suitably impressed. "Fits with what the teacher and the school psychologist told us, doesn't it? And his mother never said anything to you about it?"

"Not a word."

"I'm not surprised," Dave said. "I bet she was mighty pissed about it. Well, what do we do now?"

"I called Corey again and told him to give Jim the news. Maybe this will get him to call me back."

"Good luck. You know, this might be a good excuse to sit down with Jim and talk to him about what he's supposed to be doing on the case. I'm with you; I'd like to hear something when I call his office besides a secretary telling me he's in trial."

I felt a sick little shiver of anxiety. I hate confrontations; it's one of the reasons I live in a cabin in the redwoods writing appeals. But when we'd hung up, I rode the wavelet of resolution raised by Dave's support and dialed Jim's number again. I left a message with his secretary; we needed a strategy meeting about the IQ score, I said, and soon.

Jim's secretary called the next morning. His trial had ended in a hung jury; he could fly up to San Francisco the following week and meet us Friday at the federal public defender's office there. I was surprised that he'd gotten back to me so soon, and I felt a little silly for having asked.

18

I made the long drive into San Francisco on Thursday. Life in the country was putting a lot of wear on my poor car—but not, fortunately, on my friendship with Ed. He was as willing as ever to keep Charlie for a couple of days, even though he had his hands pretty full with a new dog. It was some sort of yellow-lab mix puppy, already half-grown, all bounding energy and big feet waiting for his body to grow into them. Ed had named him Pogo.

Pogo, seeing Charlie for the first time, had given a bark and skidded across Ed's kitchen floor. Charlie had looked at Pogo, planted his feet, and answered with a long, low growl that crescendoed into a single sharp bark that stopped the puppy two feet from him, where poor Pogo crouched, caught between curiosity and fear and whimpering hopefully.

I told Ed I owed him hugely. "Go to Baja or Greece or something, so I can take care of Pogo and make it up to you."

"Nah," he said. "Just get me a giant bag of puppy kibble on your way back."

I stayed the night in a motel on Lombard Street, near the Golden Gate Bridge. The noises of the city kept me awake, and I spent the short drive to the federal building the next morning wondering irritably what I'd been thinking when I suggested this meeting.

Outside the parking garage, I gave a dollar to a skinny old man sitting with a paper cup between his feet, because he smiled at me through rheumy eyes and because I wanted to buy myself some good karma for the day. I bought a mocha at a coffee kiosk and then joined the line of visitors snaking its way toward the metal detectors in the lobby of the federal building.

Upstairs, in the public defender's office, Dave was waiting in the reception area. We'd talked on the phone about how to approach Jim, but neither of us had had any great ideas, and now we sat next to each other in near silence, trying unsuccessfully to look assertive and confident.

Jim breezed in ten minutes later, a paper coffee cup in one hand and an ancient leather briefcase—what a prop that must be in a courtroom!—in the other. I couldn't help thinking he knew what was on our minds.

We shook hands all around, and the receptionist, a thirtyish African-American woman with very short hair and big hoop earrings, showed us to the small conference room that had been loaned to us for our meeting.

We sat at one end of the long table and made some small talk about the flight from Los Angeles and the state of the freeways. Jim pulled his phone from an inside pocket in his jacket and consulted it, then opened his briefcase, pulled out a thick file and a yellow pad, and looked from me to Dave—a look that said he wasn't exactly happy to be here. "Shall we get down to business? Tell me about this mental retardation claim."

"When Andy was in fourth grade, in Washington," I explained, "he was referred to a school psychologist, I guess because he was failing academically. The psychologist did IQ testing, and came up with an IQ score of sixty-five. Actually, sixty-three on the verbal IQ and sixty-six on performance. Full-scale IQ of sixty-five."

Jim leaned a little forward in his chair and fixed me with the look of a senior attorney quizzing his junior associate. "So. This seems like a slam dunk. With an IQ like that, any court should overturn his death sentence."

"I guess. If it wasn't an aberration. It's the only IQ test I've found in his records."

Jim sat back again. "I had a mentally retarded client a couple of years ago, in a federal death-penalty case. My client's full-scale IQ was in the low seventies. US Attorney fought it, but not that hard, and the judge found for us. This looks better than that case."

"Maybe," I said, "but we don't know how he tests now."

My hope for this meeting was beginning to evaporate, as I realized what a nasty, protracted fight we had ahead of us and how unready Jim was to roll up his sleeves and get into it. "We need to get an expert on mental retardation to evaluate him."

Jim wrote something on the pad in front of him and looked up again. "Do you know anyone good? I didn't like the guy we had in my other case."

"Who was that?" I asked.

"Hocking, or something. He was good on paper, but not on the stand; the judge didn't care for him."

"I'll see who I can find."

Jim wrote something else on his pad and looked up. "I'll need to ask for more money, won't I? I'll start on a motion when I get back to LA." He sat straight and looked at us both again. "So. Is there anything else we need to talk about today?"

I could feel Dave look over at me. I took a short breath, wishing I had thought this out better. "Well…" I began.

Jim waited.

"Well…" This time I plowed ahead. "There's the whole investigation, actually. We—Dave and I—are feeling a little adrift here. I mean, we're out here reading material, identifying claims and potential witnesses, and talking to people, but we don't really feel like we're getting much direction or feedback about what you want for the case, what you think the issues are, what leads you think we should be following up." Jim had lowered his eyes a bit; he seemed to be listening or thinking, but he didn't say anything.

Dave said, "We know there's a limited budget, and we're worried that we're going to use up the money pursuing evidence you don't think will be useful."

"That's been a real concern for both of us," I confirmed. "And I don't feel like I can make decisions about that without your input."

I hesitated, then finished with a lame peroration. "I'm getting worried, because we only have another seven months before the petition has to be filed, and I don't feel like we have a plan."

Jim looked up at me, and I was relieved to see that he didn't seem upset that we'd put him on the spot. "You're right," he said. "I've been so involved in trials that I haven't really had time to focus on this case. Right now, you both probably know it a lot better than I do."

Dave and I nodded. "Probably," I said.

"But you've been doing great, so far. Why don't you just keep at it and let me know what you're coming up with? You do what you think needs to be done; I trust your judgment."

"But—"

"Really. You and Dave both came highly recommended. You're experienced, and you know what you're doing. I'll work with you, of course. But feel free to be independent. Let me know what you're thinking. And when you need money, just give a call and let me know how much and why."

"But that's more or less just leaving the case to us," I said.

Jim looked less than pleased. "No, not completely. I'm still lead counsel, so I'm responsible for it. I just think there's a lot you can do as well as I can."

"Well, okay," I said, hesitating. "It's just—for me, at

least—I feel more comfortable being able to include you in the decisions."

Jim gave me a look he clearly meant to be reassuring. "Of course. Any questions you have, like this one"—he nodded in the general direction of the school records—"just let me know, and we'll work on them together. I think things are going great; you're doing a terrific job. If you want to talk again, let's set up a time. You let me know what works for you. So. Is there anything more?"

"No. I guess that's it," I said.

Great, I thought, *I'm a coward. Twenty-five years as a lawyer, and I can't even stand up for myself.* I was bamboozled by Jim's strategy of mixing abandonment with flattery; I was prepared to walk away from our conversation exactly where we'd started, but feeling better because he liked my work and was willing to let me do his for him. I took a breath and tried to continue, not sure what to say.

Jim stood up and started loading papers back into his briefcase. "Great. There's a Giants game this afternoon. My youngest boy is here with me, and I promised him I'd take him to it."

Oh, Christ, I thought.

Dave and I made polite noises and wished him a good weekend, and we filed out of the office, Dave and Jim talking incomprehensibly about baseball and baseball players. I knew I'd failed, and some part of me resented the fact that Jim and Dave could chat amiably about sports.

At the bottom of the steps outside the building, Jim stopped, turned to Dave and me and said, looking us in the eyes with an expression of frankness and sincerity, "You know, I appreciate all you're doing. Soon as this next trial is over, I'll make a real effort to block out some time for this case. You know, that mental retardation issue looks like a breakthrough. Let me know when you find an expert, okay? Have a good weekend!" With that, he turned and trotted down the steps. He looked like a kid at the end of his last day of school.

On the plaza, a chill, searching wind was pushing at my shoulders and blowing a parting into the back of my hair. Summer in San Francisco, I remembered it well. I looked over at Dave. "Well, do you believe him?" he asked.

"No," I answered. "I tried."

"I know."

"Did I say enough? Was there more I could have done?"

"Nah. You did what you could."

"Let's get off these steps; I'm freezing," I said.

"So what are your plans for the day?" Dave asked, as we walked down the steps.

"I'm heading for the University of California medical library, to look up some literature on intellectual disabilities."

"Well, that sounds exciting—good luck. By the way, I'm meeting some people from the public defender's office for drinks after work at this tapas place near the Hall of Justice. A friend of mine there won a murder case this week, and they're celebrating. Would you like to come? Marisol's supposed to be there; you two could meet."

"Sure," I said. "What time?"

"Six thirty or so." He pulled a pen and notebook from his pocket, wrote something down, tore the page out and gave it to me. "Here's the address. It's called Jerez; it's not too far from the Hall of Justice."

"Thanks." I was grateful for the invitation. I was starting to feel homesick, and spending another evening in my own company was looking pretty tedious.

19

I spent the afternoon at the medical library, copied some articles on psychological testing, and went back to the motel. After a vain attempt at a nap, I brushed my teeth and hair, looking disconsolately into the bathroom mirror at my badly cut bangs and the new lines around my eyes, and steeled myself for the trip to the restaurant.

Jerez was low-lit and noisy, with adobe-colored walls, accents of earthy browns, and hanging lamps with quirky art glass shades. People, mostly far younger and prettier than me, were three-deep at the bar, and a constant roar of voices rose and fell above the pulsating back beat of some indistinguishable music. I resisted an overwhelming impulse to turn and run for my car, took a deep breath, and jostled my way into the crowd. I saw Dave, standing and waving at me, at a table deep inside. He was with eight or ten men and women in suits, the public defenders, I figured, looking a little rumpled after their respective days in court.

There was an empty chair between a pretty dark-haired

woman next to Dave and a young man who seemed to be deep in conversation with the woman on the other side of him. The dark-haired woman lifted her jacket from the chair as I sat down.

"We've been saving it for you," she shouted over the din. "Dave has been absolutely fierce. I'm Marisol."

I couldn't think of what to say next. Dave had had so many girlfriends since I knew him, and it was hard to really engage with someone who was probably just passing through his life.

"Nice to meet you," I shouted above the crowd noise, then added lamely, "I guess you know I'm Janet." Clutching at a topic for conversation, I asked, "Are you a bike rider, too?"

"A little—not like him, but I'm learning."

I saw Dave looking at me and mouthing something unintelligible. At the same instant, a young woman carrying a cocktail tray materialized near me and called out to the table, in a voice that cut through the din, "Does anybody want anything else here?"

"I do." I pointed to a peachy-colored drink in a large martini glass in front of a woman at the next table. "I'll have one of those."

"A *soigné*?" the waitress said. "Okay."

I turned back to Dave, who was motioning me to come over to him. I worked my way out of my chair, with a mumbled "pardon me" to Marisol and the man on my other side, and edged over to Dave's chair.

"You need to talk to Coleman over there," he said, pointing to a young man a couple of seats away.

"I do?"

Dave gave me a "don't try to be funny" look. "Yes. He just won an Atkins hearing, and he knows a good expert. You two should talk."

I squeezed past Dave to Coleman. He was a slight Asian kid, with straight black hair brushed up in the front into some sort of compromise between a cowlick and a crew cut.

"I'm Janet Moodie," I said. "Dave says we need to talk about Atkins hearings."

"Coleman Chu." He stood and reached his hand out to shake mine, with the eager body energy of a young lawyer still fired up by his work. A man sitting next to him got up and offered me his chair. "Oh, no, that's okay," I said.

He shook his head. "Gotta go now anyway—got a dog at home to take care of."

I took the chair, and a moment later the waitress showed up with my cocktail. Dave looked down the table at it and mouthed something that looked like, "What the hell is that?"

"It's a *soigné*," I yodeled over the din.

"What the hell?" he mouthed.

I made a "get over it" face at him and took a sip. It tasted a little like a Bellini, cool and peachy, with just the merest bite of alcohol. I took a longer drink, and the booze spread through me, evaporating the worst of my anxieties. A *soigné*. A good name; one or two of these and I'd feel like anyone here who cared about my age, clothes, or weight could go to hell. I turned back to young Coleman, who was putting his glass of beer back on the table. "Dave says you know of a good expert on mental retardation."

Coleman and I spent the next half-hour or so talking about his case. He wasn't a public defender, but a private lawyer on the conflict panel, and second counsel in a death-penalty case in Alameda County, across the bay. He was totally wrapped up in it and clearly pleased to get a chance to tell the convoluted history of the mental retardation hearing to someone who hadn't heard it before.

His lead counsel had given him charge of the Atkins hearing—a pretrial hearing to determine whether their client was mentally retarded and thus ineligible for the death penalty. Both sides had presented evidence and expert testimony, and Coleman had won. "Dr. Moss— Dan Moss, from UC Davis—was a really great expert. He's a neuropsychologist. He teaches in the PhD program, and he's done both clinical work and research on mental retardation—only they don't call it that any more, the current term is intellectual disability. It's not that easy to find an expert who knows this stuff. I talked to three or four doctors before I found him."

I asked Coleman if he could send me Dr. Moss's CV and report and a transcript of his testimony in Coleman's case.

By now, the group at the table was starting to disperse. Dave, by way of apology, said that he and Marisol couldn't continue on to dinner because they were driving down the coast for a weekend cycling trip. "So," I said to Marisol, "his enthusiasm is contagious, eh?"

She shrugged. "It's the only way I get to spend any quality time with him. But I'm getting into it."

True love, I thought.

I decided to look for a quiet place to eat, followed by a movie. A theater out in the avenues was showing a French comedy I was mildly interested in seeing, and on the way I stopped at a Vietnamese storefront place on Geary Boulevard for a bowl of *pho*.

Whatever the charms of a weekend in San Francisco might once have been, they were lost on me now; in the morning I woke up early, ready to go home. At a bakery on Chestnut Street I picked up an almond croissant and a latte for breakfast and then headed gratefully north, under the big orange towers of the Golden Gate Bridge and down the grade into Marin. A few miles along the highway I had a view of San Quentin across the bay, pale sandstone buildings against the blue of the water and the sky. It looked innocuous, even attractive, in the morning light.

20

Young Coleman was on the ball. The following Monday I got an email from him with Dr. Moss's curriculum vitae attached, along with electronic files of the pleadings and transcripts from his hearing.

I called Jim's office to tell him I had found a potential expert but he was in trial, and when he called back the following afternoon, he'd forgotten that we were looking for one. When I reminded him, all he said was, "Great! Good work. Let me know if you like him. I've got a call coming in; talk to you later!"

As the realization sank in that Jim had left Dave and me to work the case up on our own, my old maladies started up. I started waking in the middle of the night, worrying about how much there was to do and what we might miss, and during the day I'd be hit with sudden moments of heartstopping fear, or a dizzying sense of being in free fall.

"I'm freaking out again," I told Dave. We were emailing and talking on the phone every day, working out details of the next months' work—his next trip to Pomo County, and the ones we would have to make to Washington and Idaho.

"What about? Jim?" Dave asked. Dave knew probably more than anyone outside my family why I had left the city and capital defense work and retreated to the remote north coast. Panic attacks and depression aren't easy things to talk about, and in the fallout that followed Terry's suicide there had been few people I felt like confiding in.

"I don't know—yes—stress, I guess."

Dave was sympathetic, concerned. "Look," he said, "there's no reason to make yourself sick over this case. If it gets too bad, just tell Christie and get out."

"Yeah, okay," I answered, already knowing that I wouldn't. To begin with, I couldn't just walk out; the judge would have to relieve me as Andy's attorney. To get off the case I'd have to have a damned good reason why I couldn't continue on it; anxiety and disenchantment with my co-counsel weren't even close. Six months to filing. I'd get through it. I'd done it before. But I was younger then, tougher and angrier. And I'd had Terry for advice and moral support and the reflection of his brilliance and confidence to get me through my crises of anxiety and self-doubt. Now, it seemed, I had nothing but guilt and the shreds of my self-regard.

Between Dave and me, I had the easier job, reading up on intellectual disability and contacting Dr. Moss, while Dave talked to cops and teachers in Shasta City. "Beautiful place, this time of year," Dave said during a check-in call. "The high today was 109." I commiserated, but the thermometer on my deck read a brisk 65 degrees.

The homicide detectives weren't talking much, Dave said. "Canevaro was pretty predictable. He has no use for Andy; thinks he and his brother should both fry. Hines has retired and lives in a trailer park out of the state. Canevaro didn't want to tell us where he was living, but I'm pretty sure I've located him in a database search. He's in Nevada, near Reno."

The courtroom bailiff at the trial, Bill Forschner, also retired, had a bit more to say. "A nice guy," Dave said. "He and his wife have this beautiful big log cabin on the mountain, with a hundred-mile view out their living-room windows. Built it himself, with his two sons, and he's real proud of it. Anyhow, he said Dobson was a good trial lawyer once, but he drank too much. He'd tried a lot of murder cases, but not for a while. Everyone was surprised he got appointed to a death-penalty case. Apparently the state had filed so many that the court was running out of defense attorneys to appoint. But Forschner didn't recall anything that made him think Dobson was impaired during the trial. He always showed up on time, no liquor smell that he remembers, seemed to act okay. He'd always hit the bars after court, though, have three or four drinks."

Dobson's ex-wife wasn't any more helpful. "She still cares about him," Dave said, "even though she left him because of his drinking. She says it never affected his work. She was a clerk in the traffic court, right in the courthouse complex, and if there had been any problem with Arnie's performance in court, she thinks she'd have heard about it. She was pretty protective of him. Said he'd been an army lieutenant in Vietnam, and he had his demons over that. But he put his heart into his cases. And no, she won't sign a declaration. She remembered this case and said Andy's a serial killer and ought to die. I got their divorce records and Dobson's death certificate, but there's not much in them."

"How did Dobson die, anyway?" I asked.

"Heart attack," Dave said. "His ex-wife said he worked himself to death."

Not on this case, I started to say, but thought better of it. *Nil nisi bonum*, and all that; not much point in getting snarky about the dead.

The jail guards Dave interviewed were a washout—not unexpected, since ninety-nine out of a hundred of them will tell you that your client was perfectly normal and faking any mental illness you may think he had. They remembered Andy and Emory only vaguely and didn't recall that they were anything but typical prisoners. "They had this mother," one of them said. "Used to visit them all the time. Was that them?" It seemed that Evie wasn't someone one forgot.

He talked to some local lawyers who remembered Dobson and his drinking, but they made him seem more like a *bon vivant* than an alcoholic.

Several days into his trip, he finally hit something like pay dirt, in the form of a former high-school counselor and a retired principal from Shasta High who remembered Andy and Emory.

In his evening phone call, Dave told me, "The principal said they weren't that memorable as students, but he remembered them because they ended up on death row. The counselor actually volunteered that he felt kind of sorry for Andy because he was so slow. Thought you'd like that. He also said Emory had a mean streak and Andy got in trouble for following his brother."

The men remembered Evie, too. "'One of those mothers whose kids can do no wrong,' was how the principal described her," Dave said. "If either of them was disciplined, she was there the next day, complaining. If they got in a fight, it was the other kid's fault. If they destroyed school property, the other kids did it, not them. Mostly, it was Emory, it seems. He seems to have been more of a troublemaker than Andy. But when they wanted to put Andy into special ed, she wouldn't hear of it. Refused to sign the papers. 'Nothing wrong with my boy. He just needs more time to learn. You need to spend more time with him.' Like that. Never rude, the counselor said, just this nice little lady who wouldn't hear a thing against her boys. But the principal called her a screwball."

"Interesting," I said. "Did he say why?"

"He just said he thought she was scary. Said he wasn't surprised that the boys ended up in prison," Dave added.

"Dave—what did she *do*?"

"Jan, I'm sorry, he really didn't say. I'll call him tomorrow, okay?" Dave sounded like he'd about had it with being on the road. Sitting in my armchair in my cool, quiet house, I felt guilty.

"I hope you've found some way to stay out of the heat," I said, trying to change the subject.

"Not hardly. I'm getting used to it. I've biked in weather almost this hot, but I've never been able to figure out why anyone would live in it."

"Me neither."

"Do you want declarations from any of these folks?"

I thought for a moment. We would need declarations eventually, signed, sworn statements from potential witnesses, reciting what they would be able to testify to if the court gave us a hearing. "Not yet," I said. "Let's wait till we have an expert who can tell us what information we need on the intellectual disability issue."

I'd read the transcripts and CV Coleman Chu had sent me and looked up Dr. Moss's faculty web page on the UC Davis website. He looked about forty, with a round baby face and metal-framed glasses. His hair was light-colored and a little disheveled, as though he had just rubbed his hands through it. In my mind's eye, I could see his wife looking at the picture on the website, shaking her head, and saying, "You couldn't have combed your hair before they took it?"

After making the decision to talk with him about

working on Andy's case, I spent twice as long as I should have composing an email that I hoped would strike the right tone of respect and professionalism.

21

Dr. Moss answered my email the next day. That's another reason I like academics; they like email. Soon we had a date to meet at his office in Davis.

The Davis campus is typically University of California—blocky post-war architecture, tall shade trees, and green lawns, except for a few additions befitting its role as the state's agricultural school, such as a department of viticulture and a dairy barn—and completely incomprehensible to navigate. In spite of Dr. Moss's very specific directions, I ended up lost on roads that circled back on themselves past barely distinguishable light-gray buildings identified by discreet, unreadable signs. After passing the dairy barn for the second time, I called for help, and he talked me in.

His building was an air-conditioned sanctuary from the steamy heat outside. Even the walk from my parking place had left me feeling wilted and sticky, and Dr. Moss suggested sodas from the machine at the end of the hall. Armed with a Diet Coke and a bottled water, both almost painfully cold, I settled in a chair near his desk, and we began talking business.

I liked him right away. He was taller and thinner than I thought he would be from his photo, and his hair, light brown with a little gray in it, was neater. His eyes were light, and his metal-framed glasses seemed almost to disappear against his face. He was wearing khakis and a pale blue Oxford shirt that looked a little worse for the heat.

A couple of framed diplomas hung on the wall over a file cabinet on one side of the office; on another wall hung a poster for a Matisse exhibition in Chicago. His desktop was fairly uninformative: photos of a smiling dark-haired woman and two brown-haired children, a small stack of file folders, a yellow pad and two or three pens, a monitor and a keyboard.

He offered me a chair in front of his desk. "I guess I should start by saying that when you contacted me I wasn't sure I ever wanted to testify in another one of these hearings. Maybe it's the stakes involved, but the level of hostility is really something else."

"It can be pretty bad," I agreed.

He nodded. "I've testified as an expert a couple of times in court and in hearings about legislation, and I've never had anyone impugn my integrity until Mr. Beasley's case. The prosecutor actually accused me to my face of tailoring my testimony because the defense was paying my fee and then made some comment about liberal experts who make up diagnoses to save criminals from the death penalty. He never even asked my views on the death penalty. He had no idea what they were."

"I saw that in the transcript," I said. "He was really over the top."

He sat upright, picked up a pen from his desk as if looking for something to do with his hands, and turned it slowly in his fingers as he spoke. "To be honest, I'm not entirely against the death penalty, at least in theory. I think there are people who deserve it." He paused for a moment as if considering what to say next. "I'm a neuropsychologist, not a lawyer. But I do agree with the Atkins decision. People who are intellectually disabled are much more compromised by it than most people think. They really can't be expected to function in the world as well as someone of normal intelligence. From what you've told me, there's a good chance Mr. Hardy fits that picture."

"I certainly think so," I said.

"It's not a foregone conclusion; there's much more testing that would need to be done. But I am interested in working with you on his case."

I thanked him.

"But you said it was on appeal, I think?" he went on. "Where do I fit in, if the trial's over?"

I made an inept attempt at explaining the intricacies of post-conviction proceedings.

"But you're going to have a hearing like the one in the Beasley case?" Dr. Moss asked.

"Maybe," I said. "Right now, what we have to do is convince the court that it should hold a hearing at all. If you evaluate Mr. Hardy and find that he's intellectually disabled, we'll put your findings into a written declaration and file that with his habeas corpus petition."

"When would the hearing be?"

"If we have one, maybe not for years. Capital habeas cases move very slowly in the court system."

"Really? Years?" he said, shaking his head. "I have so little to do with criminal law. Most of this is like a foreign language to me. To evaluate Mr. Hardy, I'd need to do quite a bit of testing—a neuropsychological battery and IQ testing. You'd need to get background information to establish that he was disabled before he was eighteen; that IQ score of his in elementary school was a good start. And we'd need to find out about his adaptive functioning—his self-care, cognitive, social skills—and that will involve interviewing him and other people—family, teachers, coworkers. When would you need this done?"

"We have to file our petition in the middle of next March."

"I could do an evaluation some time this fall. Where is Mr. Hardy?"

"San Quentin. Arranging for an evaluation there takes some time. The prison has to do a background check to clear you as a visitor, and we need to reserve the psychiatric interview room in the prison a few months in advance, because it's pretty booked up. We should be able to get the room some time in November. Are you available then?"

"As far as I know."

We spent a few minutes discussing money—Dr. Moss's hourly rate and the number of hours it was likely to take for an evaluation and report. "We'll need to make a funds request to the judge," I said, "but assuming it's granted, we should be able to get started in a month or so. I hope that's okay."

It was. But before we parted company, I had a favor to ask him. "It's about adaptive functioning," I said.

That was the hardest part. Diagnosing someone as intellectually disabled didn't just mean testing their IQ. An expert also had to determine how well the person managed the details of day-to-day life, such as cleaning, cooking, personal hygiene, getting from place to place, keeping track of money, reading, and so forth. One didn't need to be bad at all of it to be found disabled, just significantly deficient in a few areas. I had read Dr. Moss's testimony in Coleman's case, and it seemed—understandably, I guess—that people with intellectual disabilities varied tremendously in what they could and couldn't do well. Some could drive a car or hold down a simple job, while others couldn't, but might have other skills, such as the ability to cook or do simple arithmetic. But even after reading what Dr. Moss had said, along with some materials from seminars, I had only a vague idea of what adaptive functioning was and how to establish that Andy wasn't good at it.

Dr. Moss gave me a rundown of areas to look at for adaptive functioning problems. "You need to establish how he functions compared to normal people in a normal environment—which means how he did before he went to jail."

"Andy could drive a pickup truck," I said.

"Believe it or not, it's not uncommon for intellectually disabled people to know how to drive a car," Moss said. "But check whether he had a license—passing the test is harder."

I made a note to call Corey.

"Let me suggest some reading," he said, and he tossed out the titles of seven or eight books and articles. I told him I'd get back in touch as soon as we had the court's approval on our funding request.

Before heading back to the coast, I stopped at the Davis medical library—after getting lost again first—and copied the articles Dr. Moss had suggested to me.

When I turned on my cellphone after leaving the library, there was a message from Dave. He had run out of people to interview in Pomo County, and he was heading back to the Bay Area. *Just as well*, I thought. *We've got plenty of work to do.*

22

"Mr. Christie. Ms. Moodie."

"Your Honor."

Jim's response seemed to disperse, like the smoke of a cigarette, in the still air of the courtroom.

We were in the United States District Court in Sacramento, Jim and I and the magistrate assigned to Andy's case, to talk money. Being court-appointed attorneys meant that our services were paid for by the taxpayers. We, the people—including all those who'd voted for the death penalty in the first place—had paid the attorneys' legal fees and the expenses for investigators and experts for both sides, for the trial that put Andy on death row, the automatic appeal from his conviction, and now these habeas corpus proceedings. It had cost a lot of money, a lot more than if he'd just been sentenced to prison for life, like Emory. Emory had gotten a court-appointed lawyer for his appeal in the state court, but that was all—no free habeas corpus counsel, no money to investigate what might have gone wrong with his trial. He'd run out of legal moves years ago, and there was nothing left for him but to do his time.

But the elected representatives of the taxpayers had also arranged that the money we were being paid for trying to keep the state from having its way with Andy, and the money we got for expenses—for travel, investigators and expert witnesses— would be doled out by the judge in the case—or sometimes, as in Andy's case, the magistrate, a sort of assistant judge.

Judge Sally Fuentes, the magistrate assigned to Andy's case, had been a partner in a white-shoe law firm, an officer in the American Bar Association, and often showed up on the covers of lawyer's trade magazines for "top women lawyers of the year" features. A few years ago, she had taken what amounted to a well-earned retirement into a federal judgeship. Standing in the courtroom below the bench, I felt a bit like a poor relation.

Jim had told me that as judges go, Judge Fuentes had a reputation for being reasonably realistic about expenses in death-penalty cases. I'd heard horror stories about judges who had given appointed attorneys no money at all to investigate their cases, and one who had gone through the roof because an investigator on the road had rented a mid-sized car on a day when no compacts were available. Jim was responsible for handling the money issues in Andy's case, and that was fine with me. He had given Judge Fuentes a proposed budget for his investigation before he'd brought me onto the case, and she'd given him all the money he'd asked for then. With the new information we had about Andy's IQ, we were coming back to ask for more.

Until now, our status conferences with Judge Fuentes had been telephone hearings, that is to say, conference calls with the magistrate and the attorneys, a procedure that not only saved the government money and travel time for its appointed lawyers, but let me go to court in jeans and a t-shirt. Generally, they involved the briefest of progress reports and lasted only a few minutes. This time, though, we were asking both for money to retain Dr. Moss and for an extension of the deadline for the petition so that he could do his work; and the judge wanted to question us in person.

I'd never liked trial work; the courtroom isn't a place for someone like me, prone to second-guessing and after-the-fact agonizing over what I might have said or done. Appellate law doesn't involve much going to court. Oral argument, and perhaps an occasional hearing to correct the appellate record, that was all; my legal battles were fought, for the most part, from my office, where I could sharpen my arguments and get them right before launching them at the enemy.

I tried to listen to Jim as he went through the litanies of the status conference, but I found myself musing instead on the curious psychology of the courtroom. The proportions of the room, with its paneled walls and high ceiling, gave it a ceremonial feeling, like a church or a small concert hall, and the space absorbed and dissolved the human sounds and movements inside it. The air was cool and still, with a faint smell of polished wood, the lighting diffuse and shadowless. It cast a spell: the robed judge and uniformed marshal; the stately pace of the proceedings; the continual formalities of standing and sitting and the ancient forms of address; the sense of isolation from the outside world—there were no windows, I realized—all worked together to lull people into feeling that the rituals of the law, and their consequences, are not only just but inexorable. When I was working in the public defender's office, the effectiveness of the trick, even in crowded city courts, had amazed me: defendants heard themselves sentenced to long prison terms and then walked quietly out with the bailiffs as if they were about to go home. Almost no one rebelled or challenged the illusion.

From the bench, as if from a supersized pulpit, Judge Fuentes looked around the courtroom and down at Jim and me. She was about my age, I guessed. Her hair was short and dark brown, and her face, fine-featured and dark-eyed, was a mask of authority, nearly unreadable.

Jim explained why we were asking for a couple of extra months to file the petition, choosing his words carefully because the deputy attorney general, Brenda Collinson, was in the courtroom with us. She immediately objected to our getting more time. Ms. Collinson was probably in her mid-forties, with blond highlights and a taut, disapproving face. She was wearing a dark gray suit with a pencil skirt that showed off her skinny hips, and on her left hand she flashed a really serious diamond wedding ring set. When Jim had introduced us before the start of the hearing, she had given me an appraising look, assessing how I might change the dynamic of the case, before dismissing me as inconsequential and turning back to Jim, to say, "I really don't see why you need extra time just because you want to hire another expert."

Brenda made the same argument to the court, with a few flourishes. "Your Honor, this case has gone on for fourteen years. It's not fair to the victims' families or the public to drag it out any more."

Judge Fuentes thanked her and turned to Jim. "Actually, Mr. Christie, this case is over fifteen years old. You had a year from your appointment to file a petition, and nearly five months of that year is left. I'm not convinced you need additional time for your expert to finish his work. If there's some reason why you need more time after he has evaluated your client, I'll entertain a motion then. But for now, I'm denying your request."

Ouch. "Thank you, Your Honor," we all said, more or less in unison—some of us more sincerely than others.

The judge announced a date and time a month away for the next telephone status conference, and after another round of thank-yous, announced that she would proceed to the *ex parte* hearing on our request for funds. Ms. Collinson left, and the marshal cleared the courtroom of the two or three random spectators who always seem to be lounging in the audience section of even the dullest hearing.

Judge Fuentes looked around the courtroom and recited,

in the general direction of us and the court reporter, "We're here in closed session to discuss the application of petitioner's counsel for additional expert and investigative funds." That finished, she seemed to relax a little. She looked down at Jim and me.

"So. You have a potential Atkins issue in your case."

"Yes, Your Honor," Jim said, and I nodded agreement.

"I've read your application and your proposed amendment to your budget. Do you have anything additional to say on the question of funding?"

The judge's mention of our expert at the status conference had seemed like a signal that she planned to give us the funds, so Jim merely said, "No, Your Honor. Unless you have any questions, we'll submit the matter."

"Okay," Judge Fuentes said. "I'm going to grant the motion for additional funds. Is there anything else?"

"No, Your Honor. Thank you."

"All right, then. We're adjourned." We waited, standing, as she stood up, smoothed her robe with a quick gesture, turned, and left through the door behind the bench to her chambers. Gathering up our papers, we left the courtroom in silence, with a nod to the marshal.

"Well, that was pretty painless," Jim said as we waited for the elevator. "Not like my case in LA. Getting anything out of Judge Brougham is like pulling teeth. He acts like it's his own money."

"More time would have been good, though."

"Yeah, but so it goes." Jim shrugged. "I think she'll give it to us if we need it." The elevator came, and we joined a small group of suits and rode in silence to the first floor.

In the lobby, Jim picked up where he'd left off. "I'm going to be busy with a big discovery hearing in that gang case. You've been working with Dr. Moss; could you call him and let him know we can retain him?"

"I may as well," I said, feeling like an enabler. I also offered to draft a retainer letter and referral questions—our instructions to the expert—rather than leaving them to Jim.

"Great," Jim said. "I'm going to come back up and see Andy in a month or so. Couldn't on this trip because I'm in depositions this week on a civil case."

Outside, the air was hot and full of street noises and smells of car exhaust and fried food. Jim's car was parked not far from mine, and as we walked he told me about his civil case. His clients were the two small children of a couple who had been killed in a truck accident. "Little boy, five, and his sister, who's only three. Cutest kids, and their grandmother's raising them. Trucking company's insurer is trying to give them a lowball settlement because they're African American. It's just racism, pure and simple. But the company's going to settle; it has to. The trucker was completely at fault. I want to get enough to help the grandmother raise the kids and give them money for college."

People may bitch about lawyers, but we do good once in a while. "Good luck," I said.

23

It was a sweaty September day in Canfield, Washington, and the small living room, with its oversized furniture and wall-to-wall shag carpet, seemed like a hot cocoon, but one that smelled a little bit like beef stew and air freshener.

"I've got to admit, we were surprised to hear from you," Mrs. Kitteridge said. "It's been a long time since we've heard much of anything about Andy. Would you like some iced tea?" She stood uncertainly at the door between the living room and the kitchen.

"Yes, thank you," Dave and I said almost as one.

Charlene Kitteridge, the new wife of Evie Hardy's first husband, was tall and heavy, with broad shoulders and a massive torso balanced on legs that, large as they were, seemed inadequate to hold the upper part of her body. She wore tan shorts and a baggy lavender T-shirt with a faded flower design on the front. Her face was squarish, with small pale blue eyes and a helmet of short ash-blond hair. She moved her bulk deliberately through the door, seeming not so much to walk as simply to flow from one spot to the next, like a ship under sail.

Jimmy Kitteridge, as small and wiry as his wife was massive, was dressed in the rancher's uniform of new-looking jeans and a short-sleeved plaid shirt. He stood nervously in front of an armchair upholstered in a pattern of cabbage roses. Nearby, a big sofa in the same flowered pattern crowded all the other furniture into the edges of the room. Jimmy had a leather tan like an old cowboy, but his hair was full and silvery, and his face was broad in the cheekbones and pointed in the chin, giving him an almost elfin look. *In their teens*, I thought, *he and Evie must have been a cute couple. It was harder to imagine him paired with his present wife.*

He invited us to sit, waited until we settled ourselves on the sofa, and then settled into his chair. A ceiling fan above us spun its blades without much effect, and a rotating floor fan next to the television swept an intermittent breeze of warm air across the room. The television was on, showing a golf game. Jimmy picked up a remote control and muted the sound as Charlene came back with two iced teas, which she set on coasters on the shining wood of the coffee table. "Jim, honey, I forgot to ask you. Can I get you some more iced tea?" she asked, as she straightened herself.

He looked at her, and his face brightened a little with a look of solicitous kindness. "No, that's okay, Charl. Come sit down; it's a hot day to be moving around in."

She obliged, lowering herself carefully into a recliner on the other side of the sofa from Jim's armchair. "Oh, this weather!" she sighed. "Summer's supposed to be over; I don't know where it's coming from. And I hate to run the air conditioner because our power bills just go through the roof."

"So you're Andy's lawyers now?" Jimmy asked.

"I'm one of them," I said. "Dave Rothstein, here, is an investigator." I pulled out a couple of business cards and handed one each to Jimmy and Charlene. Charlene looked hers over carefully.

"He was found guilty, what, ten years ago?" she said. "What more is there to do?"

I mentally cleared my throat and gave the simplified explanation, about how Andy had the right to present evidence that might show that his trial wasn't fair and maybe get a new one on the question of whether he should really be sentenced to death row, and how we had been appointed by the court and were talking with people to see if there was helpful evidence that Andy's trial attorney could have put on but didn't. I threw in a mention of Emory, who had had a different attorney and had not gotten the death penalty.

"You're trying to get him released from prison?" Charlene asked, still suspicious. "He killed those girls, didn't he? He shouldn't ever get out, if you ask me."

Dave spoke, adding the credibility of his baritone voice to the conversation. "Frankly," he said, "it isn't likely he'll get released. Realistically, the best that's likely to happen is that his sentence could be reduced to life in prison."

Charlene nodded curtly, as if that was better than he deserved, as far as she was concerned. I took a drink of iced tea—it was home-made and sweet.

Jimmy spoke up. "Well, you know, we didn't really know Andy or his brother that well. I only saw them once in a while when they visited Ray and Margaret—Eva's aunt and uncle who raised her. They were just kids then, so I don't really know…" His voice tapered off, uncertainly, in mid-sentence.

"I understand," Dave said. "We've come to see you because we're looking for whatever we can learn about Andy's background—family history, influences, and so forth. We'd like to learn more about Eva and her side of the family, for example."

"Oh, Eva!" Charlene's big voice drew the words out in a scornful drawl. "She's a piece of work, that one."

Jimmy gave her an almost reproachful look, which she ignored. "She just left Carla—her daughter, you know?—with Jimmy's parents. Never did a thing for her. They raised her for years, until Jimmy and I got married. Every now and then Evie would come back and stir things up, talk about taking her back with her, get Carla's hopes up. Most of the time, though, she just seemed to forget the girl. We had to call her just to get her to let Carla visit for a couple of weeks in the summer. Poor kid, couldn't ever figure out why her mother didn't want her."

"I guess that's one reason we'd like to learn more about Evie," Dave said. "It's a little unusual for a mother to just give custody of her child away like that."

"Why don't you ask her? You've met her, haven't you?" Charlene asked.

"Oh yes," I said. "But there's so much we don't know about her, about Andy's family background at all, really."

Jimmy turned his head to me. "Her aunt and uncle never said much, but I believe something bad happened to Evie before she came to live with them."

"What was it—do you know?"

"I wasn't ever real sure, just that there was some big secret about why she came to live out here. Her parents were dead; I knew that. Evie said they died in a car wreck, but there was this rumor that they were murdered."

"Murdered?" Dave asked.

Jimmy shook his head. "Just small-town gossip, I think. I never believed it."

"Did Evie ever say anything?" I asked.

"No—she never talked about her parents, and I never pushed her. I thought she just wanted to have a normal life, whatever it was that had happened, and I tried to respect that. My mom and dad, I remember, they didn't want me to get engaged to her, but they never could come up with a reason why. But then Evie found out she was expecting, and they had to let us get married."

Charlene broke in. "I'm not so sure your parents weren't right. Look at how her kids came out. Carla, too."

Dave went for the opening she had made. "What happened to Carla?"

Jimmy gave a small, weary sigh. "Drugs."

"It's an awful thing," Charlene broke in, sitting up in her armchair. "Meth, cocaine, oxy—all that stuff. I don't know how many people's lives around here have been ruined by that junk. I work in social services here—just part-time these days, thank the Lord—it makes you sick seeing these women lose their kids, and the kids end up in foster homes. Same thing would have happened to Carla and her baby, except for Jimmy and me."

"Carla had a child?" Evie had never mentioned that she had a grandchild.

"Oh yes," Charlene said. "Austin. Evie never told you about him?"

"No," Dave and I said.

She sniffed. "Typical. Her only grandchild. Never even a birthday card."

"What happened to him?"

"County took him away from Carla when he was— honey, was Austin two or three when we took him in?"

Jimmy thought. "I think he wasn't quite two. I remember he had his second birthday with us."

"Oh, right. We never had kids, just miscarriages. Austin was my baby. We raised him like our own. Made Carla sign over legal guardianship of him to us."

"How old is he now?" Dave asked.

"He turned twenty-two in March."

"Oh, so he's pretty grown-up," Dave said. "Does he still live with you?"

"No," Jimmy said. "He's in Spokane. In a home." As if answering the question we hadn't the presence of mind to ask, he went on. "He's autistic. We kept him as long as we could, but he finally got too big for Charl to handle."

"And he needed help we just couldn't get for him here," Charlene added.

"He'd have tantrums," Jimmy said. "Throw himself around the room, break stuff."

Charlene's eyes filled with tears. "I hated to do it," she said.

"We go see him every month," Jimmy said. "I'm sure he's happier there," he said, as much to Charlene as to us. "Staff there take good care of him, and they can handle him when he goes off. To be honest, I don't think he misses us, really."

"I still think it was the drugs she was using that caused it," Charlene said, dabbing her eyes with a tissue.

"Oh come on, honey, we don't know that," Jimmy answered. It sounded like an old argument, half-heartedly reprised.

Dave discreetly changed the subject. "Do you know where Evie came from, originally?" he asked, in a tone of voice that made it seem almost an afterthought.

Jimmy pondered this. "Iowa, I think."

"I know this is probably a pretty personal question," Dave continued, "but can you tell me about your relationship with Evie, and why your marriage broke up?"

"Oh," Jimmy said, with a sigh, "it was just the usual, I

guess. We married too young, and we wanted different things."

"Like what?"

"Well, Evie wanted to get out and go somewhere, wanted to see more of the world. And I didn't. I grew up here, had my family, a job I liked in my dad's machine shop. I was happy, but she wasn't. And it just kind of ended. She wanted to go to community college, move to Spokane or Seattle, and that's what she did."

"Leaving Carla behind," I said.

"Yeah, well," Jimmy said, doubtfully. "I don't think she really meant to leave Carla permanently. I think she thought she could get her when she got through school and got a decent job. But then she met Len—and I guess things changed."

"Like what?"

"Well, she had the boys, and there was Len's drinking and all. I never could see how she got involved with him, but I think after a while she was kind of afraid of him."

"Len was that bad?"

"Well," Jimmy said, "not to speak ill of the man…" He hesitated, as if trying to think of a charitable way to describe Len. "But he was kind of a slick talker, not someone you felt you could trust. And you could see he had a mean streak. They came to visit, and it was like, if Len was around, Evie and the boys were always real quiet. If they said something he didn't like, he'd give them a look, and they'd just shut up. He killed a man—maybe Evie told you about that—went to prison, six or seven years, while the boys were still young."

"We did hear that," Dave said. "And we heard that he jumped parole, and no one seems to know where he is."

"Yeah, I heard that, too," Jimmy said vaguely.

"When you saw Andy back then," Dave asked, "how did he strike you?"

Jimmy paused for a few seconds, as though looking for the right words. "Quiet, I'd say. Kinda lonely. Emory was rambunctious, really a handful, but Andy always seemed to hang back."

"What kinds of things did Andy like to do?" Dave asked.

"Oh, go fishing with me. Help in the garden. Stuff like that."

"Did he read?" Dave asked.

"Oh, I'm sure he could."

"But for fun?"

"No—not that I ever saw. Neither of 'em did."

"Did he play games with other children?"

"Yeah, when they'd let him. He didn't fit in too well. Emory used to call him names, and I think the other kids picked it up."

"What kind of names?"

Jimmy thought for a moment, sifting through memories. "I'd like to say it was something like 'stupid,' but I don't remember well."

"Did he seem stupid to you?"

"Not really, maybe a little slow. He was a slow learner—I never could teach him how to cast or bait a hook right. But then I only saw him once in a while. They'd stay at Evie's aunt and uncle's when they visited."

Dave asked some more questions about Andy's limitations: could he count change, get himself a snack; did he need help with getting dressed, and so forth. Jimmy hadn't seen Andy enough to remember much. "Carla would remember," he said. "She liked him, kind of took him under her wing. And she was around him more than I ever was."

"Do you know how we can get hold of Carla?" I asked.

"Not at the moment," Jimmy said ruefully. "She never seems to stay in one place for more than a few months. Last time we heard from her, she was getting evicted from her apartment. I don't even remember where she said she was then."

"She calls sometimes," Charlene said, "asking about Austin."

"Yeah, if she calls, I'll let her know you'd like to talk to her," Jimmy said. "I think she'd want to help Andy."

"Is there anyone else around who might have known Evie?" Dave asked.

Charlene and Jimmy both thought a while. "Not many," Jimmy said. "It's been so long—people move away, pass on. And Evie didn't have a lot of friends. She kept herself apart."

We had spent part of that morning getting microfiche copies of Evie's school transcript from a secretary who'd probably found us the most interesting thing that had happened to her in months, and the early afternoon at the public library copying parts of old high-school yearbooks and city directories. Dave pulled the copies from his briefcase, and he and Jimmy went over the pages together, as Jimmy recalled teachers and fellow students, sometimes with a funny story, more often with a shake of his head and a comment. "No, he was killed in Vietnam," about one. "Died ten or so years ago—cancer," about another. He thought one of their high-school teachers, now retired, still lived in town, and a couple of girls who had been friendly with Evie had married local boys.

Charlene watched them quietly, then said to me, "I'm not much help, I'm afraid. I didn't grow up here."

The conversation between Jimmy and Dave wound down, and Dave went back to his chair. I took another sip of iced tea and made small talk while Dave and I gathered our things and stood up to leave. As we were turning to go, I saw a half-dozen photos in frames standing on a side table. "May I look at your pictures?" I asked.

"Sure," Charlene said. She glided closer to me as I picked one up. "That's Carla," she said, "when she was about twenty. She doesn't look much like that now." Carla at twenty was a wisp of a thing, with a pretty heart-shaped face, long light-colored hair, and a hopeful smile. I picked up another, a snapshot of a family. "That's Evie and Len," Charlene said, her voice a touch cooler, "with Carla and Andy and Emory." Len was tall and rangy and dark-haired, like Emory. Even in the still photo, he looked like he'd been drinking; there was something a little off-center, not quite under control, in his posture and the tilt of his head and the narrow-eyed half smile with which he looked at the camera.

"So that's Len," I said. "Does anyone know what became of him?"

"No, and I couldn't care less," Charlene said, with surprising energy. I put the photo down and turned to look at her. "I don't know if Evie ever told you, but he molested Carla," she went on. "Carla told me."

"That's terrible."

"I think it had a lot to do with Carla getting into drugs."

"I wouldn't be surprised," I agreed. "That's an awful thing to happen to a young girl." I always hate to ask people about the details of sex crimes, but as an investigator, it's one of the things you have to do. I steeled myself and went on. "Did she tell you what he did?"

Charlene didn't seem surprised by the question. "She said he'd come up and put his hands under her clothes, push against her, that sort of thing. Once he came into her bedroom drunk in the middle of the night and tried to get her to have sex with him. Laid on top of her."

Ick. I tried not to grimace. "Did he actually rape her?"

"Not as far as I know. She said she was able to make him go away."

"Good for her," I said. "How old was she when he was doing all that?"

"Fifteen, sixteen. It happened when she went to live with

them."

"Live with them?" Although Evie had already told me about this, I was keen to hear Charlene's side of the story.

"Yeah. She was in high school and fighting with us all the time, and running away. Then she decided she wanted to go live with her mother."

"She was out of control," Jimmy said, from the doorway. "She was gonna go anyway, whatever we said, so we called Evie and set things up and drove her there."

"She came back after a few months," Charlene added. "She said she felt bad leaving Andy, but she couldn't stand it there any more."

We moved toward the door, where Jimmy was waiting. As he opened it, he said, "I don't know how much help we were, but if there's anything you'd like to ask us, just give us a call."

Dave and I thanked him, and shook his hand.

"I hope you can help Andy," Jimmy said. "I know he did a terrible thing, and between you and me I don't think he should ever get out—but…" He lowered his voice, as if to keep Charlene from overhearing, "I've never really been in favor of the death penalty, to be honest."

"Me neither," I said.

He smiled a little, mostly around the eyes. "Well, do what you can for him, and good luck."

* * *

We ate burgers and fries at a McDonald's and went back to the motel, where Dave, armed with a laptop and an Internet connection, did address searches for the teachers, schoolmates, and former neighbors whose names we'd gotten from the school records, the library, and our conversation with Jimmy and Charlene.

For the rest of the afternoon we drove the streets of Canfield looking for the people who our searches said still lived there. We kept getting lost: streets meandered off into the woods or ducked off each other at angles so odd they confused even the rental car's GPS tracker. House numbers were hard to see and sometimes seemed to appear in no particular order. One house we were looking for had a weathered FOR SALE sign in front and looked as though no one had lived there for months. At another, the young man who came to the door said he had just bought the house; he had never heard of the family we asked about. Another, which had come up in Dave's search as that of one of Evie's teachers, turned out to be now owned by his son, who told us that his father had retired and moved to Florida. By that time it was dark, and I was weary and discouraged. When Dave suggested breaking for dinner, I gave a silent hallelujah.

There weren't many restaurant choices in Canfield. The diner where we'd had breakfast was closed for the day, and there didn't seem to be much else except fast food. We finally found a place with a lighted sign that said STEAKS AND SEAFOOD and a promising number of cars in its parking lot.

Inside, the place was as dim as a cave, with leatherette booths and white tablecloths. A festive crowd of customers were eating and making a buzz of conversation, and there was a heady smell of grilled steak and garlic in the air. Dave leaned down toward me. "Looks like we've found the fancy place in town," he said.

I had a green salad and part of a very good rare steak, charred on its surface from the hot grill. At the end of the meal, when the waitress asked me if I wanted a doggie bag for the rest of my steak, I felt a pang of homesickness for Charlie. A piece of beef like that would make him a very happy dog.

An hour later, I was fast asleep and dreaming in my motel bed, this time of driving endless roads in a town we didn't have a map for, trying to find someone whose name kept changing as we looked for him.

24

Things went better—sort of—the next day. I woke up early and drafted declarations for Jimmy and Charlene to sign, then printed them on the motel's printer. The weather had cooled; the pale sky, streaked with torn clouds, carried the feel of autumn and the possibility of rain.

Armed with our yearbook photos of Evie and Jimmy, we resumed our exploration of the length and breadth, such as it was, of Canfield and the farms and wheat fields around it. This time, we found several people on our list. Only one of the retired teachers remembered Evie or even recognized her yearbook photograph. He recalled Evie as a nice, quiet girl, but not much more. "Something happened to her family; her parents were killed in a car accident or something like that."

One woman who Jimmy had said had been a friend of Evie's didn't remember her at all. But another, a thin woman with tired brown eyes and iron-gray hair in a functional bob, looked at the yearbook photo for a long moment and invited us into her house. She led us through her living room, spotlessly clean but overcrowded with furniture, where a very old woman in a pink print house dress was watching a daytime talk show on the TV, and she encouraged us to sit at the dining table in an alcove between the living room and the kitchen. The table was dark wood, old, but polished to an almost mirror-like shine. Four plastic place mats, cut to imitate lace, were arranged at even intervals around it, and another place mat in the center held a bowl of plastic hydrangeas.

The woman—her maiden name had been Patty Clauson, but her married name was Cuellar—sat down with us. She held the photocopied photo for a long time, looking at it. It trembled, ever so slightly, in her hand. She shook her head slowly and looked up at us. "Oh, lord, how young we were then!" she sighed. "Why are you asking about Evie Bowden? Nothing bad has happened, has it?"

"Not to her—at least, not directly," I said. "It's about one of her sons. He's in prison in California, and we're looking for information about his background for his appeal." It was about as much of the truth, I figured, as she would care to have.

"Oh. That's a shame," Mrs. Cuellar said. "I didn't know she'd had any children after Carla. We lost touch after she and Jimmy broke up and she moved to Spokane."

She put Evie's photo down. "I don't know what you'd want to know about her," she said.

"Just whatever you can remember. What was she like?"

"Nice. A nice girl."

We waited in polite silence for her to continue. Mrs. Cuellar looked at us for a cue and when none came, she looked at the photograph on the table and then back up at us. "She was friendly to me. When no one else was." Her hands moved a little, nervously, on the table. "My dad drank and was in and out of jail a lot. The kids at school knew about him—everyone did—and some of them were cruel. You know how kids can be. Evie was kind of rejected by them, too. And we hung together. She used to laugh about it, said we both had bad blood."

"What was hers?" I asked.

"She said her brother was in a mental hospital and everyone thought she was crazy, too." Before either of us could say anything, she went on. "I don't know if it was true or not."

"Did she ever talk about what had happened to her parents?"

"I knew they'd passed away. That's why she was living with her aunt and uncle. I think I heard they were in a car wreck."

"Did you ever hear any rumor about her parents being murdered?" I asked.

"Murdered?" She looked startled for a second, but then a thought seemed to come to her. "Oh my goodness, I'd forgotten all about that."

"About what?"

"One of the boys started a rumor that Eva had killed her family. Really cruel, mean stuff, I think just because she'd come from outside. They were the kids that picked on us; a couple of them used to call her Lizzie Borden—you know, like 'Lizzie Borden took an ax, and gave her father forty whacks.'"

"That must have been terrible for her," I said.

"Yeah. I'm sure it hurt her, but she never let it show. We both knew that if they could see it was getting to you, they'd just pick on you more. She was tougher than me. Sometimes I'd cry when they'd pick on me, but she never did."

"Did she ever say anything to you about what happened to her parents?"

"I don't remember her ever talking about them. She might have—it was a long time ago," Mrs. Cuellar said, with an apologetic shake of her head.

She sighed a deep sigh, and looked up at the ceiling and then back down. "So much has probably happened to both of us since then. See? She has a son in prison—and I didn't even know she had one at all."

I gave her my business card and asked her if she knew of anyone else in the area who might have known Evie when they were young. She thought for a moment, but the only name she came up with was the other woman we'd seen that morning, who hadn't remembered Evie. "And Jimmy's still here, but I guess you've already talked to him. No—Evie and I didn't really have many friends back then. I really felt so much like I didn't belong—it's hard to believe sometimes that I've been here all these years. I guess Evie might still be, too, if she and Jimmy had stayed together."

At the door, she asked us to say hello to Evie for her. She stood at the door until we were in our rental car and waved goodbye to us as we drove off.

"Well," Dave said, as we headed down the street, "I think we've about exhausted Canfield. Shall we mosey on over to Idaho?" Dave's miraculous databases had found a sister of Len's, Gladys, married name Clancy, in a town in the Idaho Panhandle. Before leaving, we stopped at the social services office to meet Charlene and get her signature on her declaration, and then headed to their house to get Jimmy's.

"You sure got everything, just like I told you," he said after reading the declaration, and he signed it slowly and carefully, like a man who wasn't used to writing his name.

25

The drive into Idaho was a long one on lonely highways, east and then north. The landscape changed from rolling wheat fields to woods, and the sky grew darker and more gray.

It was late afternoon, and rain was falling lightly and intermittently, as if the sky itself could hardly make the effort, when we reached the place we were looking for, one of a string of small fishing resorts along the edge of a long, pine-fringed lake. There wasn't much to any of them—bait store, gas station, launching ramp, a cluster of vacation cabins. The address we had turned out to be in a trailer park dishearteningly called "Voyage's End." There was a roofed shelter with mailboxes at the entrance, and Dave got out and read the names on them until he found the one we were looking for. "Space D-12," he said as he slid back into the driver's seat.

A tired-looking dark red Ford Explorer stood in the little driveway in front of space D-12. We parked on the other side of the gravel road. Outside the car, I pulled on my jacket, shivering; we were well north of Canfield, and the damp air felt like autumn. High above us, the wind sighed in the pine branches.

The trailer house looked as though it had been there a long time. Its aluminum trim was oxidized, the white and turquoise blue of its paint chalky and faded. A step of weathered wood stood before the metal door; we climbed onto it and knocked. A television blared inside, playing what sounded like *Wheel of Fortune*.

I heard footsteps, then the rattle of a chain latch. The door opened, and a gray-haired woman in jeans and a violet sweatshirt looked out at us, obviously startled to see strangers on her doorstep.

"Hello?" she asked. I had the feeling she was sure we had come to the wrong house.

"Mrs. Clancy?" Dave asked.

"Yes?" she answered, a little hesitant. I saw her sizing us up, factoring our ages, how we were dressed, and the notebook under my arm into a quick calculation whether it was safe to keep talking with us.

I'd tucked a business card into my jacket pocket, to have it handy, and I pulled it out and offered it to her. As she reached out, a little hesitantly, to take it, I introduced myself and Dave. "I'm a criminal defense attorney, and we're working for the defense in a case involving your brother Leonard's son."

She stopped reading the business card and looked back at

us in questioning surprise. "Good heavens," she said. "You've come all the way out here?"

"Well, yes," I said.

"Well," she echoed. "I don't know what you want from me, but you might as well come in." As we followed her into a tiny, crowded living room that smelled of cigarette smoke, cooking, and cats, she continued, "I don't know how much I'd have to say to you. I haven't seen Len in forty years. I knew he had a couple of kids, but I never met 'em. Here, push some of those papers away and have a seat. Just put 'em on the floor—yeah, that's fine."

She sat down on a brown tweed sofa. Dave motioned me to the only armchair and sat on a straight-backed chair next to the couch. As I approached the chair, a calico cat jumped from its arm and ran lightly toward the kitchen. A dark tabby cat jumped from somewhere on the floor onto Mrs. Clancy's lap, looked at us, and then leapt off and vanished again under the coffee table.

The seat of the armchair seemed to sag almost to the floor, as I tried, not very successfully, to make a graceful descent into it. "You don't mind if I smoke, do you?" Mrs. Clancy said. We shook our heads, and she pulled a cigarette from a pack on the table in front of her. "Can I get you some coffee? It's a fresh pot." Coffee sounded good to both of us, and Mrs. Clancy disappeared into the kitchen, emerging a few minutes later with three mismatched mugs, which she set on the coffee table. She ducked back into the kitchen and came out again holding a carton of milk, a sugar bowl, and three spoons.

"Don't know what you take in yours," she said, after settling herself on the sofa and picking up one of the cups. "I drink it black myself. You're lucky I was here. I run the market and bait store down on the highway, but business was so slow I decided to leave my clerk in charge and come on home early. It's pretty dead here this time of year—ain't nothin' goin' on till ice-fishing season starts."

I felt at a loss where to begin. "I wonder if you can tell us about Leonard and what he was like when he was young."

"Hoo, boy," she said, shaking her head, "not a lot. He's six years older than me. I was only about ten when he left home for good."

"Sixteen is pretty young. Was there a reason why he left?" I asked.

She picked up her coffee cup and drank, then put it back down. "Oh, a lot of things, I guess. He and my dad fought all the time. Leonard was always in trouble, and my dad was pretty hard on him. Leonard ran away a few times, and once he just didn't come back."

"You say your dad," Dave asked. "Is he not Leonard's father?"

"That's right. Leonard and Walter are my mom's kids from her first marriage."

"Leonard has a brother?"

"Yep. Walt. He's a couple of years older."

"Who is their father?"

"His name was Delmore, I think. Delmore Hardy. My parents met after he died. Killed in a logging accident, I think they said."

"What was Leonard like, generally?"

"Just bad, a lot of the time. Cut school all the time. Stole things. He had kind of a mean streak, too. He used to pick on me a lot. I never liked him. Walt was a different story. He was really like a big brother to me. A good man when he grew up. Not the same after Vietnam, though. You might want to talk to him; he and Leonard were close."

"Do you know where he's living?" Dave asked.

"Not that far from here, actually. You better go see him in the morning, though. He's probably drunk by now," she said with a roll of her eyes and a short laugh.

Dave thanked her for the advice. "So are you all from around here?" I asked.

"Yes. Born and raised, all of us, in northern Idaho. My father worked his whole life in the lumber mills."

Dave asked a few more questions and got directions to Walt's place and to the nearest town with a motel. "I can't give you a phone number for him, 'cause he doesn't have a phone. Phone company cut him off for not paying his bill, and neither of us has the money right now to get his service back."

* * *

The next morning, after a night in a motel and breakfast at the diner, Dave set his GPS for Eastland Ranch Trail, where Gladys had said Walt lived. "It's not the best road," she had warned. "Better than it was, though. It's oiled now. Used to be just dirt. But the county doesn't do much to maintain it."

The roads to the trail wound gradually upward into the mountains above the lake. The area had been logged over once, but tall evergreens now grew close together around the occasional stump still visible among them. We kept missing turns for side roads barely visible in the woods, and it took the better part of an hour before we finally found our way to the road down which Walt lived. It had a green county street sign at its juncture with the paved county road. A row of battered mailboxes stood near the intersection.

Walt's was the last house in a scatter of log cabins, shabby prefab houses, double-wides, and old house trailers half hidden in the woods along the road. The clearing in which it stood was half covered in a mat of blackberry vines and other brush and littered with rusting bits of machinery, broken furniture, and old appliances. I saw a plastic cooler, a Coleman camp stove and a white china toilet. An old gray pickup truck was parked on a spot of bare earth near the cabin, and most of another, half taken apart, was rusting away in the brush nearby.

The cabin was made mostly of logs, blackened with age. At some point a room had been added to one end of it, with siding that looked like plywood, painted rust brown and stained with age and damp.

Dave turned the car around at the end of the road and parked facing back toward the county road. He and I looked at each other. "Well, at least it isn't raining," he deadpanned. Nervous, I began sputtering with laughter, hunching my shoulders and staring down at my knees, in case someone was looking out at us. When I'd recovered, we got out and walked back toward the cabin.

A couple of dogs began barking at us, interrupting each other in a syncopated duet—a big yellow mongrel of some sort and a slightly smaller, darker mutt, pulling at the ends of long chains attached to a big eyebolt next to the steps to the porch. The dogs moved between us and the steps as we approached, and as I was wondering how we were going to get past them, the door above us opened and a man shouted at them, "Shut up, you two!" He stood on the porch, squinting at us for a few seconds, and then asked, in a gravelly voice, "What can I do for you?"

He looked like a mountain man. He was about middle height, but a little stooped, as if he had a bad back. He was wearing old Levis and a faded plaid flannel shirt, half buttoned over a dingy T-shirt and a beer belly. His gray hair stood up in tufts around his head. The lower part of his face was covered by a bushy mustache and tangled beard, and the rest was wrinkled and weathered brown. He blinked in the gray daylight and kept one hand on the door frame, as if to steady himself.

"Mr. Hardy?" Dave asked. The man nodded. "My name

is Dave Rothstein, and this is Janet Moodie. Ms. Moodie is one of the defense attorneys for one of your brother Leonard's sons, Andy Hardy. Your sister, Mrs. Clancy, said you might be able to help us."

Walt stood for a moment, swaying slightly, as if absorbing the information. "Gladys sent you?"

"Yes," Dave answered.

He was silent for another second or two. "So. You're the kid's lawyers?"

Dave nodded.

"He's in trouble with the law, then." He moved to the side of the door. "Come on in. I don't know that there's much I can help you with, but you can ask."

We clumped up the sagging steps, the dogs watching us from the yard. The landing was crowded with boxes of ropes, rusting chains, jack stands, wrenches, and electrical wire. Walter waited at the door until we were inside, then closed the door behind him. I felt a stab of anxiety as it shut.

The cabin was dim inside and cold. The smell of dog and old cigarette smoke congealed in the chill air. Smoke-yellowed blinds covered the windows, and one or two had ragged curtains pulled across them as well. Clothing, tools, books, ashtrays, and empty beer cans seemed to be piled on every surface.

Walter led us down a path between small tables and bookcases heaped with the detritus of his life, to a round oak table where the debris had been shoved aside to create a clear space a little bigger than a place setting, with a coffee cup on one side and an ashtray half full of cigarette butts on the other. The smell of alcohol and unwashed clothing followed in his wake.

"Have a seat," he said. He took the chair by the cleared space, and Dave and I pulled out a couple more old wooden dining chairs and sat down. Walt pulled a pack of cigarettes and a book of matches out of his shirt pocket. He knocked a cigarette out of the pack with a practiced tap of his fingers on its bottom, put it between his lips, and lit it. On the first exhale, he bent over, coughing, for an alarming half-minute or so. I could smell his breath, an ugly compound of unbrushed and decaying teeth, tobacco, and whiskey. "Gotta stop smokin' these things," he said in a voice full of gravel, as he sat up again, his eyes watering, the cigarette in his fingers. "So Len's boy is in trouble. Which of 'em is it, again?"

"Andy—Marion—the older one," Dave said.

"Andy, huh? Wasn't he the kind of slow one? I'd've kind of pegged his brother—Emory—as the bad one. He had more of his old man in him. Must be pretty big trouble to bring you all out here."

He took another drag on his cigarette, went into another coughing fit, and then pushed heavily up from his chair. "'Scuse me," he said and walked into his kitchen. "Can I get you some coffee?" he called from inside, without turning.

"No thanks; we're good," Dave said, and I nodded in agreement. Walter picked up a glass from the overloaded counter and filled it with water from the sink tap. He took a drink and brought the glass back to the table.

"He's been convicted of capital murder in California fifteen years ago," Dave explained.

Walter's shoulders slumped, and his leathery cheeks seemed to sink a bit in his face. "Aw, shit," he said. "Who'd he kill?"

"Two women. Or so the jury said."

Walter shook his head sadly. "That's bad. I'm sorry to hear it. He about to be executed? Is that why you're here?"

"No, nothing like that. His case isn't nearly over. We're trying to get at least part of it reopened by finding mitigating evidence."

"Oh?" Walter looked uncertain, as if he didn't understand what Dave was saying.

"We're trying to find evidence about Andy's life and background that might have made jurors feel more sympathetic to him and persuaded them to give him life in prison instead of death."

"Uh. Like whether he was abused as a kid sort of thing?"

"Right."

"Well I don't know about that. Len had a temper, for sure. But I wasn't around enough to see how he treated his boys."

"You said you thought Andy was slow," Dave said. "That's something that might help him. He didn't commit the crimes alone—Emory was involved, too—and we may be able to show he was following Emory's lead."

"Emory," Walt said. "He on death row, too?"

"No, he's doing life without parole."

"Damn," Walt said. "Both of 'em in prison. That must be tough on Eva."

"It is," I said.

"You've met her then."

I nodded, and Walt turned his attention back to Dave. "Sorry," he said. "You were talking about Andy."

"We've found some evidence—tests and such—that he may be mentally retarded."

"Mentally retarded." Walter mulled that. "Well, I don't know. I didn't see them that much growing up, maybe once a year. Andy was kind of slow, but I don't know as I'd call him retarded. He seemed like a normal enough kid—just a little behind the curve, that's all."

"How was he behind?" I asked.

"I don't know—just slow."

We asked Walter a series of questions about Andy as a kid. Walter remembered trying to explain baseball to the boys and Andy not getting it at all, and he remembered Evie saying she couldn't send Andy to the store because he'd always get the wrong stuff, even when she gave him a list."

"Do you remember how old he was when she told you that?"

"Hmm—twelve or thirteen, maybe? Not long before Len got out of prison. It was when we all went to see Len together—some holiday."

I asked him some questions about his own early life, and Len's.

"We had a pretty lousy time, growing up," he said. "My dad—Len's and mine—was a logger and a drunk. Got killed falling off the back of a truck. I was old enough to remember him, but I don't think Len was.

"Then Mama married Joe—Joe Ecklund. He worked at the mill, became foreman later. He was a good man, in his way. Provided for us, treated Mama well. Didn't drink at all, which was pretty unusual up here. He'd been raised in the Mormon Church. He left it before we knew him, but I guess that part stayed with him." He paused, as if something had interrupted his train of thought.

Dave asked, "What did he do that made growing up with him so bad?"

Walter, recalled to the conversation, knit his brows and thought for a few seconds. "It was his personality, I guess. He was kind of a cold sumbitch, sort of a control freak, if you know what I mean. Didn't like us boys. I think he resented having to raise us. We was too rambunctious for him, Len especially. He and Len got into it a lot, and Joe'd lose his temper and hit him. Len started running away, and that only made things worse. After I got drafted, Len left for good, and went out on his own. We kept in touch, though. He got drafted, too, soon enough—it was the middle of the Vietnam War, and they were gettin' all of us they could." He laughed, a short, humorless chuckle, and coughed again for a while before going on. "I was in 'Nam by then; I re-upped so's he wouldn't have to go."

"That was a big sacrifice to make, even for your brother," Dave said.

Walter shrugged. "Nah—I was in country already. I knew I could handle it—or I thought I could. Young and stupid, I was then. Now I'm old and stupid. But, knowing Len, I figured he'd get out there and do something off the wall. Never could control himself, especially when he was drunk. He was always like that, even after he got out. Killed a man in a bar fight, but I guess you know about that if you've talked with Eva. He didn't treat her too well, neither. I felt for her and the boys. Used to try to talk to Len about it, but I never could make an impression on him—he was too hard-headed. I never could figure out why Eva let him move back in with her after he got out of prison." He stopped talking again for a couple of seconds, and then asked, "By the way, did you ever find out what happened to him?"

We both shook our heads. "No luck at all," Dave said. "We were hoping you might know something."

Walter looked disappointed. "I'm sure he's dead," he said.

"It seems like a good possibility at this point," Dave agreed.

"No, I mean I'm pretty sure of it. Len and I were always close. I lived with him and Eva for a few months after I got out of the army, and Len tried to help me get my disability. Didn't manage it at the time. Took fifteen years before they'd give me full disability for PTSD. But he'd go in and tell them all about how different I was after Vietnam and all the shit I was goin' through." His voice rose a little and took on an edge of old anger, for a moment, then fell back. "We stayed in touch. I'd go visit them every once in a while, and I used to call Len every couple of months or so. He asked me to call collect, let him know I was still okay, 'cause I was out on the streets a lot of the time before I got my disability." He stopped and picked up his cigarette and put it back down again. "Damn things gonna kill me," he said again, and went on.

"When Leonard was in prison, I wrote to him, and he'd write to me when I was someplace for long enough to get a letter. I visited him a couple times when I had the money, and saw Eva and the boys a few times, too. I was gonna go see him after he got out, but I was broke that winter. I knew he'd moved back in with Eva, and I called him there a couple times. Then once I called, and Eva said he'd left, just like that, after they'd had a fight. She said they found his pickup parked near the Greyhound stop. Said his parole officer was lookin' for him. I called her a couple times after that, but he never showed up, and then they all moved to California. I had my disability by then, and this place here, thanks to Gladys. I gave Eva my address so Len could write to me if he came back, but never heard a word. I wrote to her a few times, called a couple times a year for a while, just to let her know I was still here. Told her to tell me if she heard anything about Len."

"And she never did," Dave said.

"Nope, nothin'." He frowned at Dave. "It's not like him just to disappear like that. I can't believe he wouldn't have contacted any of us after all this time. That's why I think he's dead."

"Makes sense," Dave said. "Apparently he was involved with some bad people after he got out of prison."

"Huh," Walter said. He bent his head forward, as if stretching out a kink in his neck; when he raised it again, his eyes were red-rimmed and filmed with a layer of tears. "I miss the little bastard," he said. "I was kinda hopin' you'd have some word of him."

"If we hear anything, we'll let you know," Dave said.

"Yeah," Walter answered, without conviction. "But I guess you're more concerned with helping young Andy. Anything else you want to know?"

Dave shook his head. "I don't think so, at the moment," he said. "Would you be willing to sign some records releases and a declaration for Andy's habeas corpus petition?"

Walter looked puzzled. "His what?"

"It's the court paper he has to file to ask for his death sentence to be overturned," I said. "He needs to present evidence with it—paperwork and declarations from witnesses. I think what you told us about Len and your stepfather may help us explain how Andy turned out the way he did."

Walter made a face. "I don't understand all this court stuff," he said, "but if it'll help Len's boy, I'll sign whatever."

We sat in silence, Walter smoking his cigarette and coughing, while I turned my notes into a hand-printed declaration on lined paper and showed it to Dave. After rewriting a couple of pages, I gave the final draft to Walter. Walter pulled a pair of smeared eyeglasses out of his shirt pocket, put them on, and read through it, his face screwed up into a frown of effort. "Looks okay," he said finally. "What's the date today, anyway?" Dave told him, and he dated and signed the declaration and the releases and handed them back to us. Dave and I thanked him, and stood up. When Walter stood, Dave put his hand out; Walter clasped it, and they shook hands. "We may want to talk with you again," Dave said. "I hope that's okay."

"Sure," Walter said, without enthusiasm. "I don't have a phone—don't know when I will again—but you can write me or get word to me through Gladys."

After thanking him, we threaded our way to the door. In the daylight, Walter's face was a mass of seams, wrinkles, and age spots, his eyes almost lost in folds of skin. "I'm sorry about young Andy," he said, lingering in the doorway. "Wouldn't want to see nothin' bad happen to one of Len's boys—even if he did do wrong. If you see them or Eva, tell 'em Uncle Walt said hi." He backed inside and closed the weather-blackened door.

26

Back home from Idaho, I made a packet of background material about Andy for Dr. Moss and sent it to him and called to reserve the prison's psychiatric interview room for two days of testing. As usual, it was booked up for months; the earliest available date was the week after Thanksgiving. Dave flew back up to Washington and interviewed as many teachers as he could find from the schools Andy had attended. Nancy Hollister, our psychologist, read the background materials I'd given her and interviewed Andy, Evie, and Emory, with me present. I'd warned her beforehand about Emory's blowup when Dave and I had seen him, and I watched in admiration as she steered and soothed Emory through his story of his childhood and adolescence and his recollections of Andy. The anger Dave and I had seen threatened to push to the surface again when Nancy asked about Len's molesting Carla, but Nancy calmed him. "Mama said he did," he told her grudgingly. "I never saw nothin'." He managed to answer questions about Len's walking out on them without much visible emotion. "I didn't feel too bad about it," he said, almost defensively. "He wasn't any kind of father anyway."

Almost before I knew it, it was the end of October, almost eight months into the year we had to file Andy's petition. I didn't feel we'd uncovered enough new mitigation evidence to persuade a federal judge that it might have made a difference to a jury trying to decide whether or not to give Andy the death penalty. Jim was never around long enough for a real conversation about where we were with the case. The one or two times I told him I was anxious about how things were going, he brushed my worries aside. "Look," he said. "If something's out there, we'll find it. And Andy's so clearly retarded anyway, I don't think anything else is going to matter."

At home in Corbin's Landing, I had more to worry about than Andy. The last rains had been six months ago, and the warm Santa Ana winds were gusting through the Douglas firs and redwoods and pulling the last bit of moisture out of grass and branch and leaf. The air seemed charged with static electricity. The news was so full of wildfires that it seemed half the state must be burning. I was living in a board and batten shack up a dirt road next to a redwood forest, and I wasn't sleeping well.

I was working in my office late one evening, pounding out a reply brief and periodically sniffing the air at my open window for smoke, when the phone rang. It was after nine, and I figured the call was probably a wrong number, so I let it go to voicemail. The voice on the line was a woman's, flat and husky; my first reaction was *rural meth user*. But a couple of seconds into her message, I grabbed for the receiver.

"This is Janet Moodie."

"Ms. Moodie?" the voice repeated. She started over, a little tentatively, with the message she had been leaving on the voicemail tape. "My name is Carla Burrell."

I was still too surprised to answer with anything but a slightly choked "Hello."

The timid voice continued, "Andy Hardy's sister?"

Still in shock, I said the first thing that came into my head. "Oh, I'm so glad to hear from you!"

She didn't seem to react to my gushing. "My dad gave me your number and said I should call you. You're Andy's lawyer?" In the timbre of her ruined voice, I thought I heard an ever-so-slight resemblance to Evie's.

"Yes," was all I could think of to say.

"What do you need from me?"

I launched into my spiel about how we were trying to find evidence to get Andy a new trial and maybe save his life. She heard me out, and then said, "I didn't testify at Andy's trial. Or Emory's, either."

I knew that, but it seemed she wanted to tell me about it, so I asked her why.

"The investigator for Emory's lawyer found me and asked

me to come testify, but I told him I just couldn't face it. They served me with a subpoena, but I never went to court. I didn't hear from them after that. I guess they decided they didn't want me after all."

"What about Andy's trial?"

"I didn't even know about Andy's trial until it was over." She was silent for a couple of seconds. "I felt bad afterward. I should have tried to help him. But I had a lot going on in my life."

A lot going on in her life—probably shorthand for "I was using a lot of drugs."

"Things are different now. I've been making some changes, and thinking a lot. I'd like to help him—if I still can."

My mind was starting to work again after the shock of hearing from her. "I think you could be really helpful. We're investigating Andy's background, and we need as much information now as we can get."

"Like what he was like when he was a kid—that's what Dad said."

"Yes, that. And what his life was like, growing up."

"You mean whether he was abused and all that?"

"Among other things, yes," I answered.

"Like one of those trials on Court TV."

"Yes, like that," I said, thanking the media, for once, for explaining mitigation to the masses.

Carla was silent for a moment before going on. "I didn't grow up with Mama and Len and the boys," she said, a little hesitantly, "but I was there some of the time." She stopped again, as though trying to decide what to say next. "I can tell you some things."

"Anything might help," I said. It was my turn to pause before moving ahead. "I'd really like to talk with you in person. Is there someplace we can meet?"

"I think so."

"Where are you?"

"In Martinez. I'm in rehab. I got busted in Antioch. Judge told me it was this or prison."

"Can I visit you there?"

"I'm allowed to have visitors on Saturday and Sunday afternoons, from two to four."

"I could drive over this Saturday. Would that be okay?"

"Sure."

"Do you mind if I bring my investigator along?"

A second's hesitation. "Yeah. I guess it would be okay."

I asked her for the address and phone number where she was staying, and she gave them to me. Afterward, she seemed to linger at the other end of the line, as if she wasn't finished talking but didn't know how to say the next thing. I didn't want to let her go, either. What if she changed her mind before Saturday, and this was the only time I'd have to talk to her? I took a chance. "Is there something you want to talk about now?"

"No—not now." She hesitated again. Then, a little abruptly, she said, "I should go now."

"Okay," I said, trying to hit the right pitch of gratitude. "Thank you for calling; I'm really glad to hear from you. I'll see you Saturday, then."

"Okay. Bye."

"Bye."

And whatever ether it is that carried her voice, that single small thread of pulse and signal bridging the air between us, snapped into silence as the phone disconnected.

27

I left a voicemail for Dave the next morning, asking if he could come with me to interview Carla. When he called back, he was apologetic. He and his assistant Brad were both going to be in Los Angeles all weekend interviewing witnesses for another case. "I don't suppose you'd want to put the interview off?" he said.

I didn't. I wouldn't know where to find her if she left the halfway house, and I didn't want to give her a chance to get cold feet.

On Saturday I made the drive to Martinez. My car threw back plumes of pale dust as it rolled down the driveway, and the grass at the edges of the road looked brittle and bitten. The early morning air was chilly, and I saw, with relief, that the low sun was lighting a sky half full of rain clouds.

The air around the city was yellow with smog and smelled like a stale stew of truck exhaust and sulfur fumes from the oil refineries whose low round tanks hunkered along the yellow-brown hillsides. The halfway house was near the old courthouse, in a part of town that had clearly seen better days. The building was a big square Mission Revival house from the 1920s, stucco with a terracotta tile roof and a fake Spanish balcony on the second floor. It was freshly painted in a pinkish beige and landscaped with shredded redwood bark and tough-looking shrubs.

The front door was slightly open, and I could hear a vacuum cleaner running inside. I walked in and looked around for someone to speak to.

The house had been a good one, in its day. The foyer was large and ended in a wide staircase to the second-story rooms; a hallway beside it led to the back of the house. The floor was hardwood parquet, recently refinished but already showing signs of wear. Double doorways framed in beveled glass panels led to a room on the left and another on the right. The doorframes were hung with strings of paper jack-o'-lanterns, skeletons, and bats. An orange plastic pumpkin bowl full of wrapped candies sat on a small table next to the door.

The room on the right was clearly an office. In it, I saw a woman at a desk, talking on the phone. The vacuum cleaner noise came from the left, and I followed it into a living room, on the same generous scale as the foyer. One end of the room had been furnished as a children's play area, with a couple of small painted tables and kid-sized chairs and some brightly colored toys. The rest of the room was occupied by a couple of well-used sofas, coffee tables, and armchairs.

The young woman vacuuming saw me after a moment and turned off the machine.

"Whoa—you surprised me," she said. "Are you here to see someone? It's a little early; visiting doesn't start until two." She was dressed in tight jeans and a pink spandex tank top that left a bulge of firm flesh and part of a tattoo showing just above the waist of her pants. Her hair, thick and dark brown with a couple of big blond streaks bleached into it, was pulled back into a ponytail, and her eyes were outlined with a sooty ring of dark eyeliner.

"I'm here to see Carla Burrell," I explained. "She's expecting me."

"I think she's upstairs. I'll see if I can find her." She turned to go, and then turned back. "You can sit in here; it'll be okay."

She left, and I heard her footsteps on the stairs. A couple of minutes later, she was back. "Carla'll be down in a minute." She unplugged the vacuum cleaner, wound up its cord, and wheeled it out.

Not long after she'd left, another woman came into the room. "Are you Mrs. Moodie?" she asked, a little hesitantly.

I stood up. "Yes. Mrs. Burrell?"

She rolled her eyes. "Please, call me Carla."

"Okay. And I'm Janet."

"Okay."

Carla looked like she'd lived hard. She was thin, almost spare, and the skin on her arms and the half circle of chest that showed above her scoop-necked T-shirt was freckled and brown. She was taller than me, maybe five foot five, and her long, straight hair, light brown mixed with gray, was held away from her face with a couple of barrettes. She had three or four stud earrings in each earlobe. Her eyes were like Evie's, but paler, and the small features of her thin face recalled Jimmy's.

She looked around the room. "This isn't a good place to talk. There's visiting today. Always a bunch of aunties and kids. Mrs. Evans gave me a pass to go to the park by the church. Would you mind that?"

I shook my head. "No, that seems fine."

"Good. Wait, and I'll tell her I'm going."

She turned away quickly, and I watched as she walked into the office across the hall. A woman at a desk gave me a quick, appraising look and said something to Carla. Carla nodded, turned, and came back to meet me in the foyer. We walked out to the street, Carla leading the way.

"The park is just down the street and across," she said. She walked with a little swing to her hips that made me wonder if she had waited tables. Her jeans were loose around her thighs, and her shirt hung straight from her shoulders.

There wasn't much to the park: a play structure with a couple of slides, some swings, and a sand box, and next to them a small lawn with garden beds, graveled paths and metal mesh benches. It was bounded on one side by the wall of the church and surrounded on the others by a heavy wire fence with signs prohibiting pets and drugs and proclaiming that the park closed at 6 p.m.

A half-dozen small children, one or two in parts of Hallowe'en costumes, were sitting on the swings or climbing on the structure, and a couple of women—mothers or grandmothers—sat nearby watching them. In the garden, an old Asian man and a younger woman who looked as if she might be his daughter were sitting on one of the benches. Carla walked ahead of me to another bench farther in, and we sat down. We were in the shade of the church wall, and the air, which had been sultry in the sunlight, felt cooler and smelled faintly of damp earth.

"Mind if I smoke?" Carla said. I shook my head, and she pulled a pack of cigarettes and a disposable lighter from a small black nylon shoulder bag and lit up. She took a drag on her cigarette, holding it in her thumb and forefinger, exhaled tendrils of grayish white smoke into the barely moving air, and shook her head as if shaking something out of her hair. She seemed to be, at the same time, tired and full of nervous movement. In the daylight, the skin on her face and hands looked thin and papery.

"It's okay here," she said, looking around at the garden and the playground. "I get a little crazy in that house—all the noise and shit that goes on there."

"How is it going?" I asked. "The rehab."

"Okay." She shrugged. "I'm really trying to clean up this time. I'm hoping to get a job or get on disability, move someplace away from where I was. You get too old for all that drinking and doping shit after a while—'scuse my language."

"No problem."

She began to speak again, looking at a place on the ground a couple of yards from her feet. "I've made a real mess of my life. I'm hoping to do better with what's left of it. I don't know how much that's gonna be—I have hepatitis C and lupus. My teeth are all gone to hell. They sent me to a dentist here; he filled some, pulled some, but he says I'm really gonna need dentures. I have no idea how I'd pay for them." She shook her head, with a brief throaty chuckle that turned into a cough, and then fell silent, looking out at nothing in particular and rocking slightly back and forth on the bench. She took another pull at her cigarette, looked at it in her hand, dropped it and ground it out under her shoe. Then she looked up at me, her face serious. "How is Andy?"

How is your son, nephew, cousin, brother, on death row? It was one of those questions I never had a good answer for.

"He's holding up," I said. It was a meaningless phrase, but it seemed to satisfy most people.

"I always meant to visit him," she said, "but I just couldn't handle it, and now I've got this drug conviction, so I guess I can't anyway. How is his case going?"

I decided not to sugarcoat it for her. It might motivate her to be a little more helpful if she thought there wasn't much standing between Andy and lethal injection.

"Not as well as we'd like," I said.

She looked at me, worried. "What's the matter?"

I tried to read her expression, not sure what she was

waiting to hear. "Trouble is, we're not having much luck finding evidence that might have made a jury see him more sympathetically."

"Andy?" she said, surprised. "God, who wouldn't feel sorry for him?" She pulled her pack of cigarettes out of her purse and lit another one, leaning back on the bench as she exhaled a plume of blue-white smoke. "You know, I never understood why Andy got the death penalty and not Emory. Emory—he's the mean one. But not Andy. I never believed he killed them girls."

I debated how much to tell her. "The police seemed to think right from the beginning that it was Andy," I said. "I think Emory told them a better story, and they believed it."

"Damn," she said. "That's Andy's luck. No one ever cut him a break." She looked up and paused for a moment as if deciding whether to say something. "I'll bet it was Mama."

"What was?" I asked, nonplussed.

"She and Emory, they were close. They had an understanding. I think she'd have told the police Andy did it, to save Emory."

This was new to me. Evie's devotion to Andy had seemed almost obsessive; certainly, I'd never felt she loved him any less than his brother.

"An understanding?" I asked, genuinely puzzled.

Carla looked at me as though debating what to say next. "About Len," she said. A second or two passed, and probably seeing my blank look, she said, with a short, humorless laugh,

"You don't know about our little secret, then." Another pause, and she continued quietly, almost as if thinking aloud. "I guess you wouldn't if Andy didn't tell you."

"I don't know that much about Len," I said, baffled. "I know he went to prison. And that he lived with Evie and the boys for a while and then disappeared." I didn't mention what we'd heard about his molesting Carla; it seemed too early in the conversation to get into that. "We haven't been able to find him. I was going to ask you if you knew anything about where he might be."

"Oh, he's dead," she said.

"Really? Do you know for sure?" I asked.

Carla looked away. She took another drag on her cigarette and dropped it on the gravel next to the first one, then pulled the pack from her nylon bag and tapped another cigarette from it. She seemed unnerved and shaky; it took her several tries to flick a small flame from her lighter, and when she looked at me again from behind a barely visible veil of smoke, her face looked tense. *Oh, damn,* I thought, *she's going to blow up and leave.*

Instead, she took a deep pull on her cigarette and turned away to exhale the smoke. When she turned back toward me, the strain in her face was gone, and she looked worn and sad. "So Andy really didn't say anything, then."

I shook my head, hoping she would believe that I really didn't know what she meant.

"I guess he wouldn't." She looked around the park, and

seeing no one in earshot, leaned toward me. "Mama and Emory killed him."

I felt my stomach jump into my chest, as though I'd just stepped off a cliff. In the next second I decided she really hadn't meant it quite that way, that she was exaggerating and that there had been some accident that the family had, for some reason, not wanted to talk about.

"Killed him?" I asked. "What happened?"

She sat straight again, took another puff of her cigarette, and turned aside to exhale the smoke. When she turned back, her eyes seemed a little red, whether from smoke or held-back tears I couldn't tell. "I guess Andy didn't tell you because he's afraid for Mama. I guess we all are. But—well, I've said it now. I don't know, maybe it'll help Andy in some way for you to know. He was there when they did it—we both were." She spoke the words quietly, looking past my shoulder into some middle distance of memory.

For a moment I couldn't think of anything to say, so I just nodded. The sounds around us—the little children's voices and the squeaking of the swings on the playground, the hum and rush of cars on the street—seemed far away and unreal. I felt a faint cool breeze and noticed for the first time that the sky was mottled with darker gray clouds. "What happened?" I asked again.

Carla went on in a low, almost detached voice, breathing a faint acrid smell of cigarette smoke as she spoke. "Andy was always my little buddy." The expression in her eyes softened.

"You talked to my dad, so I guess you know I was raised by my grandparents and then Dad and Charlene. But I used to visit Mama for a few weeks every summer. Andy was the sweetest little boy. I just loved him; he was so good-hearted. But he was always being picked on by Emory and the other kids. I kind of took him under my wing. I used to give Emory and his friends hell for messing with him." She smiled a little at the memory. "They were all scared shitless of me."

"Did you ever get the sense that Andy was mentally slow?"

"Yeah. That's why Emory and the others were so mean to him. He couldn't keep up with them. They'd play games, and he'd mess up because he'd forget the rules—that kind of thing. They played mean jokes on him, and Emory called him dumb-ass and retard in front of his friends. It was really sad. I remember Emory would do things to ditch Andy like send him into the house to get them cans of soda, and then he and his friends would split. I can still see Andy standing there in the doorway, holding all the soda cans—" She shivered, as if trying to shake the image from her mind.

"How did Evie and Len treat him?"

"Len treated him like shit—but then Len treated everyone like shit. Mama acted like nothing was wrong. I think she was always that way with Andy and Emory; she just refused to see. She protected those boys too much. They couldn't do anything wrong in her eyes. But I should finish telling you about Len. When I was fifteen I got sent to live with Mama because I was getting in a lot of trouble at home.

"Len was out of prison by then, and staying at her house. Mama wasn't happy about it. She told me he showed up one day after he was paroled and asked to stay for a few days until he could find a place, and then he wouldn't leave. He wasn't working; he just hung around the house and drank. When Mama was at work and we were home from school he'd smack the boys around and try to mess with me. And then one night he snuck into my room in the middle of the night. I yelled out, and Mama and the boys woke up. Len and Mama had a huge fight. He went after her, and Andy and Emory and I all jumped him. He shook us all off, then he just slammed out of the house saying he was gonna come back and blow us all away. Mama sat up all night in the living room, with a big kitchen knife on the table next to her, and we all sat up with her because we were too scared to sleep.

"The next day when I got home from school, Len was there, sitting in his chair in the living room and drinking his usual, cheap bourbon and coke. He had a sawn-off shotgun across his lap. When Mama came home she told him he needed to leave, but he said no one was going anywhere. He just sat there and kept on drinking, and we all stayed out of his way.

"It was the weirdest night. I remember it was a Friday night in January and snowing out. We were all scared to move, with Len sitting there with that shotgun and drinking his whisky and cokes. I kept thinking we could all just sneak away out the back door, but Mama kept going out to the kitchen and filling his glass, and I remember thinking at the time that was weird. I went into the kitchen for something, once, and I saw her crushing some sort of pill with a knife and putting it into his glass. I asked her what she was doing, and she said, 'Giving him what he wants.' She sent us all to bed early, even though it was a Friday night. I couldn't sleep because I was so afraid."

She dropped her cigarette and crushed it absently under her shoe, and stood up.

I got up, too. "Are you okay?" I asked.

She seemed to sway a little. "Yeah. I think I need a drink of water or something. There's a fountain here somewhere." She looked around, a little vaguely, saw it, and walked over to it. I wondered if she had decided not to go on with her story—not that I could blame her. But she came back and sat again on the bench. She reached into her purse, found her pack of cigarettes, glanced at them, and put them back with a shake of her head.

"Sorry," she said. "I'm trying to remember where I was. Oh, yeah—I was in bed, and I heard some noises from the living room—like something falling over—and I got up to see what was going on. Emory came out of his and Andy's room, too.

"Mama was in the living room with a pillow, holding it over Len's face and kind of leaning on it. And I guess Len had kicked out or something, because the coffee table was on its side. We both just stood there, and Mama looked up after a while and saw us and said, 'You both get back to bed!' And that kind of snapped me out of it, and I said, 'Mama, what are you doing?' And she said, 'What does it look like?' And I wanted to say, 'Like you're smothering Len,' except I couldn't say the words. He was just laying in the chair with his legs and arms kind of splayed out. I think he was moving around a little, but I'm not sure. I must have been in shock or something, because it felt like time had just stopped. I was thinking I should try to stop her, but I didn't really believe what I was seeing, so I just stood there.

"Emory ran over to her, and I thought he was going to pull her away, but he didn't. Instead, he got a plastic bag from the kitchen and moved the pillow away and stuck the bag over Len's face. Then he told Mama to hold Len's arms and took over holding the pillow down on Len's face with the bag under it until he completely stopped moving. He made some noises, like he was choking, and he kept moving around for a while. It seemed to go on forever. I just kept watching; I couldn't stop. It felt unreal, like a movie playing in front of me. It was so strange."

Carla had been looking down at her knees, as if concentrating on remembering. While telling the story her voice had been flat and almost emotionless, a reaction I recognized from interviewing other people about traumatic experiences. Psychologists I'd worked with said it was a sign of someone dissociating—separating their descriptions of what happened from the emotions associated with them as a way of avoiding re-experiencing a trauma.

"Anyhow, after a while, Mama stood up and checked Len's wrist for a pulse. Then she moved the pillow away from his face, leaned down close to his nose and mouth—checking for breath, I guess—and felt for a pulse in the side of his neck. His eyes were closed, and his face was kind of puffy and red; that's about all I remember about him. She looked at Emory and said, 'Well, since you've done this much, you may as well help get rid of him.' And Emory said, 'Oh, yuck, he barfed in the bag.' Mama must have seen me move or something, because she looked over at me, and said, 'You'd better come help, too.'

"So Emory and I helped her put Len's body into a sleeping bag and carry it out of the house. I didn't want to touch it, and the vomit smell made me sick to my stomach. Emory was pretty strong, but Mama and I had a lot of trouble holding Len's legs up so his butt didn't drag on the ground. I remember being surprised at how heavy he was. Emory was kind of excited by it all, but I think that's because he was a kid and hated Len, and it didn't really sink in what we'd done. We put him in the trunk of her car outside. Something happened when we loaded his body into the trunk—a thunk the head made or something—and I just suddenly started throwing up, and Emory started laughing and just kept laughing, like he couldn't stop—it was nerves, I guess. Mama told him to shut up or the neighbors would hear, and she put her arm around me, and helped me back inside.

"Inside the house, I started crying—I guess I was having an attack of hysterics or something. Mama was shushing me, saying, 'You'll wake Andy up,' and she gave me a glass of water with some bourbon in it to calm me down. Then she said, 'We're gonna have to pack Len's stuff, make it look like he left.' She and Emory and I took Len's belongings and loaded them into his duffle bag and took it out to the car. Then she told us to go back to bed.

"Early the next morning, she woke me up and told me she and Emory were going to drive somewhere and get rid of the body and Len's truck and stuff. She told me to stay and look after Andy. They were gone all day until after dark. And while they were gone I found out that Andy had seen and heard a lot of what happened. He'd been afraid to come out into the living room, but he stood behind the door of his room and watched. I told him never, ever to tell anyone, because they'd send Mama to prison forever.

"Things were really strange with us after that. I mean, it was like we kept living a normal life on the surface, but I felt like I was looking at it from some other place. I had this huge, awful secret I couldn't tell anyone except Mama and Emory. It kind of tied us together. Emory and Mama seemed to kind of bond after that; it was like they were together in some sort of conspiracy. I felt like I was in jail. We all seemed to be watching each other all the time, checking each other out to see if we were gonna stay true. I begged Dad and Charlene to let me come back, and they did, but I ran away after a couple of months, started using speed and coke because it made me feel less depressed.

"I was scared, too. I asked Emory what they'd done with the body, and he said they'd driven way up into the mountains and pushed it over a cliff by the side of a road. He said it was really hard to move it from the trunk because it was stiff, and he slipped on the snow as they were pushing it down and almost went over the edge after it. I kept thinking someone was going to find him and it would all come back to us, and we'd all go to prison." She hunched her thin shoulders. "I still have nightmares about it happening."

"I guess no one found him?" I asked.

"Not that I know of. The only thing that happened was that Len's parole officer came by a couple of times looking for him. Mama told him Len had just up and left, and I don't think he came around after that. Oh, and Uncle Walter called. I remember because I answered the phone. He seemed kind of surprised that Len was gone like that, but nothing else." She stopped talking and looked ahead of her, as if she had grown tired of thinking.

It was chilling to think that a family of children could carry such a terrible secret. And that a man could break his connections to other people so utterly that he could disappear one day and no one would try to find out what happened to him. I thought of what Evie had done to her children—desensitized Emory to killing and burdened Andy and Carla with the terrible secret of Len's murder. I wanted to do something to comfort Carla, take her in my arms and rock her like a forlorn child. The barrier between people, between strangers, felt like a thick glass wall, transparent but impenetrable. Feeling awkward, I just watched her, wishing I could somehow project compassion and strength. "I'm so sorry," I said.

Her eyes snapped back into focus, and she shivered and turned to me. "I don't know why I've told you all this," she said, her voice tired. "I don't even know if it will make a difference."

"I'm glad you told me," I said, though I wasn't sure why I should be.

I knew I had to—for Andy's sake—at least ask her to help. "I know this is rough," I said, "but we can't really do anything with what you've told us unless we can present it to a judge."

She hunched her shoulders and looked at me, shaking her head rapidly, emphatically. "I can't tell anyone else—no way I could do that. You can see why, can't you?"

I had to say yes. Without much hope, I asked her if she would sign a records release. She took the copies from me and studied the top one for a moment. "This is just for stuff about me, right?"

"Yes," I answered.

She reached for the pen I was holding, set the releases

down beside her on the park bench and signed all three copies, then gave them back to me decisively, as if she wanted to make sure she didn't change her mind. "There. Maybe you'll find something that will help him. I'm so sorry."

She looked at me again. "What time is it?" she asked.

I checked my watch. "A little before three."

"I've gotta get back." She stood up, a little stiffly, and I got up also. As we walked past the play structure, she paused and looked for a moment at a little boy hitching himself along a set of parallel bars. On our way back we saw a couple of small groups of children: ghosts in sheets, superheroes, a vampire or two in ghoulish makeup and black capes lined in purple, a fairy princess in silver gauze and sequins. The light was starting to fade. While we had been talking the sky had grown darker, and the air was cooler, with a breath of moisture in it.

"Looks like it might rain," Carla said.

28

After saying goodbye to Carla at the halfway house, I drove around the town until I found a coffee shop. I ordered coffee and pie, and after the waitress left with my order, I opened my iPad and started writing down everything I could remember of what Carla had told me. By the time I'd finished, night had fallen.

Outside, it was raining, and the dark streets glittered with reflected light. There were no little trick-or-treaters here, and the sidewalks were nearly empty.

In the parking lot I sat in my car for a few minutes, thinking of Carla and feeling like a visitor in the world of normal holidays and happy children. The burden of what she knew weighed on me; by comparison, my life and my son's, even with Terry's suicide, seemed prosaic. Suddenly I remembered sitting, sobbing, in a convulsion of heart-emptying grief, in a rental car in a strange city, a couple of months after Terry died, and for a few seconds the same feeling came over me again. This time I squeezed my eyes until the bone-deep ache subsided and then threaded my way through dark streets to the freeway, cursing Terry, Andy, Emory, Jim Christie, Evie, and fucked-up fate in general.

The drive home seemed endless, and I took the last stretch of Highway One, along the cliff edge, in second gear, afraid of the wet road and the murky darkness. For the last twenty miles I didn't see another car.

The dark house felt damp and cold; the kitchen light, when I turned it on, saturated the room with a shadowless light that seemed to expose everything that hurt—each dent in the cabinet doors, every scratch and stain on the counter and floor. I poured some kibble for Charlie and the cats and went to the living room. I built a fire in the wood stove, feeling more at home in the quieter lamplight and the valiant, hopeful glow from the kindling. For several minutes I stood in front of the stove, shivering, watching the fire through the glass, and absorbing the heat. When I was sure the fire had caught well, I put a couple of big logs on it to keep it going overnight, made myself a hot milk and brandy and went to bed. The clock showed half past midnight—the Feast of All Saints.

I woke up at three in the morning with a sense of tumblers clicking into place. No one had ever determined the cause of death of the two young women whose bodies had been found on the ranch. Andy told Canevaro, with considerable prompting, that he had strangled them with his hands. The bodies were so decomposed that it wasn't possible to see most of the signs a pathologist looks for in such cases, such as fingermarks on the neck and tiny burst blood vessels in the eyes. But the women's hyoid bones—a small bone in the throat almost always broken during manual strangling—were intact. What if they had been killed the way Len had been—drugged in some way, and then smothered?

Later that morning I called Jim's office and left a message to call me as soon as possible. He called back himself, for once, that afternoon, and I told him what Carla had said to me. His reaction was a cold splash of reality. "How do we know she's telling the truth?" he asked, dubious. "No one else has said anything about this. What do we know about her?"

"Not much," I said.

"That's the trouble. She could be lying or delusional—we don't know, and there's nothing to corroborate her story. I can't even see how we could check it out. She's vague about what they did with the body. There's nothing here we could take to a judge."

I had to admit he was right. It was a bizarre story that could have been nothing more than a complete fiction—though it was hard to see what her motive might have been in telling me but refusing to put it in writing. I didn't know Carla well enough to rule out the possibility. Even if she was telling the truth, we had no other evidence to confirm it. It was hard to imagine a judge finding the story credible on her word alone.

2 9

The next week, I paid another visit to Andy.

The Hallowe'en rain storm had lasted a couple of days, long enough to wash the dust off trees and hedges and raise a barely visible wash of green above last summer's brown grass. The morning was silvery with changeable light, as one mass of clouds after another moved in front of the sun and past it. At San Quentin, a damp, penetrating breeze off the water seeped under the neck and sleeves of my jacket, and I was almost grateful for the overheated visiting area.

I bought a cheeseburger, coke and chips for Andy and a coffee for me before he appeared, handcuffed and flanked by guards in drab olive, at the door from the cell blocks. As I moved food off the tray and onto paper towels on the scuffed table, I asked Andy how he'd been. "Okay," he said. "Nothing much happening."

"I met Carla," I said. "We had a pretty long talk."

Andy looked up at me and let go of the wrapper of the cheeseburger. He hesitated a minute, as if deciding whether to go on. "She told you about my dad, didn't she." It wasn't a question.

I was caught completely off guard. Trying desperately to figure out what to say, I asked, "What about your dad?"

"That they killed him."

I'd made the wrong move. If I said now that I couldn't tell him what Carla had said to me, I was as good as telling him he was right. I could lie and deny she had said it, but he would know I was lying; there was some reason why he was so sure she had talked about it. So I lied ambiguously. "They what?" I said.

Andy looked puzzled, as if he couldn't understand the turn the conversation had taken.

"I saw them," he said. "Carla knew it. She wrote me a letter and said she told you all about Len."

Jeez, I thought. It would never have occurred to me that Carla would write to Andy about our meeting. His crazy family always seemed to be a step ahead of me. But for better or worse, it seemed Carla's story was the truth. "Tell me what you saw," I asked him.

He looked around and leaned toward me, his forearms resting on the edge of the table and his hands clasped in front of him. In a quiet, almost monotonous voice, looking sometimes at my face and sometimes at the table in front of him, he began. "I heard noises and I woke up in the middle of the night. I looked over at Emory's bed and he was gone. So after a while I got up and went out in the hallway and kind of hid and looked around the corner because I knew Mama'd get mad at me if she knew I wasn't in bed. And—and—I could see my dad in his chair, and Mama and Emory standing by him." He stopped and looked at me as though waiting for permission to go on.

"What was happening?" I asked.

"My dad wasn't sayin' nothin or moving, like he was passed out. Carla was just standing there in front of me in the hall, watching. And Mama said, 'I think that's done it.' Then she and Em tried to lift Dad out of the chair, but I guess he was too heavy. So Mama saw that Carla was up and told her to come over there and help. And I ducked back into my room. But I heard them in the kitchen, and they went out the back door."

He hesitated again. "What happened after that?" I asked.

"Em and Mama went away that night—Em told me later they went to get rid of the body—and Carla and I were by ourselves, and I asked her if Mama and Em killed Dad, and she got all upset and cried and said, 'Andy, you weren't supposed to know about it.' And I cried, too. And she told me I shouldn't ever tell anyone because Mama could go to prison for the rest of her life or maybe even death row.

"And when Mama and Em got back, Em was all crazy and excited, and was going on about how they went way up in the mountains down these little mountain roads, and the car got stuck on this really lonely road and he didn't think they were gonna be able to get out. And Mama shushed him, and Carla said, 'It don't matter, Mama; Andy saw you.' And Mama told me they had to do it because my dad was a bad man and she was afraid he was going to kill us, but no one would understand, and they'd put her and Emory in prison, maybe forever. And later when she wasn't around, Emory told me that if I ever told anyone they'd just say I was crazy and have me locked up in a hospital. So I never told nobody—except now you."

As he finished, he was watching me as if waiting to see how I would react.

I was as speechless as I had been with Carla. "Oh, God, Andy," I said, finally. "I'm so sorry."

"We didn't want anyone to know about it," Andy said. "We don't want Mama to be hurt."

"I understand," I said.

"But then Carla wrote me a letter and said she'd told you about Len—so's I'd know you knew."

"I didn't know Carla wrote to you."

"Yeah. She always sends me a birthday card with a money order, and sometimes a Christmas card. She used to write more letters. This was the first one in a long time. She told me she was in rehab."

"She is."

"How is she doing?" Andy asked. "Her letter said she'd been sick."

"Kind of thin," I said, "but I think she's feeling better."

"Good." He noticed the burger in front of him and touched it. "Cold," he said.

"Think they'll let me warm it up for you?"

"It's okay." He picked it up and took a bite, and then another, until it was gone, then wiped his hands and mouth carefully with a paper towel. "That was good," he said.

We spent the rest of the visit talking about Len. "Mama hates for me to talk about him," Andy said. "Carla used to say Mama never wanted to talk about anything bad."

Before Len went to prison, he remembered, "We were all afraid of him. He had a really bad temper. He'd hit Mama. Emory used to run at him and yell at him to stop, but he'd just hit him, too. I used to hide in the back of the closet, so's he wouldn't see me."

While Len was in prison, Andy recalled, things were quieter. "We lived in Spokane for a while, and Pullman. It was good not having to be afraid of my dad. And we used to visit Aunt Margaret and Uncle Ray and Carla, and Carla would come and visit in the summer for a couple weeks. Mama took us to see Len in prison a couple of times a year. We didn't want to go, but Mama said he was our dad and he had a right. Emory just wouldn't go after a while. He'd run away."

He didn't know why Evie had let Len come back after he was paroled. "He just sat around the house drinking and calling everyone names. He called me stupid and Em a mama's boy and Carla a slut. And then he and Mama got into that big fight about something he did to Carla, and we was all afraid he was going to kill us. That's when they killed him."

Only then did it occur to me to ask, "Andy, did anyone ever tell you how your dad died?"

He looked at me, puzzled. "I told you, they killed him."

"Sorry—I mean, did anyone say how they killed him?"

He thought for a second or two. "No—I don't think they did."

"Not even Emory?"

"No. He didn't talk about that part."

"So you don't know how he died?"

"No. I think maybe Emory hit him on the head or something."

I had come to talk to Andy about Dr. Moss and his appointment for the neuropsychological evaluation, and I still needed to deal with that. After Andy's revelation, though, it seemed oddly anticlimactic.

Andy had been seen before his trial by a psychologist hired by Dobson. The psychologist was a local hack who picked up extra money doing one-hour examinations of defendants whose lawyers had questioned their sanity at the time of the crime or their mental competence to stand trial, or who, like Dobson, knew that a lawyer representing a capital client should have him evaluated by a mental-health expert and wanted to be able to check that off their list of things to do.

The examination had been a drive-by: an interview lasting about an hour and a couple of almost valueless personality tests. One of them was a written, multiple-choice test that required the subject to be able to read at an eighth-grade level. The psychologist didn't check Andy's reading ability and decided that the strange answers he gave to some of the test questions were an attempt to fake symptoms of mental illness. In the end, he told Dobson that there was nothing wrong with Andy.

Dr. Moss's tests, I told Andy, would be different. For one thing, they'd go on a lot longer: two six-hour sessions. For another, a lot of neuropsychological testing isn't just pencil-and-paper stuff, but more like puzzles. Dr. Moss would interview Andy, more or less as Dr. Hollister had done. But he would also play sounds to find out how well Andy could listen, give him wooden puzzles with pieces to insert while blindfolded, connect-the-dots games to play, sequences of numbers to remember, and cards to read. I told him I'd be coming to the prison that morning with Dr. Moss and would stay long enough to introduce him.

When I asked Andy if he had any questions, he told me about the football pool that some of the inmates had organized, entirely against the rules, using stamps for money. "I won it last week," he said proudly. "Seventy bucks in stamps."

3 0

Dr. Moss's visit was scheduled for the week after Thanksgiving. While I waited for it, I began rough-drafting the parts of the habeas corpus petitions that I could put together without his conclusions. The weather didn't leave much else to do: rain, on and off, obscured the view toward the ocean, and morning frosts withered the tomato plants in my garden.

Thanksgiving came, and Gavin sent funny emails from Sydney about how strange it felt to remember it in a country where it wasn't a holiday. He sent photos of their dinner; his girlfriend, Rita, had risen to the occasion by roasting a turkey with a bread and chestnut stuffing and baking a lemon pie, which they both preferred to pumpkin.

Harriet, my garden mentor, invited me to join her and her partner Bill, serving dinners to the poor at a church in Santa Rosa. We spent the morning laying turkey-patterned paper tablecloths and centerpieces of artificial autumn leaves and flowers on long tables in the basement meeting room and the afternoon filling plates with slices of steamy turkey, scoops of mashed potatoes and yams, green bean casserole, and salad, and then handing out slices of sticky pumpkin pie with dollops of sweet whipped cream, to what seemed like a never-ending line of old people, homeless men, and poor families. We bantered with the people we were serving, or just smiled at the shy ones, and I found myself wondering if this would be me someday, old and lonely, trying to make a holiday of steam table food and a smile from a stranger.

And I kept writing. Legal boilerplate for the introduction; claim after claim based on the ineffectiveness of Dobson's performance as Andy's lawyer; declarations for the signatures of teachers and old acquaintances whom Dave was visiting one more time.

On the day of Dr. Moss's appointment with Andy, I hauled myself out of bed in the small hours after a night of fitful sleep, and left home in darkness that didn't lift until I was nearly at the prison.

Dr. Moss was waiting for me with his laptop and a box of cards and board puzzle tests, all of which were opened and peered at by a pair of guards at the gate. They looked at his credentials with suspicion before we were allowed to pass through.

"Is it always like this?" he asked, as we walked down the long sidewalk toward the prison buildings.

"Or worse," I said.

Inside, we waited as lawyers and investigators emerged, shaking off the rain, through the sally port from outside, and guards brought inmates one at a time, in their denims and handcuffs, through the metal door from the back. After about ten minutes, the guard in the glassed-in office motioned to us, and I went to the window. "Your client refused the visit," he said.

I went numb. "Did he say why?" I asked.

"They didn't say. I'll call up and ask," the guard said.

"What's happening?" Dr. Moss asked me.

"Andy is refusing to come down to see us," I answered. "I'm trying to find out what's up." Embarrassed, I nattered on, feeling more foolish with every word. "I don't know what the problem is. He knows what this is for, and he seemed to be looking forward to it."

The guard waved at me to get my attention and called through the window, "He said he didn't want to see the doctor."

"I don't know what happened," I said lamely, as the outer gate of the visiting area slid shut, and we started back to the parking lot under a wet and lowering sky. "A couple of weeks ago he was really enthusiastic about seeing you."

Dr. Moss seemed remarkably patient under the circumstances. "He could have gotten cold feet, I guess," he said. "Does this happen often?"

"Not that much," I said. "Some guys are apprehensive about psych testing of any kind. But Andy wasn't. I really don't know what's up with him. Can you make time to come back when we can get another appointment? Assuming I can get Andy back on track, of course."

"In another couple of months? I imagine so. It's a shame this happened; if I remember, you said you were working to a deadline."

I nodded; the thought made me feel like crying on the spot.

In the parking lot, I kept apologizing, effusively, compulsively, until Dr. Moss was practically in his car. Even the thought that he would be paid for his trip down here didn't keep me from feeling as though I were personally responsible for failing to make it work.

I dreaded calling Jim, so I called him right away on my cellphone, to get it over with. I needn't have worried; he was in court, and I broke the news to Corey, who was sympathetic.

"I'll call Moss," he said, "and find out when he's available and reserve the psych interview room again. I sent you some more vital records," he added. "Interesting stuff."

"Thanks," I said. "I'm going to call Evie tonight. She'll know what's going on with Andy if anyone does."

My car bounced up the potholed road to my house, reminding me that the driveway needed grading and a new coat of gravel. "God damn it," I said out loud. I felt defeated and in no mood to deal with anything else going wrong.

In the house, I turned on my computer and wrote and printed a letter to Andy, asking, as kindly as I could, what the hell he thought he was doing. I signed it and stuck it into an envelope, on which I printed CONFIDENTIAL: ATTORNEY–CLIENT MAIL. I saw Corey's email, but didn't open the attachments; Andy's case was not high on the list of things I wanted to think about. I made a pot of coffee and thought about making some bread, to take out some of my frustration on something that would actually benefit from being repeatedly punched.

My second cup of coffee was three-quarters empty when I finally opened the files Corey had sent. There were some court records of cases involving some of the witnesses and jurors—a divorce, a civil suit over a car accident, nothing particularly useful. Then there were some death certificates. The first was for Robert Bowden, Jr., born February 23 1954, showing he had died of pneumonia in 1994, in the Iowa State Hospital in Davenport. Evie's brother, I figured. The next was for Marilyn Bowden. It took me a second to recognize the name as Evie's mother's. The information on the certificate was sparse and to the point. She was born in Jefferson City, Missouri in September 1927 and had died on February 12 1965, in Corydon, Iowa, aged thirty-eight. At the time of her death she was married, her occupation "homemaker." The cause of death was given as evulsion of the brain from a gunshot wound. The manner of death was listed as homicide. She was buried in the Millbrook

Presbyterian Cemetery, Corydon, Iowa. The informant listed in the certificate was someone whose name I didn't recognize.

Behind Marilyn's death certificate was that of Robert Bowden, aged forty. Robert had died on the same date of multiple gunshot wounds to the heart and lungs. His death was also described as a homicide. The same informant was listed on his death certificate as on Marilyn's, and he was buried in the same cemetery.

And behind Robert Bowden's was another: Susan Bowden. Dead the same day of loss of blood from a gunshot wound that severed her carotid artery. Age: fifteen years.

The rumors Jimmy had heard were true: Evie's family had been murdered.

31

I called Dave.

"Christ, what a morning!" I said, when he answered. "Andy refused Dr. Moss's visit."

"Oh, shit. Do you know why?"

"No. I'm going to call Evie this evening, to see if she knows anything about it."

Dave commiserated as I agonized over how we were going to meet our deadline for filing the petition or, worse, how we were going to make a case to get Andy off death row if he wouldn't cooperate with our experts.

"But wait," I added. "It gets stranger."

"How?"

"Remember what Jimmy and Charlene said about 'some big secret,' about the death of Evie's family?"

"Yeah?"

"Well, the rumors were true."

"Really!"

"Evie's parents and her older sister were murdered—

shot—all on the same date."

"Damn!" Dave said. Then silence on his end of the line.

"Dave?"

"Nothing—I'm thinking. Didn't she have a brother?"

"Yeah, she did. Corey got his death certificate, too. He died in a state mental hospital."

"We need to plan a trip to Iowa," Dave said.

"Speak for yourself," I said. "I have to get Andy off whatever limb he's put himself out on and get him to see Dr. Moss."

Dave snorted. "You just want the glamorous assignments."

"That's me. Oh, to be in Quentin, now that April's here."

"Christmas in Iowa—I got you beat."

I told him I'd send him the death certificates, and let him go to look into plane reservations.

In the early evening, I called Evie. "I need your help," I said. "Dr. Moss, the neuropsychologist, came to see him today, and he refused to meet with him."

She was silent for a moment, like a child confronted with some bad behavior, before answering, in a tight little voice, "Maybe he didn't want to."

Oh, bullshit, I thought. "Evie, Andy *wanted* to see Dr. Moss. Something changed in the past two weeks. Have you seen him recently? Do you have any idea what's on his mind?"

Again, she hesitated before answering. "He doesn't want to see any psychologists. He's not crazy."

"Evie, did you talk to him about it?"

"Yes."

"Did you tell him not to see Dr. Moss?"

She paused again, and when she spoke, her voice had an edge. "Nobody's going to say my boy is wrong in the head. There's nothing wrong with Andy."

"Evie, that isn't what Dr. Moss's evaluation was about."

"He's not retarded, either, if that's what you mean."

"Evie," I went on, trying to keep my voice calm, "we're trying to save his life."

"By lying about him, that's what you're doing. Like they did with Emory. He isn't crazy, either. They just tried to pretend he was and the jury didn't buy any of it."

"They didn't give him the death penalty, did they?"

"That didn't have anything to do with it."

I struggled to think of something I could say that would persuade her. "Evie, don't you want to save Andy's life?"

"Not by letting them lie that he's wrong in the head. You have other things you can do."

"This is important. This is probably the only thing that will save him."

Again, she was silent for a moment, before speaking. "There's nothing wrong with my boy, and I told him so. Now, goodbye."

The line went dead.

Jim called her the next evening, but he had no better luck than I did. I called again, too, and asked her to meet me the next time she was at San Quentin.

"I don't see any reason to talk about it," she said.

When I begged her again to rethink her decision and told her Andy would probably lose his appeals and be executed if he didn't go through with the evaluation, she listened without a word. When I'd finished, she said, "I know what's right and wrong with my boys. You need to find some other way besides telling lies about Andy."

So I made an appointment to see Andy the next week, and wrote to him to tell him I was coming. He refused the visit. When I got home that day, there was a letter from him in my mailbox, dated two days earlier. In blocky printing, he had written,

**I DO NOT WANT TO SEE YOU OR DR MOOS.
I AM NOT A RETARD OR CRAZY, AND THER
IS NOTHING WRONG WITH MY MIND.**

I wrote him another letter, struggling to think of what to say to him. "I know your mother loves you," I tried, "but her advice will hurt her as much as you. She would be very sad if you lost your appeals and were executed, because she would lose you. If you let Dr. Moss do his testing, he may be able to tell the judge something that will get you a new trial and save your life."

I made another appointment, drove again to San Quentin to see him, and again he wouldn't see me. To keep the trip from being a complete waste, I also scheduled a holiday visit the same morning to my ex-client Henry Fontaine, who, sensing I was anxious and down over something, plied me with evangelical encouragements and advice to find comfort in the Lord, gave me copies of some hymns he had written, and went on in detail about the prison doctors' attempts to adjust his medication and the various symptoms that had worsened each time. Nevertheless, I was cheered enough by his "you have a merry Christmas, Ms. Janet, and don't let the things of the world get you down," and his final smile and wave as he was led through the iron door, that I took Andy's refusal, when it came, with a resigned sigh and went home to try to follow Henry's advice.

Because it was, after all, the holiday season, I wrapped and mailed Christmas presents for my sisters and their husbands and kids (I had sent Gavin's by sea mail in October) and shopped for things for my few friends—Ed, Harriet, Bill, Dave. To ward off the darkness of the winter and my thoughts, I put up strings of multicolored lights outdoors and in, around the front door and living-room windows and framing the doorway to the kitchen. I bought a little potted spruce tree and set it up on the coffee table with lights and miniature ornaments.

When I had the heart for it, I continued drafting the petitions, feeling acutely and painfully the huge gap that would have been filled by Dr. Moss's results. Even if he had not found that Andy was mentally retarded, his evaluation would almost certainly have shown that Andy's intelligence was low, and he would have been able to use his personal evaluation of Andy, the information from Andy's school records, and the statements of the people who had known him, to explain Andy's limitations and his personality. Without the concrete information from his observations and tests, we didn't have much except speculation. And when it came out—as it had to at some point—that Andy himself had refused to cooperate with the defense's expert, there was probably no judge sitting who wouldn't hold that against him.

It occurred to me to call Carla, in the hope that Andy had kept a lifeline open to her, but when I called the halfway house, my call was transferred to a counselor who told me Carla was no longer there. When I asked how I could reach her, she gave me the name and phone number of Carla's probation officer.

The probation officer, citing confidentiality, wouldn't tell me where she was until I emailed him a copy of Carla's records release. After receiving it, he called back and told me she had just completed the residential part of the drug program and was living on her own. He gave me a number he said was her cellphone. "She applied for permission to make a visit over Christmas to her father and stepmother in Washington," he added. "That was a couple of days ago. I just approved it today."

I called the phone number he'd given me and got an automated message. Then I called Jimmy and Charlene.

Jimmy answered. "How are you doing?" he asked. "We've

been thinking about you, Charl and I, wondering how you're doing with Andy's case."

"Not so well," I said, and without stopping to elaborate, I went on. "I'm really sorry to bother you so close to the holidays and all…"

"Don't worry about it. We're pretty quiet here."

"I heard that Carla is coming up there for a visit," I said.

"That's true," Jimmy said. "She's coming on the bus. I'm supposed to pick her up in Walla Walla tomorrow. I wish I'd known sooner; we'd a bought her a plane ticket. But we couldn't find anything we could afford this close to Christmas. Do you need to talk to her? I'll tell her to call you when she gets in."

"That would be great," I said.

"She was in the hospital last month—her liver," Jimmy went on. "She must be doing better now, 'cause the doctor okayed her coming up here. But she was feelin' pretty bad for a while. She wanted to see us and Austin this Christmas, be near her family."

That didn't sound good. "I hope she's feeling better," I said. "And ask her to call me, if you would, please—it's about Andy."

"Sure will," Jimmy said. "He's okay, I hope."

"Oh, yes," I lied.

"Glad to hear it. Well, Merry Christmas."

"Merry Christmas," I said, feeling how uncomfortably the syllables fell from my mouth.

* * *

Carla called two days later.

"I'd have called when I got in," she said, "but I was too tired."

"How are you doing?" I asked. "I heard you were in the hospital."

"Pretty bad," she said. "They thought I might have liver cancer, but it turned out to be a false alarm."

"Yikes!" I said, sympathizing. "That must have been a scare."

"Yeah. I'm not ready to kick it just yet. I quit smoking, though. Hardest thing I've done in my life so far. So what's up with Andy?"

I told her. After I'd finished, there was silence on the line for a few seconds before she said, quietly, "Shit, Mama." She said nothing else for a second or two, then asked, "What can I do?"

"I'm not sure," I admitted. "I guess you can't get into the prison to see Andy."

"No, I asked. I'm on probation for a drug conviction, and I guess that's the end of it, as far as they're concerned. I'll write to him, though, tell him to see you and cooperate."

"That might help," I said.

"Maybe if I talked to Mama—"

"Do you think it would do any good?"

"I don't know. I may as well try. I don't want to see Andy hurt."

"Do you have any idea why she's so against him getting evaluated?"

"She never wanted to believe that there was anything wrong with Andy," Carla said.

"We'd have to go up to Redbud," I said. "I asked to meet her down here, and she said no."

"Okay."

We arranged to talk on the phone after Carla was back in California, and I wished her a merry Christmas. "Take care of yourself," I added.

After that, there wasn't much else for me to do, except take everyone's advice and try to enjoy the holidays.

Not that there was much to be merry about. The courts have a Scrooge-like disrespect for the Christmas season, and after another unsuccessful try to visit Andy and holiday visits to a couple more former clients, I spent several ten-hour days finishing the reply brief in a non-capital appeal that had to be filed by December 23. Dave hadn't been able to get an affordable flight to Davenport, Iowa, until New Year's Eve. "Seems like as good a day as any," he'd said, when I commiserated. "I don't generally do anything on New Year's Eve any more; do you?" I wondered where Marisol was these days, but didn't want to ask.

32

I spent Christmas doling out holiday dinners again with Bill and Harriet because it was better than staying home alone. Two days later, I woke up with chills and a fever. My throat was sore, my head felt as though someone was hitting it repeatedly with a cymbal, and all my bones felt clenched with pain. I spent the next couple of days sleeping as much as I could, leaving my bed only to use the bathroom and make an occasional cup of weak, sweet tea.

·   On the thirtieth, Dave called for a last-minute briefing on his trip to Iowa to investigate the murders of Evie's family, the Bowdens. "You sound awful," he said, after the first sentence I tried to speak.

"I'm a goner; you'll have to go on without me," I croaked, then coughed and cursed exhaustedly as the muscles in my raw throat contracted.

"I hate to laugh; you sound so miserable," he said. "I'll call as soon as I find out anything."

* * *

By New Year's Day I was feeling a lot better. I called Dave on his cellphone, figuring that a motel in Iowa was a pretty cheerless place to ring in the new year. Dave told me he was staying in the county seat, a town called Commerce, about ten miles from Corydon, and the weather was actually pretty nice, cold, with a lot of snow on the ground, but sunny. "It's a pretty sad place, though," he said. "Most of the buildings downtown are boarded up. I guess the only thing that keeps it going are the county offices. I drove out to Corydon this morning, and there's nothing left there at all. Even the church is closed." He had spent New Year's Eve at a sports bar near the courthouse, among a festive crowd of locals. He had mentioned to a couple of people that he was investigating a murder that had taken place in Corydon in the 1960s. No one there remembered anything about it, but his story had created a certain interest. "People assumed I was writing some sort of true crime book, and everyone was interested in helping out." He had gotten leads to some potentially useful resources—the local historical society, the names of some of the local newspapers.

The next afternoon I was working on a brief at my computer when Dave called.

"Well," he said, and I could hear the satisfaction in his voice, "I've found out more about the murders."

"Tell me about it."

"Here's what happened. A guy named Steve Persson heard I was asking about the Bowden murders on New Year's Eve and asked his father about them. His father's a retired deputy sheriff. He was in the department when they happened, and he remembered the case. Steve got hold of my cellphone number from a friend of his who'd gotten one of my business cards—I guess I was handing them out pretty freely. Anyhow, he called me on my cell and invited me to meet his dad.

"I spent this morning in the county library looking for newspaper articles about the case. It was a big story at the time, as you might guess, so there was quite a bit of coverage, a dozen pieces at least.

"Then this afternoon I met Steve at his father's place. The elder Mr. Persson was a young deputy then—he's in his mid-seventies, I'd say—and he remembered a good deal about the case. 'It wasn't something you forget,' he said. 'It was our own *In Cold Blood*, you might say.'

"The Bowden family lived on a farm outside of Corydon. Mr. Persson said Robert Bowden was a little eccentric; he was some sort of religious fanatic, a lay preacher. The two girls went to high school in Commerce; Persson had a younger sister who was classmates with the older girl, Evie's sister Susan. The boy, Bob Bowden, Jr., wasn't in school because he was feebleminded."

"Really!"

"Yeah. Made me think of Andy and his nephew—Austin, right?"

"Yes."

"Anyhow, the story as Mr. Persson remembered it was that Evie showed up in the middle of the night at a neighboring farm and woke the people there. It was winter, and she had walked all the way there in her nightgown with a coat over it. She told them something had happened at her parents' place and her parents, sister, and brother had been shot. The Bowdens didn't have a phone. The neighbor and his oldest boy drove over there and found the bodies. Father, mother, and the other girl were all dead. Bob, Jr. was shot, too, but he was alive.

"As Persson remembered it, the police and the prosecutor pieced the story together from Evie's account and the crime scene. What happened, it seems, was that Evie's father went crazy and shot his wife Marilyn and his daughter Susan with a shotgun in the kitchen of the house. Evie and Bob, Jr. were upstairs asleep, but were wakened by the screaming and gunshots. Evie ran to her parents' room and got a .38 pistol her father kept loaded on a shelf in the closet. She heard him coming up the stairs yelling for her and Bob. Bob came to the door of his room, and her father shot him and then reloaded and started looking around for her. As he was standing in the upstairs hallway, she shot him with the pistol. Not just once, either. She emptied the chamber, all six rounds. Mr. Persson remembered that detail, because it kind of shocked everyone. 'Once or twice you could see,' he said. 'But to keep shooting like that after the man was down.

It was the coldness of it, the calculation.'"

"Actually, it sounds like a panic reaction," I said.

"That's what I thought, too, but I guess it didn't occur to anyone then. Anyhow, there was a big investigation because the prosecutor was trying to decide whether to bring a case against her in juvenile court. The neighbor whose house she went to said she'd seemed real cool-headed when she was there, not as upset as he figured a child should be under the circumstances."

"How did she know how to shoot a gun like that?" I asked. A .38 was a lot for a child to handle.

"Interesting question. I guess they asked how she knew the gun was on the shelf, and she said her father had taught all the kids to shoot, rifles and handguns, and she'd seen her father take that one from the closet before. Some of this was in the newspapers, too, because it came out at the inquest. But there was another detail that didn't make it into the papers. Probably too scandalous for the times."

"What was that?"

"The autopsy of Susan showed she was about four months pregnant. The police tried to find who the father was, to see if Susan had a boyfriend who could shed some light on what was going on in the family. But they didn't find anyone. Everyone who knew the family said both girls were extremely well behaved, and their parents kept them on a tight leash. They never went to any dances or even after-school activities like sports. No one ever saw Susan show an interest in any boy, or vice versa. If anything, the other kids more or less shunned her and Evie because they were a little odd and dressed strangely. So with that and the other facts the police were learning about the family—the father's craziness, the family's strangeness and isolation—they began to suspect the worst. Mr. Persson didn't know what Evie told them, if anything, but the upshot was, the state dropped everything, called the killing of the father self-defense, and let Evie go live with her aunt in Washington."

"And Bob ended up dying in a mental hospital in Davenport."

"I guess."

"Well, it does shed some light on Evie. God, what an awful story."

Dave made a grunt of agreement. "I'm going to check around tomorrow to see if I can find any police reports or court records from the case, and then see if I can get hold of records from the state hospital in Davenport. Apparently, it's still in operation."

"Good luck," I said.

"Any movement on Andy's part?"

"Nothing. I haven't heard a word from him."

"Damn."

33

Carla would be back from Washington, I thought, so after Dave hung up, I called her cellphone. She answered on the second ring. After a little small talk about how we'd spent the holidays, I took a deep breath and asked, "Are you still okay with talking to your mother about Andy?"

There was a pause on the line. I felt my heart start beating faster, and I realized how much I'd been counting on her help.

"Yeah," she said, finally. When she spoke, I realized I'd been holding my breath.

"Are you free next Sunday?"

"Oh yes. I've got nothin' but time these days. My doctor declared me totally disabled, and I'm on state disability, waiting for Social Security to kick in. Believe it or not, I wish I could work."

She was living in Sacramento, near the university hospital where she was being treated. We arranged that I would pick her up at about nine the following Sunday. Redbud was fairly far into the mountains, so I reserved a rental car with snow tires in Shasta City.

The morning of our trip was dark and wet, and I hoped the weather on the coast didn't mean it was snowing in the mountains. I was out of practice driving in snow, and even a rental car with snow tires wasn't going to cure that.

The house where Carla was living was a tidy bungalow in a slightly seedy-looking neighborhood not far from downtown Sacramento. As soon as I pulled up, the door of the house opened, and Carla walked down the steps. She was wearing a lavender ski jacket that looked a couple of sizes too big for her and carrying a denim-blue overnight bag. There was something stooped and tired in her walk, and I got out of the car to take the bag from her and lift it into the back. She shrugged the jacket off and laid it on the back seat. "My landlady loaned it to me," she said. Her face was thin and her skin had a pallor which showed every small line and freckle as if in relief.

"You can recline the seat," I said, feeling suddenly solicitous for her as she settled into the passenger seat. "Are you feeling okay?"

She looked over at me with something that seemed more of a brightening of her face than a smile. "Yeah. I think I look worse than I feel."

As we drove, Carla talked a little about her life. "I was a

wild kid," she said. "I always had a chip on my shoulder. I don't blame anybody, except maybe Mama. Everyone was good to me, my great-aunt and uncle, Dad and Charlene, but I always felt hurt because Mama never took me back with her. I used to wonder why she didn't want me. I think I resented Emory the most; he was always kind of a little shit, but he got to live with her and I didn't."

She drank from a cup of coffee we'd bought on our way out of Sacramento, and went on talking, holding the styrofoam cup in both hands as if to warm them. "In high school, I got in with a bad bunch of kids. I was sneaking out of the house at night to go hang out with my friends and smoke weed. Dad and Charlene tried different things—grounding me, taking away privileges—but nothing worked. That's when they decided to try sending me to Mama.

"I told you about the rest—what happened there. When I went back home to my dad's, I was completely freaked out, and I couldn't stop thinking about it, but I was afraid to talk to anyone. I used to dream about it and wake up with the shakes. I left high school, and I started using drugs big time. Then I ran away with this older guy, who got me into speed. I just more or less wasted my life—getting high, working to get money to get high some more. I tried to kick it a few times and stayed clean for a while, but I kept going back. I got pregnant with Austin and waited too long to get an abortion, so I ended up having the baby, and Dad and Charlene raised him. I guess you know how he turned out.

"I lived in California, Oregon, Las Vegas, even Hawaii for a while; got married a couple of times. Bob Burrell, the last one, wasn't a bad guy, but he was older than me, and he was a drinker. We split up, and he died of a heart attack a few years ago.

"People around me got busted, went to prison, died in accidents, died of overdoses. I was blessed or something; I just seemed to sail past it all, until I got popped last year. Even then I was lucky; it was simple possession and I got drug court and probation and that halfway house. Probably saved my life, actually. I knew I had hep C, but I wasn't sick and I didn't have medical insurance, so I was just cruising along, not thinking about it. In denial, I guess."

I made some comment about how lucky breaks come in strange ways.

"Yeah, maybe," she said.

I asked her what Evie was like when Carla was a child.

"Like a little bird. Always busy, doing this little thing or that. Not a cuddly kind of mother—she'd give you a quick kiss at bedtime, but that was about it. But under that cuteness she was tough. Those boys were afraid of her. Emory might run wild away from home, but around her he always behaved himself."

"Did she ever tell you about herself?"

"Not really. I knew she was from somewhere else and her mother and father—my grandparents, I guess—had died in some kind of accident when she was a kid, but that's all."

I told her what we'd learned about the Bowdens and how they had died.

"Oh, sweet Jesus," she said quietly. "Poor Mama."

"I think that may be why she doesn't want to have Andy examined by a psychologist. Some fear of bad blood, that sort of thing. Or at least that's what I'm hoping, and that we can talk her out of it."

"I hope so," Carla said. "But she never would hear anyone say there was anything wrong with Andy or Emory. And you know," she continued, "she has never said a word about Austin. He's her only grandson, and he lived with Dad and Charlene for years, but since we found out he was autistic she has never even asked about him. It's as if in her mind he was never born."

I said I'd decided to call on Evie unannounced. "I don't want to make it easy for her to say no," I explained. If she wasn't home, we might have to try more than once.

"That's okay," she said. "I don't mind staying an extra day or two. I lived up in Tahoe for a few years. It'll be kind of nice to see snow again."

Our conversation drifted on, into comments about the rain and the flooded ranch lands and rice fields we were passing, and then into near silence. Carla asked me if I'd mind if she turned on the radio, and she found a country-western station, which she listened to with occasional wry comments, until we lost the signal in the Sierra foothills near Shasta City.

In Shasta City we picked up the rental car, a small

SUV with snow tires, which we'd need for a trip into the mountains in winter.

As we drove out of town, I asked Carla, over the grumble of the tires, "What were you thinking of saying to her?"

"I don't know," she said. "Whatever it takes, I guess. What do you need her to do?"

"Write to Andy. Tell him he needs to see Dr. Moss. Promise not to interfere any more in Andy's defense."

"Okay."

Snow began falling gently in a darkening gray sky as we drove along the two-lane highway from Shasta City to Redbud. During the latter part of the drive we were climbing, and the landscape changed from snow-covered hills dotted with gray-black rock outcroppings and occasional ranch buildings to stands of evergreens half-dissolved into the whiteness of the snowfall. Then buildings began to appear by the roadside, the usual small businesses that line country highways—a small grocery store, an auto body shop, a couple of gas stations, a used car lot. There were churches: Jehovah's Witness, Assembly of God, and a couple with evangelical-sounding names I'd never heard of. Eventually a sign reading WELCOME TO REDBUD, with the usual list of fraternal organizations and churches in the town, marked a road that forked away from the highway. About a quarter-mile down it we reached the old downtown.

It was prettier than I thought it would be. The little main street was lined with Victorian and Craftsman-era houses half hidden behind bare-branched cottonwoods and tall pine trees. The business district, a couple of blocks long, was almost all wood or brick storefronts from the 1920s or before. Multicolored Christmas lights still glittered festively on stores and houses. Side streets led off into the woods, and the houses on some of them looked a little like civilized log cabins. There were several signs for campgrounds and RV parks. Back in the days before air conditioning, Redbud had been a resort for families escaping the summer heat in the San Joaquin Valley. Now the visitors were campers, hunters and fishermen and some cross-country skiers, and the little downtown looked quiet, but not depressed. The street parking was about three-quarters full, and most of the storefronts looked occupied.

Past a little shopping center with a small supermarket, I saw a motel with an AAA approval sign. It called itself the Mountain Home Lodge and carried on the mountain cabin theme with redwood siding and dark green shutters framing the windows of the rooms. "Does this look okay to you?" I asked Carla, and she nodded.

I took two rooms for the night, drove around to them, and carted in our bags. Carla got out of the car and walked around, stiff-legged, for a minute before following me into the building.

Standing in the doorway of her room, she looked inside for a long minute, leaning on the door jamb. "Jeez, I'm tired. That bed looks awfully nice."

I felt suddenly guilty; I'd forgotten how sick she was. "Do

you want to lie down for an hour? We don't need to go see her just yet."

She turned away from the room. "No, that's okay. A cup of coffee would be good, though."

On the main street, we passed a couple of breakfast and lunch places that were closed for the day before finding one whose lights were still on. Signs in the window advertised daily dinner specials. Tonight's was spaghetti and meatballs, and as we walked through the doors the warm air was heavy with the smell of meaty tomato sauce and garlic. It was a little early for dinner, and the only other customers were two elderly couples in the booths and an old man seated at the counter. A plump, fiftyish woman in a waitress's uniform behind the counter looked up at us. "Just sit anywhere you like," she said.

We slid into one of the booths, sinking into dark-red padded plastic seats.

"You should eat something," I said to Carla. "Would you like some dinner now?"

She was reading her menu, without much interest, and she shook her head. "I'm okay."

I ordered two coffees and a piece of apple pie and persuaded Carla to try some ice cream. She ate about half of it and pushed the bowl away. After her second cup of black coffee, she put the cup down decisively. "Okay," she said. "I'm ready."

I followed the car's GPS to Evie's address, a couple of blocks off the main street. The apartment complex where she lived was a barracks-like pair of tan-colored two-story buildings set in a wide, snow-covered lawn. A sign at the entrance of the private parking lot said PINECREST SENIOR APARTMENTS.

Evie's apartment was on the first floor. Several pots of dead geraniums, their leaves brown and crumpled, lined the cement landing in front of her door, and a wreath of artificial Christmas greenery surrounded the peephole. I rang the bell, and Evie opened the door a few seconds later.

She looked from me to Carla. I tried to keep my expression bland, but I felt she could tell from the fact that we had shown up without calling first that this was not going to be a visit she wanted to have.

"Ms. Moodie—Carla. This is a surprise," she said, and I felt that she was buying time while she tried to figure out what we had come for. After a second or two she continued. "Come in."

We stepped into the apartment, and she closed the door behind us. She glanced at me and then looked long into Carla's face. "You don't look well," she said. She reached out a hand as if to touch her, then let it drop.

Carla looked down at her. "I've been sick, Mama. Hepatitis C."

"I'm not surprised," Evie said. I was shocked by the matter-of-factness of her comment, but Carla took it without any reaction. Evie looked again at me. "What did you come here for?"

"Andy," Carla said, without waiting for me to speak.

"What about Andy? Why are you interested in him?" Evie asked.

"What difference does it make?" Carla shot back, and then stopped and sighed. "Oh, Christ, Mama, he's my little brother. You know I always cared about him. Mama, can we sit down?"

Evie seemed to remember that we were, after all, guests. "Okay," she said, almost absently, and led us into the living room. The room was spotlessly clean and plain, even bland, with off-white walls and light beige wall-to-wall carpet. We walked past a small maple dining table, bare except for a coffee mug and a few papers that looked like mail. Beyond it a sofa, upholstered in a blue and white flower print, stood against the wall to our right, with a matching armchair at an angle to it and a glass-topped coffee table in front. On the table stood a small Christmas tree, with a few little glass ornaments and several more that I recognized as inmate craft projects—a small heart woven of shiny red paper, a beadwork wreath. A dozen or so holiday cards were arranged behind it. The apartment smelled faintly of furniture polish and toast.

As we approached the sofa, my eye was drawn to a glass-fronted cabinet on the far wall. It was the kind with glass shelves and lights inside to highlight the objects displayed. The back of the cabinet was a mirror, and against it miniature glass animals, porcelain dancers, French baroque shepherdesses, and cut-crystal candy bowls, doubled by their reflections, threw beams of reflected silvery light like diamonds in a jewelry store display. Carla walked over to the cabinet and studied the glittering objects inside for a moment. She turned back to Evie as if she were about to say something, but stopped, looked away, and came back to where Evie and I were standing.

Evie sat in the armchair, and Carla and I sat on the couch. Carla took the side closer to the chair, making herself, it seemed, a buffer of sorts between me and Evie.

Evie sat upright, looking suspiciously from one of us to the other. "What did you come here for?" she asked again; this time the question was directed to both of us.

"To talk to you about Andy's refusal to see Dr. Moss," I answered.

"What about it? He made his decision." Her face was set, pinched, closed.

"Evie," I said, "you know that wasn't his decision. I talked to Andy a few weeks ago, and he was looking forward to seeing Dr. Moss. I don't know what you told him, but I know you changed his mind. Why did you do that?"

"It's what he wants," she said, as if that put an end to the discussion.

"No," I answered. "It's what you want."

"I've already told you Andy doesn't need a psychiatrist."

I felt an opening and took it. "Evie, we found out about your parents and sister and what happened to them. Are you afraid they'll find that Andy's like your brother? Or your father?"

She stiffened and glanced at Carla, as if to see whether she knew what I was talking about, and then looked back at me, but said nothing.

"Andy's not psychotic," I went on, "and he's not feebleminded. What Andy is, is probably mildly mentally retarded, and if we can prove that it will save his life. Don't you understand that?"

She looked at me, her face expressionless, for a long moment, before answering. "I don't want him talking to no psychiatrists. Mr. Dobson did that before his trial without my permission, and when I found out I told him off. There's nothing they're going to find out."

"Evie, it's not like that. It's IQ testing and testing for brain functioning."

That was the wrong thing to say. "There's nothing wrong with his brain," she snapped.

Then Carla spoke. "Mama."

Evie turned to look at her, and I saw flash across her rigid face a look of questioning and, I thought, of apprehension.

"What is it?" she asked. "Why are you here anyway?"

Carla looked at her for a second or two and then took a deep breath, as though she had reached some certainty or resolve. "Ms. Moodie knows about Len. I told her."

Evie sat silent for a second, looking fixedly at Carla. When she spoke, her voice was flat and tense.

"What about Len? There's nothing to know about him."

Carla shook her head. "It's too late for that, Mama. I told her the whole story. And I told Andy to tell her, too."

"What story?" Evie was bluffing, and the expression of rapid calculation on her face showed it. "There's nothing to tell. Anything you'd say would be a lie."

"You know what story," Carla said, levelly, "and you know it's true. You want me to tell it here again?"

Evie said nothing, but the sullen tension in her look at Carla made it clear that she was in check, at least for the moment.

"Mama, it's all out now. There's nothing left to hide."

"I don't know what you're talking about. You're lying. Len walked out, and you know it."

"Mama, I don't want to go to the police, but I will if you don't help save Andy."

"You can't do anything. It's just your word."

Something—anger, I suppose, at being lied to—made me decide to take a risk, to jump to a conclusion. "Evie," I said, and she turned to me again. "Carla told me how Len was killed. Those girls that Emory and Andy kidnapped could have been killed the same way—given some kind of drug to knock them out and then suffocated."

I was guessing. The similarities between Carla's account of Len's death and the murders of the two girls didn't amount to that much—just the lack of any signs of violence on their bodies. But Evie froze, and her expression told me

I had hit home. I was almost as surprised as she was that I had guessed right.

She began shaking her head. Outraged at what she was doing to Andy, I pressed our advantage. "There are still tissue samples from the victims," I said. "They can be tested for drugs." The movement of her head stopped, and she looked from me to Carla.

Carla looked back at her, and when she spoke, her voice was low, almost thoughtful. "Jesus, Mama, you mean you knew? What happened? Did you kill those girls?"

Evie's eyes narrowed in anger. "What do you think I am?"

"I don't know, Mama," Carla said. "I don't know if it was you or Emory or the two of you. But I think you're in some trouble here."

I didn't necessarily agree, but I wasn't about to correct her.

"Are you going to try to turn me in?" she said sarcastically.

"I might," Carla said.

"They wouldn't believe you," she said, but there was less conviction in her voice.

"You don't know that," Carla said.

Evie stared at her for a moment, almost absently, as if denying her own thoughts, and then looked at me. The defiance drained from her face and her expression became calculating as she weighed her options. "What do you want?" she asked.

I spoke up. "Tell Andy he needs to see his lawyers and Dr. Moss."

She thought for a few seconds, then nodded once. "Okay, if you say so."

"I need you to write to him, and tell him it's okay for him to see us and get tested."

"Okay," she said again.

"I need you to write it now," I said, "so I can see it."

Evie looked at me angrily, but said nothing. She pulled herself out of the armchair, walked out of the living room, and returned a minute later with a pen, some writing paper, and an envelope. She laid them on the dining table, sat in one of the wooden chairs, and picked up the pen.

I dictated a letter, watching over her shoulder as she wrote, signed it, put it into an envelope, and addressed the envelope to Andy. She handed the envelope to me.

"In case this doesn't reach him before he calls next," I said, "tell him what you said in this letter."

"Yes, yes," Evie said, irritably.

Carla spoke up. "Andy calls me, too, and I'll ask him." Evie looked up at her, and I thought for a moment she was going to call her a bad name, but she said nothing. *No mother should look at her own child like that,* I thought.

Carla and I moved away from the table, and Evie stood up.

"I guess that's it," Carla said, as much to me as to her. "We'll be on our way."

The three of us walked together to the door, Carla zipping up her oversized ski jacket. Evie opened it for us and stood by it, stone-faced, as we walked past her into the cold night.

I went out first, and as I waited on the step, Carla stopped and turned back to her mother. "Goodbye, Mama," she said, reaching a hand out to touch Evie's arm. Evie looked at her blankly, but did not move. "You did the right thing," Carla said, her voice kind, but with an undertone that promised consequences if Evie changed her mind. She bent her head down toward her mother and added, more gently and a little regretfully, "Good night, Mama. Take care of yourself. And be good to Andy."

We had almost reached the car before I heard the door close behind us.

34

Carla sat silent for a couple of minutes as we drove back downtown, looking ahead into the bright halo the headlights made in the darkness. Just after we turned onto the little main street, she said, "She's always had those little glass animals and things. I remember some of them from when I was a kid. I just loved to look at them, the way they sparkled like ice or diamonds. Some of them were presents I gave her. Charlene used to help me pick them out." She stopped for a moment, as if uncertain what to say next, and then asked, "Do you really think Mama might have helped kill those girls?"

"I don't know," I said. I hadn't thought much about my suspicion, because it seemed so unlikely that Jim and I would ever be able to find out the truth from the only three people who would know. I was shaken by the confrontation with Evie, and I felt guilty that I'd brought the subject up at all. I had all but accused Evie of two more murders in front of her own daughter. And I'd just been an accomplice in something uncomfortably close to extortion, a crime that could get a lawyer disbarred. Unless you're a prosecutor, it's a serious breach of legal ethics to use a threat to report a crime as a bargaining tool. Not that Evie was likely to complain to anyone, but that didn't stop me from feeling unnerved at what I'd done, at how easy it had been to cross the line when the opening came.

"Andy confessed to the police and said he strangled them," I said.

"But you said they could have been killed the way Len was."

I backtracked. "I was guessing," I said. "But the bodies really didn't show any signs they'd been strangled. No signs of violence at all, in fact."

"But Mama knew," Carla said. "I could see it." She went silent, and out of the corner of my eye I saw her bend her head forward and press a closed hand to her mouth.

We arrived at the motel, and I pulled into the parking lot and stopped the car. I put a hand tentatively on her shoulder in an inept attempt to comfort her. She didn't seem to notice, but after a few seconds she relaxed a little and wiped her eyes and cheeks on the sleeves of her jacket. "I'm sorry," she said. "I guess I'm just tired."

"It was my fault. I shouldn't have said what I did." At a loss for words, I added, "Would you like to go inside and rest, or have some dinner?"

"Let's go someplace," she said. "I don't want to just sit in a room right now."

The café we'd been to that afternoon was still open, but in the dark the bare-bones decor and fluorescent lights were a little too Edward Hopper for my present mood. I opted for an Italian restaurant farther down the street that had an encouraging number of cars parked in its lot. It was dimly lit inside, but warm and cheerful, with wood-paneled walls, hokey fifties pop music on the sound system, and a little group of regulars laughing and telling stories at the bar. We both ate, bread with olive oil and big plates of pasta, as though we'd been starved all day, as if food would fill some hollow, trembling place inside us and make us solid and strong again.

As we drove back to the motel, Carla returned to the subject of Evie. "If she did it, I guess it was because she was desperate," she said thoughtfully, her profile a silhouette against the points of multicolored light moving past beyond the window. "Those boys were all she had. And if you've done it twice already, the idea of killing someone else isn't as hard."

"It makes sense," I said.

"Yeah—but it's still crazy." She shook her head. "There really is something wrong with her. She's—I don't know. I guess you don't see these things in your parents when you're young."

I agreed. "You don't have a frame of reference when you're a kid to know what's normal and what isn't."

"But with what happened to her family—and having to

shoot her own father—I guess that would leave just about anyone a little bent."

"We don't know if she had anything to do with those women; it still could have been Emory."

"Uh-uh." She shook her head again, slowly, as if emphasizing the point. "Emory doesn't think. He wouldn't plan something like that. God—my own mother. It makes you wonder about yourself."

"I don't think you need to worry."

"No. I'm more like my dad. Just spent my life letting people walk all over me." She laughed, a one-syllable grunt of air. "Do you think she'll leave Andy alone now?"

"I don't know; I don't know her that well. But I think she was afraid of you."

"I hope so."

35

When I saw Carla the next morning, she looked ill, her face sallow, and there were dark smudges under her eyes. "Are you okay?" I asked, alarmed.

She shrugged. "I've been worse. I didn't sleep much last night."

She spent most of the drive back to Sacramento leaning back against the headrest, her eyes closed. "Do you need me to stay a while?" I asked her as I carried her little overnight bag up the walk to the house. "Take you to the doctor?"

"No, that's okay. I'm having a bad day, that's all."

When I got home that evening, after picking Charlie up from Ed's, I called Carla's cellphone, but she didn't answer. I left a message on her voicemail, saying I'd just called to make sure she was all right and asking her to call if she needed anything.

The next morning I called Jim and left a message with Corey that Evie had promised to tell Andy to go ahead with the examination. I faxed a request to the prison for a visit with Andy the next week, and when the confirmation came, I wrote him a longer-than-usual letter, explaining that Carla and I had met with Evie and that she had agreed with us that he should be tested after all.

Carla didn't return my call, and Andy didn't call me, either; I wondered whether Evie would find some way to derail the testing again. But when I made the long dark drive to the prison the week after our visit to Evie, Andy came down to see me.

"I got a letter from Mama," he said, when the guard had locked the visiting cage and left. "She says it's okay for me to see that doctor." He seemed baffled but also relieved—I supposed because he was no longer between his mother's intentions and mine. "Will you be there?"

"Yes," I said.

"Okay." He hesitated, as if he were trying to remember something he'd meant to say. "Oh, yeah, I've been making bead necklaces. Can I make one for you? I made one for Mama for Christmas, but I don't know if she got it."

I said I'd ask her about it when I next talked to her, and that I'd really appreciate getting one from him. He smiled. "Good. I'll start working on it right away."

36

During our trip to Redbud, I'd told Carla about Nancy Hollister, the psychologist working with us, and had asked if she would be willing to meet with her. Carla had agreed, and I'd given her phone number to Nancy.

A week or so after my visit to Andy, Nancy called.

"Well," she said, "I drove up to Sacramento yesterday and saw Carla for about three hours. Poor woman; I really felt for her. Did you know that she has liver cancer?"

"Oh, God, really?" I said, shocked. "No, the last thing she told me about it was that there'd been a cancer scare but it turned out to be a false alarm."

"Not so false, I guess. I think she found out after you and she went to see Eva. She says they've told her there isn't much they can do—chemotherapy may give her a few more months, but there aren't many options, apparently, given her other medical problems."

"Damn," I said.

"Yeah," Nancy agreed. "She also told me about Leonard.

But she's still worried about protecting Andy and Eva. She wants to talk to you."

I called Carla the next day and left a voicemail; she called me back within the hour. "Dr. Hollister told me about your diagnosis," I said. "I'm so sorry."

"Yeah—it was kind of a shock," she said, with a short, nervous laugh. "You think your life is finally starting to come together, and then…" She sighed, and gave another weak laugh. "Oh, well. I haven't started smoking again, though."

"Good for you," I said.

"Yeah, I guess. Especially since I don't have to worry about it killing me any more, do I?" She paused for a moment, then went on. "I need to figure out what I can do to help Andy, you know, because of what's happening. I know you all want me to sign a deposition of some sort."

"Yes, we need a declaration from you for the habeas petition."

"And you'll send that to the other side and the judge?"

"I think we'll have to, yes."

"And Dr. Hollister said I might have to testify at a hearing."

"Maybe." Given the glacial slowness of capital cases, an evidentiary hearing on Andy's petition, if there even was one, wouldn't happen for years. It seemed unlikely Carla would live that long.

"That's the problem. I know I told you about Mama and Emory and Len. But I just don't see how all that coming out is going to help Andy. I mean, it was all so long ago, and it didn't have nothin' to do with what him and Emory did."

"Not quite," I said. "It helps explain Andy, to some degree. It's the kind of thing that might have made a jury more sympathetic to him—to know that he'd gone through something so terrible."

Carla wasn't convinced. "I don't see how it has anything to do with what he's in jail for," she said. Her voice became more tentative, as if she was thinking something through as she spoke. "I'm worried about what'll happen to him if Mama goes to jail."

"I don't think she's in any legal trouble over this," I said, trying to reassure her. "I believe what you've told me, but there's not nearly enough evidence to prosecute her—no body, nothing at all to even say there was a murder except what you've told me." *And in a reasonable world*, I thought, *Evie's act would be seen as defending herself and her children from a man who'd been holding them hostage at gunpoint.* But I knew of too many women doing long prison terms for killing abusive husbands out of fear for their own lives to trust that the justice system would take the reasonable view.

"Yeah," Carla answered, hesitantly. "But what if they look for Len's body? And what if they put two and two together, like you did, and start to think she had something to do with killing those girls?"

So this was the unintended consequence of confronting Evie with my speculations. "I really don't think they'll do that," I said. "And it's the same problem—no evidence. And they have a confession from Andy. The prosecution's got their man; the last thing they want to do is reopen the guilt part of the case—especially since it would mean admitting that Andy's confession wasn't true."

"But what if Mama gets scared and moves away? She's all Andy has in the world. I don't want to take her from him."

I had to admit I didn't know what Evie might do if she felt threatened. I made the only suggestion I could think of. "Why don't I write up a declaration of everything you told me except the part about Len's death? Then we'd have that much, at least, and you'd have time to think about the rest."

She thought the idea over for a moment and then said, "Yes—I think I could do that."

A couple of days later I made the drive to Sacramento. Hoping Carla might relent, I'd written two declarations. One recounted what Carla had told me and Nancy Hollister about her life with Evie, her grandparents, Jimmy, Charlene, and Len, her son Austin, and her observations about Andy's slowness. The other, a supplemental declaration, told about the murder of Leonard Hardy.

Over lunch at a deli, we talked more about her living situation. Her landlords were a retired couple whose son was a friend of Carla's probation officer. "They've been okay," she said. "I have this little granny unit in the back of their house. Doreen brings me cookies and stuff. They belong to some little church, and they keep trying to get me to go with them. Maybe I will some time. I may be moving up to Washington, though."

"Really? Why?"

"Dad and Charlene want me to come up there where they can look after me. Charlene can't stand the idea of me being so far away and sick. It's crazy, after all those years when I never said boo to them, didn't help them with Austin, anything."

After we'd eaten, I gave her the two declarations. "I wrote them both up," I said. "You can sign both or just the one and maybe keep the other in case you feel differently about signing it in the future. At least you'll know what it would say."

She read the longer one, frowning in concentration, corrected an incorrect place name and a spelling mistake, filled in the date at the end, and signed it decisively, pushing it back to me across the table. Then she studied the second one for a minute or two, her face unreadable, before folding it in thirds and putting it into her purse. She looked up at me. "I'll think about it," she said. "I don't know."

I hated to go into particulars about her illness, but we needed to know whether she was likely to live to testify at a hearing. "Is your doctor saying there's no possibility of recovery, then?" I asked.

"That's about it."

"No possibility of a transplant."

"No—I've got too many other things wrong with me."

"Are they going to try any therapies—chemo, radiation?"

"He said there are some things they can do to kill some of the tumors and slow the rest down—but he said they're risky. I'll probably try anyway, though. Not much point in just sitting around waiting to die."

"Sure," I agreed. "You're too young for that anyway."

She made a face and shrugged. "Not really. I've lived a lot. Not much to live for when I think about it." Her gaze shifted to a spot in the middle of the table between us. "It's funny," she said thoughtfully. "I thought I'd be really afraid of dying, but I'm not."

I wished I could say the same. "Some people say that's a sign of wisdom."

"First one ever," she said, with a rueful smile.

After I'd paid for our lunches, she asked if I'd mind driving her to Wal-Mart, so she could pick up some prescriptions and groceries. She bought only a few things: a quart of milk, some cans of soup, peanut butter, cookies, crackers, a loaf of bread and some butter. At the pharmacy counter, she wrote a check and then turned to me, holding her small paper bag of prescription jars and bottles. "Damn—that about cleaned me out until the end of the month."

"Do you need some cash to tide you over?" I asked her. "I can help you."

She shook her head. "No, I'll be all right."

On the short ride home, she said almost nothing. Her face looked tired and strained, as if by pain. Back at her place, I offered to carry her groceries in, but she said, "No, I'll be okay. Think I'll take a nap, though."

"Stay in touch with me, will you?" I asked her. "Let me know if you move, so we can reach you if anything develops in Andy's case."

I waited while she walked up the little path, carrying her plastic grocery bags, and unlocked the door. Before going inside, she turned and waved to me, and I waved back.

37

Dan Moss liked Andy. "He was pretty low key," he said, between bites of a wedge of quesadilla. The wind outside had pushed up a couple of tufts of brown-gray hair near the crown of his head, and he looked tired. "Not what I expected. The other case I worked on—Mr. Chu's—the client was more in line with my preconceptions—streetwise kid, into being a gangbanger. Andy just seems like—well, kind of a schlemiel." He picked up another piece. "I'm really hungry," he said almost apologetically. "We were there from eight to two with only one bathroom break."

It was well after two in the afternoon, a late lunch for both of us. Dan had finished his evaluation of Andy, two six-hour days at the prison. I'd spent part of the first day with him and Andy, making introductions and sitting quietly in a corner of the interview room for the first couple of hours, just to be there in case Andy got stressed by the clinical interview and the testing. The second day, to stay nearby, I made visits to a couple of former clients.

Our marathons finished, Dan and I had headed off to lunch at a brewpub. It was late enough that we were able to get one of the booths along a wall, apart from the echoing center of the room, where we could talk with some quiet and privacy.

"Not the best conditions for testing, that's for sure," Dan went on, after swallowing another bite. "He held up well, though. I was impressed."

"It's standard operating procedure at the prison," I said. "No one's been able to get them to change it. It took ten years of arguing with the warden's office to get a psych testing room at all."

Dan shook his head in disbelief. "What a system."

He took a drink of his Diet Pepsi. "You know," he said, shaking his head, "obviously I haven't met anyone else on death row, but Andy doesn't seem capable of the crimes he's accused of. Unless he's just showing me a front."

"Personally, I think his brother Emory was the heavy," I said, "and Andy was just following along."

"And his brother isn't on death row. Why is that?"

"They weren't tried together. Different lawyers, different juries. Emory got life without parole."

Our server appeared and set our main courses down. Dan took a bite of his sandwich and looked over at me again. "I imagine you'd like to hear some more about how the evaluation went?"

I nodded, and he went on. "Well, you were there for the

clinical interview. He was very cooperative, generally. But you saw how he reacted when I asked him about his father. I let it go, because it seemed to be making him upset."

"I think his mother must have warned him away," I said.

"Maybe; I don't know. But this morning he brought it up again. This time he said he didn't really think his sister would tell a lie like that, but that she must have just had a bad dream or something. Obviously, he feels some loyalty to his sister; he didn't want to call her a liar. But at the same time he wasn't telling me it had happened. I could still put something about the incident and what he said into my report, but you said yesterday you didn't think I should, if Andy doesn't endorse it. Is that still how you want to go?"

"Yes," I said. "I wish he were willing to confirm what he told me. But since he isn't, there doesn't seem to be much we can do. I'll check with Jim, but I think he'll agree with me."

"Okay," Dan said. "I'll let it go unless I hear from you. As for the IQ testing, I scored it last night, and he's definitely in the mildly mentally retarded range." He explained how Andy had done on the subtests that measured a person's skills in different types of brain functioning: verbal, math, short-term recall, longer-term memory, mental flexibility.

"And for the neuropsychological testing, I'll need to score it and get back to you with the full picture. But I can tell you it's likely he has some pretty substantial deficits. He had trouble with all but the simplest sets. I'm figuring his overall score will be in at least the moderately impaired range. I'm surprised no one did neuropsychological testing before his trial."

I'm never sure how to react to news that a client has shown evidence of brain damage. On the one hand, brain damage can save your client's life. When the prosecutor argues that your client chose to use drugs and commit murder and other crimes simply because he's antisocial, cold-blooded, pleasure-seeking, and selfish, you can counter with expert testimony that he has a defect in his brain that keeps defeating his attempts to control his impulses and make good choices in life. On the other hand, it means your client has what amounts to a permanent and crippling mental illness and will live his life in a chaos of mistaken perceptions and unpredictable compulsions. Not exactly a cause for wild cheering.

As we waited for the check, Dan said, "I'm supposed to go skiing with the kids this weekend. Is it okay if I finish analyzing my data after that and call you early next week? I know you need it pretty quickly."

I swallowed a mouthful of salad. "Should be okay. Our filing deadline is the middle of next month."

In the parking lot, watching Dan's car pull away, I felt suddenly empty with exhaustion. I'd made the long drive from Corbin's Landing two days in a row, but beyond that, I realized I'd been tense with waiting: worrying whether Andy would refuse to see Dan again; whether something else would go wrong—some bureaucratic snafu in the prison, a sudden lockdown of prisoners—that would derail the examination; whether the testing would show that Andy wasn't mentally retarded after all. Everything had gone well, and the results seemed even more favorable than I'd expected, but my body had stopped pumping adrenalin, leaving me feeling depleted and knocked down. I sat for a minute or two, contemplating the long drive home. Then I got out of the car and walked back into the shopping center and into a chocolate store I'd seen on our way to the pub.

When I drove out of the lot, ten minutes later, I was armed with a very hot latte (with low-fat milk to soothe my itching conscience) and a quarter-pound of buttery caramels and dark chocolate-covered orange peel. When the habeas petition was finished, I told myself, I would go on many hikes up in the hills. Maybe I'd even get a mountain bike. In the car, I ate a caramel and wondered what the possibilities were for going into business making candy. No more negligent lawyers, no more painful interviews in trailer parks and small sad towns, no more grim visits to San Quentin. I took a sip of the latte. The coffee was good, and its toasted, slightly bitter edge brought my senses back to reality as I started the engine of my car.

38

No candy store, no bakery. During the next few weeks I griped about my choice of careers, and my decision to get back into this one, as I wrote page after page of legal boilerplate and factual narrative for the petition, and Jim and I edited the declarations of Nancy Hollister and Dan Moss.

Nancy had worked on habeas cases before, and she knew what we needed; her declaration didn't require much work. But Dan was new to litigation and had never written a report for a case. I wrote most of his declaration for him, working from my notes of what he told me, calling him almost daily as I tried to translate the jargon of psychology and neuropsychology into language a judge or law clerk would understand and a jury might have found meaningful and sympathetic. Dan quickly understood what I was looking for, but it still took a lot of hours before we got everything right and had a declaration he felt was accurate and something he could stand behind. "My wife's starting to wonder what's going on between us," he joked one weekend, after my third call in a day.

March blew in with rainstorms that collapsed hillsides and sent boulders and chunks of dirt calving like icebergs from the cliffs of the coastal range. A section of Highway One south of us was closed for a week after a rock slide, and a downed power line left Corbin's Landing without electricity for two days.

Before the electricity went out, I had emailed what I hoped would be the final draft of the petition to Jim. Nevertheless, during the power failure I drove north each day through sheeting rain to Gualala, the nearest actual town, where I set up my laptop in a coffee house with Wi-Fi, worked while nursing a succession of lattes, and exchanged emails with Corey about margins, titles, and the naming and numbering of exhibits.

Dr. Moss's findings had been as helpful as he'd anticipated. Our phone conversations about them had been awash in technical terms—lateralization, executive function, crystallized knowledge, the Halstead Impairment Index—but the bottom line was where Andy needed it to be. His full-scale IQ was 68, and the functioning of the parts of his brain that process and remember information was well below normal. Translating the findings into a written declaration in support of the petition had been slow but satisfying work, and in the end we had what I hoped was a fairly clear explanation of what wasn't working right in Andy's brain and how his disabilities left him adrift in the world, bewildered by the everyday complexities of life.

Dr. Moss's findings and opinions supported a suite of arguments in the petition: that the constitution prohibited the state from executing Andy because executing a mentally retarded defendant would be cruel and unusual punishment; that even if Andy didn't meet the test for mental retardation the evidence of his low intelligence and other brain deficits might have moved the jury to doubt the prosecution's claim that he was the ringleader in the crimes and show him the relative mercy of a sentence of life without possibility of parole; and that Andy's trial lawyer provided him with ineffective assistance because he could have found all this out by looking at his school records and hiring a neuropsychologist.

The day Corey emailed me to tell me the petition had been filed, I thought I ought to celebrate, but I couldn't think of anything to do. In the end I drove down to Vlad's pub on the highway and marked the occasion with a pint of hard cider and a plate of brie and crackers.

After finishing the petition, my mind felt drained of words and any ability to put them together. I spent the next several weeks repairing deer fencing, grafting and planting apple and pear trees, repotting lemon trees, digging compost into the garden beds, and writing up billing claims itemizing my work on Andy's cases and the other appeals I'd been too busy to bill on. Because I'd stopped taking new work to finish Andy's petition, I made a few phone calls to the agencies in charge of appointing lawyers to criminal appeals, to let them know I was available again. My life began to look a lot like what it had been before I took Andy's case.

Jim and I visited Andy together, to give him a copy of the petition and exhibits and explain to him, as best we could, the case we had tried to make for getting him a new trial. Andy made a show of looking through the papers, but he didn't seem to notice the claims based on mental retardation. Once I reassured him that we hadn't included anything about Evie killing Len, he seemed content to put it aside and make small talk.

Afterward, I talked with Jim about Carla and suggested asking Judge Fuentes for an order allowing us to take a videotaped deposition of her testimony. If Andy received an evidentiary hearing on his habeas petition, and Carla wasn't around to testify in person, her written declaration wouldn't work as a substitute; it would be considered hearsay. It wasn't completely useless: mental-health experts, like Nancy Hollister or Dan Moss, could refer to her declaration as part of the basis for their opinions about Andy's psychological and intellectual functioning. But the judge wouldn't be able to consider Carla's declaration as direct evidence of the facts in it, unless the attorney general agreed to allow it. And in the bitter gamesmanship of capital litigation, for the attorney general to stipulate to anything that might help a defendant get a new trial was practically unheard of.

A court-approved deposition, on the other hand, where the attorney general could cross-examine the witness, would be the equivalent of presenting testimony in advance of the hearing, and the videotape of it would be admissible evidence. Motions for depositions were commonly granted by the federal courts for witnesses who were very old or ill, so Jim had a good shot at getting the court to approve deposing Carla.

For a couple of months after the petition was filed, I didn't hear anything from Jim or Corey, except an email telling me the unsurprising news that the attorney general had requested and received an extension of time to file a responsive pleading to the petition. From experience, I guessed it would probably take nearly a year for Brenda Collinson, the attorney general in Andy's case, to read what we'd written and write an answer. Even Dave had stopped emailing. It was as though we were all too tired of the case to deal with each other.

Ed went on a fishing trip to Baja, finally giving me the chance to repay him for all his dog-sitting by keeping Pogo for two weeks. It was two weeks of doggy day camp, with long walks with Charlie and Pogo every day and trips to dog-friendly beaches where Pogo could work off some of his boundless energy chasing tennis balls and seagulls.

I got appointed to a few more appeals, and I decided to take another one in a capital case—just the appeal. No witnesses to interview, no traveling to exotic locales—just reading and research and writing and visiting my client every now and then to touch base. It was a three-defendant gang case from Los Angeles County, involving two crimes:

a robbery and murder at an ATM and a drive-by shooting that left two bystanders dead. My new client had been arrested a day after the drive-by carrying a Glock that was later identified as the murder weapon in the robbery. That, a blurred photo from the ATM camera, and the testimony of one of his codefendants in the drive-by, who was allowed to plead guilty to second-degree murder for his cooperation with the prosecution, were the major evidence against him—though it didn't help his defense that he'd been caught in a taped phone conversation trying—allegedly—to arrange to have the snitching codefendant killed before the trial.

The client himself, Arturo Villegas, was short, tattooed, and painfully young, puffed up with immature swagger and bravado. He had been eighteen when he was arrested, and twenty-one when he was sentenced. Four years on death row waiting for a lawyer and a few months in the hole for fighting with a rival gang member hadn't calmed him down much, though it had given him a better grip on the reality of prison life than he'd probably had at the time of his trial. After I'd visited him a couple of times, called his parents, and put forty dollars on his books for the canteen, it seemed we'd have a decent working relationship.

3 9

From time to time, Dave's assistant Brad ("my database maven," Dave called him, with the marvel of the middle-aged at the technical proficiency of the young) had worked at finding a possible address for Nicole Shumate, the girl Andy had let go. Nicole had been essentially homeless before and during the two trials, squatting in vacant buildings or living with one group or another of drug-using friends and moving from place to place as her welcome, or their rent, ran out. All we had for her was her name, a couple of temporary addresses, a date of birth from a police report, and a photograph from the trial exhibits. Using those, Brad had found court records showing that she had been convicted of possession of marijuana and cocaine in California a year after the trial. She had pled guilty and received a short jail sentence and probation. After that, it seemed, she had moved to Las Vegas, where she had picked up arrests for shoplifting and using a stolen credit card. She had served another jail sentence, and, after being released on probation, had successfully completed a drug program. After that, the trail disappeared.

She wasn't in prison, at least not in California or Nevada, and she didn't show up on any of the databases tracking residence or credit histories. The absence of any more references could mean that she'd died somewhere without being identified or, more likely, had married. Marriage is the bane of skip tracers; a woman can change her last name overnight and disappear from the databases more effectively than if she had died. A search for the record of her marriage would require searching fifty states (assuming she'd stayed in the United States), some of which had laws making access to marriage records difficult for anyone but the couple themselves.

Eventually, Brad found a marriage record from Arizona showing that a Nicole Shumate and a David Madison had been married in Phoenix about ten years ago. After that Brad found other databases showing the couple at two different addresses in Arizona and Nevada. But the most recent address was in California, where credit reporting records showed Nicole Madison, aged thirty-two, and David Madison, thirty-five, residing with Joshua Madison, seven, and Lisa Madison, five, in a single family dwelling on Edelweiss Drive in La Cresta, a small town in the mountains north of San Bernardino.

"Bingo!" Dave emailed, with the information.

The petition was filed, but I knew we had to interview her, or at least try. She was the only surviving victim of Andy and Emory's crimes, better able than anyone else to describe what had happened in the barn and to help us figure out why Andy had let her go. The police had written her story in their reports, and she had testified at both trials. But we had to question her ourselves, if possible, to find out if there was anything omitted from the police reports or left unasked at trial. It's not unknown for police investigators and prosecutors to deep-six interesting bits of information that might muddy their cases against a defendant.

"Can you come with me?" Dave asked. "It may be easier for her to talk to a woman—assuming she's willing to talk to us at all."

I dreaded the interview, but I had an oral argument coming up in Riverside and no excuse not to make a side trip to La Cresta. Dave was free that weekend, so on a Friday afternoon we flew down to San Bernardino together.

We both knew San Bernardino pretty well. The county probably had more of its population on death row than any other except Los Angeles. Eventually everyone who worked on death-penalty appeals had a case, or more than one, from San Bernardino, and we had both done our share of time there.

There was a pretty decent Hilton hotel near the freeway, with a Japanese restaurant across the street. Over salmon teriyaki and Kirin beer, Dave and I plotted our approach to Nicole. We had both read everything the file contained about her. Her statements to the police and her testimony at the two trials had been consistent, varying only where memory might naturally falter. She had been a good witness, answering questions well and clearly: no exaggerations, theatrics, or verbal potshots at the defendant or his lawyers.

She had been a sixteen-year-old runaway, turning tricks downtown for money for food and drugs, when she had had the bad luck to flag down Emory's truck. Once she was inside, she testified, Andy had grabbed her and pushed her head down below the dashboard while Emory drove the truck out of town and out to the farm. They'd walked her to the barn, and into a room inside it where there was an old sofa and a television set. They'd taken turns raping her and making her go down on them for a couple of hours. Afterward, Emory had tied her to a chair, with a gag made out of a towel in her mouth, and left her in the barn.

Some time late that night, they'd come back with food. They'd untied her and let her eat, telling her that they would kill her if she made any noise, and after she'd eaten, they both had sex with her again, and tied her up. The next day Andy brought her breakfast and lunch and had let her come into the house to take a shower. He'd wanted to have sex with her, she said, but she started crying, and he stopped. In the evening he'd brought her dinner again. Exhausted from fear, she had fallen asleep, and she wasn't sure how much later it was that he'd reappeared alone, untied her real fast, and told her to hurry up and get into the truck. She believed he was taking her someplace to kill her.

Out on the highway, she pushed the truck door open, jumped out, and ran into the woods. He said something about not meaning to hurt her, but she didn't believe him. She saw the truck make a k-turn and head back toward the ranch.

She walked down the road for a couple of miles, ducking into the trees whenever she saw headlights, and when she was too tired to go on, she hid in the woods near the road until morning. When it was light enough to see what the cars approaching looked like, she flagged down a passing pickup truck and told the driver what had happened to her, and he took her to the police station in Shasta City.

After Andy and Emory were arrested, she identified them in a lineup and identified their truck. The police had taken her to the ranch, where she pointed out the room in the barn where she had been kept. On the witness stand, she identified Andy and Emory and photographs of the truck and the room.

At their penalty phases, she had taken the stand again and had testified about how being kidnapped, sexually assaulted, and held prisoner for two days, convinced she would be murdered, had changed her. She told of being placed in a group home for troubled teens, which she left for the streets as soon as she turned eighteen, of being afraid to sleep alone in a room, of overdosing on codeine, feeling numb, ashamed, and afraid. She had lost a lot of weight at first, had been in therapy for post-traumatic stress disorder, and was taking medication for anxiety.

"What courage," the prosecutor had argued. "What bravery this young girl has shown, coming to this courtroom again and again, to have to look at this man, this monster who subjected her to the worst nightmare imaginable, raped her, kept her tied up like an animal, and was prepared to kill her. You saw what he and his brother did to Lisa Greenman and Brandy Ontiveros, ladies and gentleman. This young woman was the Hardys' next victim. She would have been strangled and buried in the woods with the others. We'll never know why she was released. Maybe Mr. Hardy here got cold feet. Maybe he was afraid his mother would find this girl and turn him and his brother in to the police. Or maybe he had an argument with his brother over her and decided to let her go to get back at him. Who knows? Whatever the reason, she is the lucky one; she wasn't killed and buried in the woods. Nicole survived to speak here for herself and for Brandy and Lisa. She told you what these animals did and what her life has been like because of it. It was hard for her to relive the horror of those days and nights, but she came here and she faced the man who did that to her, and she told you what he did. What do you do, ladies and gentleman, what should society do, to a man who can do such sadistic things to a young woman like that—and not just her but all those young women? What penalty is severe enough to punish him for what he has done to Nicole Shumate, to Lisa Greenman and her mother and stepfather, to Brandy Ontiveros and her mother and her little daughter, who will have to grow up knowing her mother was murdered and live her life in the shadow of such evil?"

And so on.

That had been fifteen years ago. Nicole was twice as old as she had been when she was kidnapped, with a husband and children. Other than that and her criminal record, we knew nothing of her life since the trial. I knew what I wanted to ask her—sort of: more detail, more specifics of what was said and done by whom—anything not in the police reports which might shed some light on what Andy and Emory's actual roles had been in the crimes—and why Andy had released her.

Dave and I didn't talk much as we drove the winding road from the valley floor into the mountains. I don't know what was on Dave's mind, but I was thinking of the fact that we were about to walk in on Nicole's Saturday morning and ask her to reminisce with us about the most horrible experience of her life, to help one of the men who inflicted it on her. And the many ways, each unkinder and more humiliating than the last, in which she could say no to us, tell us to take a hike and that our murdering son-of-a-bitch client should rot in hell. *It's interviews like this one*, I thought, *that make me glad not to be an investigator*.

Wildfires had burned through this country in some

recent summer, and as the road climbed, we saw canyons and valleys where nothing remained of the pine forest, as far as the eye could see, but row upon row of blackened tree trunks. The presence, here and there, of a bit of green—a young evergreen or a patch of brush—seemed less a message of hope and renewal than a comment by nature about all that had been destroyed.

Part of La Cresta had been burned over in that fire, and we drove past streets of cleared lots with concrete pads. On some of the lots stood new houses, complete or under construction. We were relieved to find that Edelweiss Drive was in an area that the fires had missed.

The Madisons' house was set well back from the street, on at least a half-acre. It was sort of a cross between mountain cabin and mid-twentieth-century split level, with redwood siding, a bay window, and a two-car garage. The area around it had been cleared of trees and bushes as a defense against forest fires, but beyond that, big pines cast shade partway into the cleared area. A soccer ball and a few colorful plastic toys were scattered in the yard, and a child's pink bicycle with training wheels stood next to the steps to the door. A dark green SUV was parked in the driveway. My heart sank to see it; I realized I'd been hoping no one would be home.

We parked on the street in front of the house and walked to the front door. The spring morning was chilly, and the air felt sharper and thinner at this altitude. Three big unglazed pots filled with petunias and geraniums stood on the concrete pad in front of the door, and the musky scent of petunias and the faint, sharp taste of geranium leaves mingled with the scent of dry pine needles and wood smoke in the air.

I rang the doorbell and waited. In a minute, a deadbolt clicked, and the door opened a few inches, releasing a faint smell of coffee and cooked bacon. A woman, half visible in the opening, looked out at us. "May I help you?" she asked—the kind of "may I help you" that means, "What are you doing here?"

"My name is Janet Moodie," I said, floundering ineffectually for the right tone, the right expression. "I'm one of the attorneys for Marion Hardy." The woman stood still, saying nothing. She was a few inches taller than me and slender, with red-brown hair. I nodded toward Dave. "This is Dave Rothstein, an investigator in Mr. Hardy's case."

I held out a business card, and she reached a faintly tanned hand, trimmed nails shiny with clear polish, outside the door and took it. She looked at the card, then from me to Dave and back to me. From inside the house I could hear the indistinct sound of a television playing a children's program, then running footsteps and a child's voice behind her. "Mommy, who is it? Is it Aaron?"

She turned her head away from us and looked down. "No, honey, it isn't Aaron. Go back inside and watch *Magic Schoolbus* for a while, okay?"

"Okay." I heard the child move away into the house, and the young woman turned back to us, reached up and undid the chain latch, then walked outside, closing the door behind her.

She was slender, with a soft, pretty face, gray eyes, and long light-brown hair pulled back into a ponytail. She wore tight jeans and a pink hooded sweatshirt. She looked at the two of us, her expression tense and watchful. "I thought he'd be dead by now," she said.

I shook my head. "No, he isn't," I said, as neutrally as I could, trying to convey in those words that I understood why she would think that after all these years, but not to hint either that I sympathized with her for wanting him dead or that I didn't. "We're working on a habeas corpus petition for him."

"You're not trying to get him freed, are you?"

I hedged. "Well, to be honest, there's not really much chance of that. We're more focused on the penalty in his case."

She looked at me intently. "You don't think he deserves the death penalty, after what he did?"

"We think there was mitigating evidence that should have been presented in his case and wasn't. We've got some reason to think that maybe his brother was more responsible for the crimes."

"Yeah. He should have been executed for sure." She seemed to relax a little at the idea that we shared at least that bit of common ground.

"Why—do you think he was worse?"

"They both deserved it. I don't know why he didn't get

it, too." She stopped, looked down at my card in her hand, then back to me. "He was—he was worse. His brother—your client, I guess—was kind of a dope. The dark-haired one—Emory—he was a real creep."

"Kind of a dope? How?"

She thought for a second before answering. "I don't know. It just seemed that his brother kept ordering him around and griping at him. And he hit us."

"Emory?"

"Yeah."

"You and Andy both?"

"Yeah."

"So did he—Andy—seem slow?"

"No, not really. But his brother treated him like he was. That's what it was, I guess. He acted like he didn't have any respect for him." She stopped again to think, and looked up again, her expression in some barely perceptible way more open to us. "I remember that the district attorney, Mr. Dannemeier, kept saying that Andy was the leader in the murders and all that. I guess because he was older and he was the one who let me go. I remember it seemed strange. But I figured he knew something I didn't."

"Did you ever tell Mr. Dannemeier that Andy didn't seem to be the leader?"

"We talked about it. I told him what I saw—about Emory's attitude and all."

"Did you tell him how he treated Andy?"

"Yes."

"How did he respond?"

"He didn't seem to think it made any difference. He said Andy killed the two girls, that he'd confessed to the police."

Dave asked the next question. "Did anyone from the defense ever talk to you before the trials?"

"I remember someone tried to, but I wouldn't talk to him. I just wanted them both dead." I recalled from the trial transcripts that she had been asked by Emory's lawyer if she had refused to speak with his investigator.

"No one before Andy's trial?"

She thought for a moment before answering. "No, I don't remember anyone else."

"Did anyone tell you not to speak to the defense?"

"No. Mr. Dannemeier said someone might try to question me, but it was my decision whether or not to talk to them."

She glanced back toward the door. Dave asked the next question. "Do you have any idea why Andy Hardy let you go?"

She looked back at us and then down again, her eyebrows knitted into a frown, shook her head and looked up. "No. I've thought about it a lot. You do, you know. Why me, and why not them? I used to keep running it over in my mind, trying to figure it out."

"Do you remember how it happened?"

She stood silent for a moment, obviously thinking, before answering. "I remember he came to the shed where I was earlier that evening with some food and later a glass of juice. The juice tasted bitter, and it was grainy, as if some coffee grounds had gotten into it. I told him it tasted bad. He said he'd get some other juice, and left. But he came back after just a minute and said we had to hurry and that he wasn't going to hurt me. We went out and got in the truck, and he kept whispering to me to be quiet. After I was in the truck he tried to close the door real quietly, and it didn't close completely. That's when I thought about jumping out."

"What happened then?"

"I think he had some trouble with the truck, backing it up and making the turn in the driveway. Like he wasn't really used to driving it."

"Which direction did he turn on the road?"

"Left. Back the way we came."

"Toward town?"

"Yeah."

"Did he say anything in the truck?"

"Not until I opened the door. Then he said, 'Don't jump; I'm not going to hurt you.'"

"What happened then?"

"I told him I didn't believe him, or something like that. And then I jumped."

"Did he try to grab you and pull you back in?"

She closed her eyes and thought for a few seconds. "Not that I could see," she said.

"What did he do then?"

"Just pulled out, made kind of a k-turn, and drove away back toward the house."

"He didn't get out and look for you?"

"No."

"What did you do after that?"

"I ran into the woods and hid for a while and then started walking along the edge of the road in the direction we were going—back toward town, I guess. I remember a couple of times I saw headlights coming from the direction of their place, and I got scared that he was coming back for me and ran into the woods and hid."

"Could you tell whether it was him?"

"One of them might have been the truck. It was moving kind of slow. When it was past I came out and kept walking along the edge of the road, but then I thought I saw the headlights coming from the other direction, and I hid again. I decided then that I wouldn't try to hitch a ride with anyone until it was light, and I just kept walking and hiding until morning. Then I flagged down a truck with some kind of contractor's logo on it and told the guy in it I'd been kidnapped and asked him to take me to the police."

It was Dave who asked her the hard question. "Would you be willing to sign a declaration about what you've told us?"

She shook her head. "No. I'm not about to do anything that would help him get away with what he did." She looked behind her at the door and then back at us. "I need to go back inside; my little girl is in there." She reached her hand for the door knob and shivered as if shaking off a spasm of pain. "It's hard talking about this, you know. I've done all I can to forget it. It's a good thing my husband's off fishing today, or I wouldn't be out here talking to you at all. He's had to deal with what they did to me. I don't know where I'd be if it weren't for him. Probably dead by now. Certainly not here." With a gesture and a turn of her head she indicated the tidy house, the car in the driveway.

"I'm sorry to bother you," I said.

"It's your job, I guess," she said. "I wouldn't want to have it. I really have to go now."

She opened the door as we were thanking her and edged inside with a nod and a small dismissive gesture. The door closed behind her, and I heard the chain latch slide into place.

Dave and I walked back to the car in silence, conscious that Nicole might be watching us from the house.

As we drove away, I said to Dave, "You should probably have gone alone. You might have figured out a way to put her at ease more, get her to talk."

"I doubt it," Dave said. "I don't think she'd have talked to me at all if I'd shown up alone when her husband wasn't there."

"Maybe." I wasn't sure I agreed with him.

"What are we going to do with what she told us?" Dave asked. "She'll never sign a declaration to help Andy."

I agreed. "But she did confirm that Andy wasn't calling the shots, and it looks as though Andy meant to let her go, she didn't just escape."

"Did she say at the trial that Andy was the leader?" Dave asked.

"No, she didn't. That was the DA's theory, but he didn't ask her. I guess he knew she wouldn't go there."

"Smart man."

"And a little unscrupulous. He knew she wouldn't support his theory and was hiding it from the defense."

"No one from the defense thought to ask either, then."

"No. Dobson wouldn't, because he never talked to her and didn't know what she might say. And Mark Levenson didn't at Emory's trial, because the DA's theory was good for Emory."

"That story she told about the juice," Dave said. "I've never read anything about that before."

"Neither have I."

"Rings a bell, doesn't it?"

"Yes," I said. "I just wonder how much Andy knew."

40

Jim called me in July to let me know the court had granted his motion to depose Carla. It took a few weeks to find a court reporter and work out a date when Jim, Deputy Attorney General Brenda Collinson, and the court reporter could all meet in Canfield, but they eventually arranged for a deposition at the Holiday Inn, on a date around the middle of September.

Not much else happened that summer. Andy called about once a week, and we talked about inconsequential things. The case of one of my former clients, Dwayne Orton, lurched another step forward—his federal attorney emailed me to say that the district court magistrate assigned to the case had ordered an evidentiary hearing on the question of whether Dwayne's trial attorney had acted ineffectively when he had advised Dwayne to refuse a plea bargain offer of a life sentence—and then stopped again, when the attorney general asked the judge in charge of the case to overturn the magistrate's order. And in another old case of mine that

I'd given up when I left the state defender's office, the state Supreme Court issued its inevitable decision affirming the death judgment.

The week after Labor Day, I flew up to Alaska, my first trip there in two years. When my mother was alive, I'd made a point of visiting a couple of times a year, but she died, and then Terry died, and I stopped wanting to travel anywhere for a long time. I'd never liked Anchorage while growing up anyway, and after my mother's death I felt as if one string that had kept me tied to Alaska had given way.

I flew into Fairbanks and spent a couple of days with my younger sister Maggie, and we drove to visit my older sister Candace for her birthday. Candace and her husband Emil lived in the mountains outside Anchorage, in an alpine house with cathedral ceilings and awesome views out the tall windows. Astrid, their older daughter, was living in Seattle, and the younger one, Rachel, had flown in from Dutch Harbor. Astrid couldn't get home for her mother's birthday, Candace explained, a little smugly, because she was eight months pregnant and wasn't supposed to fly. It was a comment on Gavin's unmarried state and my lack of grandmotherly fecundity; I let it pass.

Maggie and I sometimes rolled our eyes about Candace and Emil, who'd settled early into safe civil service jobs and the big house in Eagle River, raised three well-adjusted children, and, with glum earnestness, taken on the responsibility of looking out for Mom after Dad died. They were estimable and well off, but Candace seemed to feel resentfully that Maggie and I had somehow gotten a better deal in life.

By the time I left for home, after Candace's birthday party and a couple of days hiking and berry picking with my sisters and Rachel, I felt about as good as I ever had since Terry died. "You've got to come home more often," Maggie said, as we said goodbye at the airport. "We really miss you. Even Candace does, you know."

On the plane trip, I felt lonely and desolate. I tried to cheer myself up by thinking of seeing Charlie and the cats again, and how happy Charlie would be to see me. But my spirits didn't really lift until I'd left the urban blight of the East Bay and the suburban sprawl of Marin County and was driving once again toward the coast among the tan and dark green of the late-summer hills.

The air in my house felt cold and smelled musty. The cats, fed by Ed while I was gone, came to the door, made a small show of acknowledging me, satisfied themselves that I had no food for them, and retreated to the bedroom. I set my suitcase down, put away the inevitable groceries I'd picked up on the drive home, opened every window I could reach, and, looking disconsolately at the pile of mail Ed had left on my dining table, called to let him know I was back. Then

I walked to his house with a slab of smoked salmon and a bottle of birch syrup.

Ed had made enchiladas for dinner, and his house smelled like green chilies and corn tortillas. Charlie rushed up, vibrating all over, and stopped to sniff my boots and jeans while I scratched his ears. "Have you eaten?" Ed asked. "I'll fix you a plate."

It hadn't occurred to me that I might be hungry until I'd smelled the food. Ed brought me a plate with about twice as much as I could eat. We talked about Alaska—Ed had spent a couple of summers up there working on fishing boats when he was young. By the time I finished eating, I felt almost too tired to talk. I thanked Ed effusively and headed home in the dark with a borrowed flashlight, a dish of enchiladas, and Charlie.

Besides the mail, there were messages on my answering machine, and I hadn't bothered to check my email for a couple of days. I knew I wouldn't be able to sleep until I'd found out what was waiting for me behind that blinking red light and in the heap of envelopes on the table.

I started with the phone messages—a couple from the prison operator, some solicitations and hang-ups, and then one from Jim. "I have bad news," he said. "Carla Burrell had a sudden downturn and passed away yesterday. Give me a call when you get back." There was a message from Charlene, whose voice sounded sad and tired. "Carla passed on yesterday. I told Mr. Christie, but I wanted to tell you myself, too. She always spoke well of you and wanted you to know she was grateful for everything you and Mr. Christie were doing for Andy."

Oh, God, I thought. *Poor Carla*. I felt like crying, and suddenly drained of energy, I walked out of my office and sat down at the table full of mail. I sat for a while with elbows on the table and my head in my hands and let the rush of sadness and pity wash over me. How little life had given her—a mother who deserted her, an autistic child she barely knew, her brothers in prison, her own best years lost to the drug addiction that had finally killed her. After a while, I sat up and, looking for something to keep me busy, began sorting, dully and mechanically, through the week's accumulation of paper.

Most of it was junk mail, which I tossed into a bag to recycle or burn. I opened a few of the work-related letters and put the rest and the bills into a pile to open later. About halfway through, I uncovered a worn-looking envelope addressed to the private mailbox at the realtor's office on the highway that I use for business mail. The handwriting was unfamiliar; the return address, on one of those free address labels charities send by the hundreds, was that of Jimmy and Charlene Kitteridge.

Without picking up my letter opener, I opened it right away, running my thumb along the inside top of the envelope. The paper shredded along its length, like a jagged wound. I pulled out the paper inside and unfolded it. There was no note and no cover letter; it was simply the declaration I had given Carla in February, the one that told of the murder of Len Hardy. I turned the pages, which were wrinkled and scuffed as though they had been carried around for a while. She had initialed each one at the bottom, and signed and dated it at the end in a shaky hand. I looked at the postmark on the envelope; it had been mailed on the day I left for Alaska.

"Oh, Christ—oh, Carla," I murmured. I wished I had someone—Terry, Ed, Gavin, my parents—there just to hold onto—anything but loneliness and night. Instead, I got up and fixed myself a brandy and hot water and drank it, and then another one. Then I put on a CD of Samuel Barber's violin concerto and lay on my couch in a dark, dull haze of alcohol, sadness and exhaustion until I fell asleep.

41

The next morning, I scanned the declaration and envelope and emailed it to Corey. Later, I called Jimmy and Charlene with my condolences. Charlene was at work, but Jimmy was home and seemed grateful for the chance to talk about Carla. "She had kind of an unexpected downturn at the end," he said. "She had so much wrong with her; I guess everything just went at once. In a way it was merciful; she didn't suffer much."

I said I was sorry and that I'd hoped to see her again. Jimmy went on, as if he'd hardly heard my response. "It was good to have her here, though. It's so sad the Lord had to take her just at that time." He stopped, and when he spoke again, his voice was thick. "It seems wrong somehow, you know; your children should outlive you." He paused. "But I should let you go; you have work to do. I'll let Charlene know you called. And tell Andy I pray for him every day."

Jim called me that afternoon. "So—what can we do with this?" he asked.

I was tired from the trip, hung over, and sad about Carla,

and Jim's all-business insouciance irritated me. "Oh, Christ," I said, "I don't know."

"It's going to be a tough one," Jim said, "but it'll get the judge's attention, all right. We don't have to deal with the issue yet, though, do we? I mean, we can just file it as an exhibit and fight the admissibility thing out if some court orders a hearing."

I was worried about what else would happen if we filed the declaration. Would Evie cut off our contact with Andy again, or would she realize that whatever damage it could do had been done by filing it, and there would be no point in keeping Andy from us? Even if she and Andy did cut us off, would we be okay? Dan Moss's evaluation was finished, and we'd gotten about all we were going to get from Evie. It could be years before any court might order a hearing on Andy's petition; and a hearing, with its promise of getting Andy off death row, might make him more willing to cooperate in spite of Evie.

And where did Carla's statement leave us, anyway? Jim and I couldn't tell anyone that Andy had once told me her story was true, because of the attorney–client privilege. And as long as Andy, Emory and Evie denied it, it was easily dismissed as a lie told against Evie by her hostile, drug-addicted daughter.

"Maybe we should look for Len's body," Dave replied, with a copy to Jim, when I emailed him the news about Carla's declaration.

"And how would we do that?" I wrote back.

"Unidentified recovered bodies." Dave had read a newspaper article about a coroner's office somewhere in Nevada that kept a storeroom full of unidentified skeletal remains found in the desert. "I met an investigator from Washington at a conference last summer," he went on. "I think we may be able to narrow down the area where Evie and Emory must have dumped Len's body to a few counties. From what Carla and Andy told us, it has to be in the mountains and within a day's drive of where they were living. We could hire this guy to check with the local police departments and coroner's offices."

"And what do we do if we find a possible hit?"

"DNA testing."

Jim liked the idea, and he left Dave to arrange things with the investigator in Seattle, Steve Bardelli. I didn't think much about it; the chance of Len's remains being found and identified after all this time seemed vanishingly small.

With a sense of dread, I called San Quentin and asked for visits with Andy and, since I would be there anyway, Arturo Villegas.

42

Arturo came through the door with as much of a roll and swagger as a short man in badly fitting prison blues and handcuffs—flanked by guards and hugging a manila folder of papers between his arm and ribcage—could manage. On his way to the visiting cage, he called out, "Hello, bro," to a couple of buddies.

Between bites of microwave popcorn, he peppered me with information and questions about his case, and issues he thought I should be arguing in his appeal. The attorney for the codefendant who was tried with him had made a motion for a mistrial during jury selection because the district attorney was selectively challenging Hispanics on the jury panel. The district attorney had gotten an order keeping Arturo's sister and two cousins out of the courtroom because they were supposedly gang members and their presence might intimidate witnesses. A witness who testified she heard him bragging about the drive-by at a party was the girlfriend of another suspect and had accused Arturo to keep her boyfriend out of jail.

I'd only read about half the trial transcript, but it was pretty obvious that Arturo's court-appointed lawyer had decided early on that the case was a loser and had pretty much phoned it in at trial. He was Arturo's third lawyer on the case. A deputy public defender had been the first, but had withdrawn when he found out that the office had represented one of the prosecution witnesses on an unrelated robbery charge. The alternate defender who replaced him dropped out after being appointed to a judgeship. Joe Brasile, the lawyer who finally represented Arturo—if you could call it that—through his trial, was appointed from a panel of attorneys who were willing to try capital cases for the low-ball fee the county was willing to pay. Brasile, it seemed, made up for the low profit margin by dealing in volume. A lot of judges approve of lawyers who move their cases through the system efficiently, and Brasile aimed to please. Six months after his appointment, and two weeks after finishing another capital trial, he announced himself ready for trial in Arturo's case. A jury was picked in a week, and the whole trial, guilt and penalty phases, took another three. Brasile filed no pretrial motions and, up to the point I'd reached in the transcript, had made only one objection.

After the trial, Arturo told me, he had gotten some help from another prisoner and filed a motion asking the judge to appoint him a new attorney for a new trial motion. At the hearing he'd presented a list of witnesses whom Brasile had never interviewed or called to the stand. Brasile had explained he didn't bother with them because they were all gangbangers and the jury wouldn't believe them, and the judge had denied the motion on the spot, lecturing Arturo for trying to game the system by waiting until after the penalty phase of his trial to bring up the issue of the uncalled witnesses.

It might be easy to say that it didn't matter because Arturo was almost certainly guilty of at least aiding a brutal double murder for the stupidest of motives. In spite of his protests, there was plenty of evidence that he was in the car, and some evidence that he was the shooter; and there's nothing sympathetic about a gang vendetta, particularly when it involves carloads of not very bright young men spraying a neighborhood with automatic gunfire. But paying snitches, hiding evidence, threatening witnesses, and turning a trial against a defendant with one-sided rulings work just as well to convict the innocent as the guilty. And they create distrust, cynicism, and disrespect for the system among everyone involved in it: defendants, cops, lawyers, and judges.

So we spent an exhausting hour and a half as Arturo, semi-literate jailhouse lawyer, tested my good faith with questions and demands, trying to decide whether he could trust me to know what I was doing and care about his case or whether I was another dumptruck like his trial attorney.

By the time Arturo was taken back to East Block, after extracting from me a promise to send him another forty dollars for canteen, Andy was waiting beyond the iron door.

The guards brought him in a minute later and put him in the visiting cage, and a guard waited outside it while I fumbled with quarters and pushed dollar bills into the food and drink machines.

Andy had asked for only a candy bar and a Coke. His shoulders were even more slumped than usual, and he looked somber and tired. After the cuffs were taken from his hands, he sat wearily in the plastic chair.

"Are you doing okay?" I asked.

"Yeah," he said. He looked at his Coke as if deciding whether to open it, and then back to me. "I feel really bad about Carla. I keep thinking now I'll never get to see her."

I reached across the table and put a hand on his forearm. "Andy, I'm so sorry," I said.

He looked down again, then back at me, and his eyes welled up with tears. He pulled his arm away, bent down, and wiped his eyes with the hem of his shirt. "I'm going to miss her," he said in a muffled voice.

"I know. I will, too. I really liked her."

Andy looked up and nodded. "She was good to me," he said. "My neighbor, Lindstrom—they call him Shaky, 'cause his hands shake—his mom died last month. He was pretty broken up about it. We've talked some."

"Has that helped you?"

"Yeah, some. That would be the worst," Andy said, with a deep breath and a sigh, "if it was Mama. I don't know what I'd do. Shaky hadn't even seen his mom in years."

I'd brought a copy of Carla's second declaration. That was part of the purpose of the visit, after all, to show it to Andy and let him know our plan. I wished there were a better time to bring it up. Reluctantly, I opened the manila folder I'd brought, pulled out the copy I'd made of Carla's declaration, and set it in front of Andy.

"Andy," I said. "Before she died, Carla sent us this."

He read it through, slowly, silently, turning the pages, his lips moving now and then to form a word. I felt as though I were inside a bell, the sounds of the prison reverberating from its sides: individual words of conversations or a laugh from the cells around us, the occasional shouted command from a guard, thumps of doors closing, the harsh jingling of keys and handcuff chains. Eventually, Andy reached the end of the declaration and looked up at me. His face was tense with misery and confusion.

"Why did she write this?" he asked.

"To try to save your life, Andy," I said. "Because she loved you. She didn't want to, you know. She didn't want to hurt your mother, either. But in the end, you won out with her. She signed this just a few days before she died."

"Did you show it to the judge?"

"Not yet, but Jim is going to."

The angry protest I expected from Andy didn't happen. Instead, he looked at me almost pleadingly and asked, "What's going to happen?"

"Probably nothing, at least not for a long time," I said.

Andy shifted uncomfortably in his chair. "Mama said if we ever told about it she'd have to go to prison forever."

"That was almost thirty years ago," I said, trying to be reassuring. "Nothing's going to happen to Evie now. I don't think she would go to prison anyway; she was trying to save your lives."

"Yeah," he said, "it was just like Carla said. But what if you're wrong, and they put Mama in prison? Why do you have to tell about it?"

I struggled for an explanation. "Well," I said, "it's part of the mitigation evidence in your case. It's an awful thing that happened to you and your family; if the jury had known about it they might have felt more sympathetic toward you, and maybe not have given you the death penalty." The more I tried to explain it, I thought, the lamer it sounded.

Andy didn't seem to notice. "What's going to happen to Mama when the judge sees this?" he asked.

"Nothing," I said. "Really. They don't have any other proof that Len is even dead."

"But what if they find his body?"

"After all these years," I said, "the chances are slim to none. And I really think anyone reading what Carla says will see that Evie did it to keep Len from hurting all of you." I felt hardly more confident about that than I did about the mitigating effect of Carla's revelation.

There was one more thing I had to find out, though, that had weighed on my mind since our meeting with Nicole.

"Andy," I asked, "do you remember the night you let that girl go?"

"Yes," he said, without hesitation.

"Do you remember bringing her a cup of juice that had something funny about it?"

He looked at me and nodded. "Yeah—how did you know about that?"

"We interviewed her back in the spring, remember? And she remembered it."

"Oh."

"Did someone give it to you to give to her?"

"Yeah, Emory."

"How did that happen?"

Andy thought for a moment. "It was when I came back from seeing her—the girl. It was in the evening, and I brought her something to eat. And I came back with the dishes. I walked into the kitchen, and he and Mama were both there. And Mama asked, 'Where are you coming from with those dishes?' And I didn't know what to say, and she looked at me and Emory. And she was really angry."

"About what?"

"She figured out about the girl."

"You mean she knew you had her there?"

"No—I guess she figured it out just then."

"How do you know?"

He paused, thinking. "She told me to go into the living room and watch TV, and I did, and she told Emory to wait and went upstairs and came down again. I wondered what was happening, so I went over near the kitchen door to hear, and she was reading Emory out, calling him stupid, telling him she'd told him never to do that again. I think she gave him something, 'cause she said, 'You give her this and make her drink it.' Then I went back into the living room and sat down again so they wouldn't know I heard. And then Emory came in and said to me, 'You moron; you've messed everything up.'"

"So did he give her whatever it was your mom had mixed up?"

"No—he made me do it."

"What was it he made you do?"

"He said to take the glass of juice out to the barn and tell her to drink it."

"What happened after that?"

"I went out to the barn, and she tasted the juice and wouldn't drink it. That's when I decided we needed to get out of there. I went back to the house and got the truck keys and then put her in the truck and left."

"Why did you do that?"

Andy looked down at the table. "I was scared."

"Of what?"

"I was thinking Emory was trying to give her some kind of poison."

I remembered what Nicole had said about the truck headlights. "Did anyone go looking for her after you came back?"

"Em did. I think he heard us leave in the truck, 'cause he was waiting at the door when I got back. He asked me where I'd been. I didn't want to tell him, but I guess he figured it out, 'cause he went out to the barn and looked and then jumped into the truck and left. When he came back, that's when he told me we were dead men and it was all my fault. And then we packed up and left."

"Did you know at the time what had happened to the other girls?"

"No. Just what I told you, that Em said he drove them someplace and dropped them off."

"But Evie knew about the others," I said.

Andy was silent, frowning, for a long moment. "Yeah, I guess she did," he said, finally. "That's why she was so mad."

He looked at me, pleading. "You're not going to tell anyone, are you?"

"No," I said. "I can't unless you give me permission."

"I don't want you to tell anyone." He shivered. "I shouldn't have said it." He closed his eyes and rocked back and forth, his head bent forward, his hands clasping each other in his lap.

"Are you okay?" I asked.

The rocking stopped, and he looked up at me. "Yeah," he said, without conviction. "Just scared." His eyes found the candy bar on the table. "I never ate that," he said, and he reached for it and offered it to me. "I don't feel hungry any more. Do you want it?"

"I can't take it away from here," I said. "Prison rules."

"Okay. Shame to waste it." He opened the wrapper and broke a piece off the bar from one end. "Would you like some?" he asked.

"I got it for you."

"I'm not that hungry. Please?" He held out the piece of chocolate bar, and I took it from him and took a small bite, tasting cheap milk chocolate and sweet caramel. Food was about the last thing I wanted just then, and the candy felt like cardboard in my mouth.

43

When I got home, there was a voicemail from Dave on my answering machine. I called him right away.

"I have news," I said, "but what did you call about?"

"You won't believe this," he said.

"What?"

"Remember Steve Bardelli, up in Washington?"

It took me a moment. "Was he the guy looking for Len's remains?"

"That's him. Well, he may have found them."

"That fast?"

"Looks like," Dave said. "He rang around police departments and coroner's offices in the areas where we figured Evie and Emory might have gone to, asking about unidentified remains. Said he was working for relatives of the disappeared man. There weren't that many places to call, and one of them phoned back with what seemed like a possible hit. So he had them fax their report. And damned if some loggers didn't find some bones and the remains of a sleeping bag in a little mountain valley about ten years ago."

"Damn!"

"Apparently they're in a storeroom in the morgue. Not much left, it seems. No skull, for example. I guess animals carry bones away and scatter them."

"So now what?"

"I am so glad you asked that question," Dave said, with exaggerated pride. "As it happens, Brad and I worked on a case not long ago where we had to arrange for post-conviction DNA testing. I have an expert you can talk to."

"Let Jim do it," I said.

"Okay, Jim. And I know a good lab. So we just have to get the coroner to release the bones, or enough of them to test."

"That shouldn't be hard," I said. "We'll be asking on behalf of Len's sister and brother, not Andy. Now let me tell you my news." And I told him Andy's story of the night he released Nicole.

"Shit," Dave said.

"And there's nothing we can do with it," I said. "Even if Andy were willing to talk about it, who'd believe him?"

44

Judge Fuentes wasn't nearly as impressed as we were with the possibility that we'd found Len's body. "So it supports—maybe—his late sister's declaration that his mother killed his father," she said in the telephone hearing she had set so that we could explain our request for money for the DNA testing. "The declaration is still hearsay, and what is the relevance of it, if no one else, including your client, confirms it?" In the end, though, she agreed that Carla's declaration was not entirely without value and that the evidence that Andy had witnessed his father's murder might have been seen as mitigating by a jury, had Dobson managed to find it. "Given this family's reluctance to come forward," she warned, "I don't see how you're going to show that trial counsel was ineffective for not unearthing this." In the end, though, she approved the money, possibly because she was curious, too, whether the bones in the morgue were really Len's.

Dave and Brad arranged to get the necessary samples to the lab Dave had mentioned. Dave called Len's sister

Gladys Clancy with the news that they might have found Leonard's body and sent saliva sample kits, one each for her and her brother Walt. Because of the age of the bones and the fact that we had no known sample from Leonard, the lab could do only mitochondrial DNA testing. The DNA profile wouldn't be unique to the owner of the remains, but would be one he shared with his mother and all his maternal relatives. Even so, if the mitochondrial DNA in the bones was a match with that of Gladys and Walt, it would be strong evidence that the bones were Len's.

45

The phone rang on a Friday night as I was watching a Hercule Poirot TV movie and wishing my own cases would resolve themself as tidily as Agatha Christie mysteries.

"Mom?"

I was startled by Gavin's voice on the phone. "Gavin, what is it? Is everything okay?"

He laughed, that grown-man's laugh that always surprised me a little, a stranger's baritone evolved from the piping voice of my little boy. "I guess I should call more often."

"No, no, it's okay. I understand the time difference and all. And we email each other a lot. I guess—a phone call seems so—*fraught* or something."

I was chatting a little crazily, overcome with surprise and with missing him.

"Well," he said, "I called because I have big news. Two things, in fact. I've been offered a job—a professorship—at the University of Idaho, starting in January. And—" a dramatic pause—"Rita and I are getting married."

"Oh my God," I burbled. "Oh, sweetie, I'm so happy for you. Have you set a date yet?"

"The second Saturday in December—I think it's the twelfth."

I heard a woman's voice say, "No, it's the tenth," and something else.

"Rita's saying it would be just like me to get you here two days after the wedding."

"You're getting married over there?" Saying that, I felt stupid, and I backtracked. "I guess it doesn't matter whether it's there or here, really."

"Not to us, so much. But we're doing it for Rita's family. They're going to be losing her when she leaves with me, so we figured we'd have it here, as the big send-off. Which brings me to my next point. You're invited, of course. And we want you to come and see Australia while we're still here to show you around."

I hadn't done any traveling for pleasure since Terry died, except to Alaska. I felt uncomfortable going places alone and reluctant to share a tour with a bunch of strangers. And, though it pained me to admit it, I seemed to have lost the joyous resilience I'd had when I was younger. I felt fragile and brittle, as if instead of bouncing back from the little surprises and irritations of travel, I might chip or break like a dried weed stem or a bit of old bone.

Over the phone, Gavin reacted to my hesitation. "Here," he said. "Let me put Rita on."

A second later, a young woman's voice said, "Hello—Mrs. Moodie?" The "hello" sounded wonderfully Australian, and I liked Rita's voice immediately.

"Please," I said, "call me Janet."

"Okay—Janet, then. I'm looking forward so much to meeting you. Gavin and I have been working out travel plans for while you're here. We thought we might go to Melbourne and maybe over to Tasmania."

I was a bit overcome. "I don't know much about Australia," was all I could think of to say.

"Gavin thought you'd like seeing the ruins of the old prison at Port Arthur. Professional interest and all. You will come, won't you? My mum and dad would love to meet you, and the wedding won't be complete without you." I heard Gavin say something in the background, and Rita laughing. "He says he needs you there to give him away," she said to me. "Here, I'll give the phone back to him."

"You're planning to take me on a trip right after your wedding?" I asked Gavin. "What about a honeymoon?"

"We didn't think we needed the usual honeymoon. We've been living together for almost a year. We both decided it would be more fun to make it a vacation, and while you're here you really should get to see a little of the country. Rita loves showing visitors around."

I felt myself getting tearful. "Oh, honey, thank you," was all I could say.

"So," he said, "you're coming here, right?"

"Of course," I said.

"Really?"

"Yes."

We talked some more about his new job and the move, travel dates and so forth, until he and Rita had to leave to meet some friends for lunch. "We'll be in touch about arrangements," he said before signing off. "I love you, Mom."

"I love you, too," I said. "I'm so happy for you." After hanging up the phone, I stood still for a long time and listened to the empty silence left by the absence of his voice.

"Buy the ticket," Ed said, when I told him about Gavin's phone call.

"Good heavens! Go!" Harriet and Bill said, almost in unison.

Dave emailed me every day, with one word, "So?" until I'd gone onto the Qantas website and made my reservation.

46

October seemed to end a week after it began, and there was hardly enough time to prepare for the trip. I rushed to get briefs in my other cases written and invoices sent to various courts before I left, and dealt with what amounted to harvest season, even in my young and slapdash garden, picking apples and pears from the trees I'd planted four years ago, making jam, drying apples, freezing applesauce and cooked pears. In my spare time, I shopped for wedding gifts for Gavin and Rita and Christmas presents for Rita's family, and for a dress and jacket for the wedding. I'd half forgotten about the DNA testing when Corey's email came. "Jim wants you to see this," he wrote, attaching the lab report.

I opened the attachment and read it. The report described the samples, the testing that had been done on them, and the results. The mitochondrial DNA sequenced from the bones matched that of Gladys Clancy and Walt Hardy. *Bingo*, I thought—and then, *Now what?*

47

I had my answer soon enough. On a drizzly November morning, as I was cleaning up the table of authorities on a reply brief that had to be mailed that day, the phone rang. Muttering an unprintable word or two, I picked it up and was startled to hear Jim on the line.

"Janet, hi," Jim said. From the tone of his voice, it was clear something had happened, and it wasn't good.

"Jim—what's up?" I said.

"It's Andy. He's in the prison hospital."

"Oh dear—what for?"

"They're saying it was a suicide attempt."

"What? You're kidding." Andy was about the last person I could think of who might try to kill himself. "What happened?"

"Apparently he got hold of a lot of pills."

"Is he going to be okay?"

"They think so. He's still pretty sick, though. Do you have any idea why he would try to kill himself? He calls you a lot, doesn't he? Did he say anything about feeling depressed?"

"No," I said, "but now that you mention it, I haven't heard from him in a couple of weeks. Does Evie have any idea why he did it?"

"That's even stranger," Jim said. "She seems to have disappeared. Her phone is disconnected. I had Corey call the nursing home, and they told him she just suddenly said she was retiring and left with only a few days' notice. The supervisor there didn't know where she was; she said all Evie said was that she planned to do some traveling for a while."

"Do you have any idea what happened? Did she learn about the DNA testing, do you think?"

"She may have. We sent Andy a copy of the brief we filed with the court about the report."

"That's probably it," I said. "Andy told her, and she's gone on the run." No wonder Andy had tried to kill himself. I wondered what would happen to him now. I asked how Jim had found out about Andy.

"A neighbor of his in the prison called his own lawyer, and she phoned me."

"I should go see him," I said, and regretted it instantly. I had too much to do, and there was no reason why Jim couldn't get his ass up to San Francisco to see his client.

"That would be great," he said.

So I dragged myself out of bed on one more dark fall morning, put on my prison-visiting uniform, and made the long drive.

"Mr. Hardy's Grade B," the guard in the gatehouse said, as she stamped my visitor form.

Oh, great, I thought. Grade B meant that Andy was in the "hole," probably as punishment for having the pills on which he'd overdosed. Inmates in Grade B were not allowed contact visits, even with their attorneys. Instead of Plexiglas cages, we were given booths the size of closets, where we had to talk over a telephone to our clients, with a heavy glass window between us. It isn't an arrangement that encourages free conversation.

On the drizzly walk to the visiting building, I was too cranky to pay much attention to whatever view of the bay might be visible behind the curtain of fog and rain. Morosely, I gave my ID to the guard in the window and went to wait for Andy in one of the booths.

After a while the door into the room on Andy's side of the window opened, and he emerged, unshaven, pale and bewildered. A guard, half-visible behind him, unlocked his handcuffs, and Andy sat. He picked up his phone, looking dully at me through the glass, and I put the receiver on my side to my ear.

"Hi, Andy," I said.

"Hello," he answered, his voice trailing off as if he wasn't sure where the conversation would go from there. He looked his age, for once. The skin on his face was yellowish and flaccid-looking, and lines were visible on his forehead and around his eyes.

"I see you got rolled up," I said. "Was it because of the pills?"

"Yeah." His voice over the phone sounded tired and expressionless. "I didn't fight the disciplinary. I think I'll only get ninety days in the hole, though."

"How are you doing?"

"Better."

His one-word answers and the tired flatness of his voice nonplussed me. "Are you on medication now?" I asked.

"Yeah. Something to make me feel less depressed. Mostly it makes me want to sleep." He squinted for a few seconds, as if trying to think of something. "I can't remember what it's called," he said, finally.

"So what happened to you? I was really shocked when Jim called and said you were in the hospital."

A slight grimace, like a shadow of pain, crossed Andy's face. "Mama's gone," he said.

"I heard that," I said. "We tried to call her when we heard about you. Do you know where she went?"

"No."

Andy stared blankly at the sill of the window and swayed a little back and forth.

"What happened? Do you know?"

"She wrote me a letter. She said she had to do it because of me and Carla—because Carla wrote that deposition and because I told you about that night."

"What night?"

"The night I let the girl go. She said she couldn't stay around here any more because the police might come after her. She told me I let her down." He stopped speaking for a moment, as if he was trying to find the energy or strength to continue.

"Let her down? How?" I asked.

"She said…" His eyes were wet, and a couple of tears rolled onto his cheekbones. "She said she sacrificed everything for me and Emory, and Carla and I went and accused her of terrible things. She said, 'You don't know anything.' And she said she was going away, and I'd never see her again." Andy shuddered, wiped his arm across his face, and drew a deep breath, then looked up at me, bewildered. "I don't know what I'm going to do," he said.

With the glass window between us, I felt helpless to reassure him. "We'll be there for you. We'll try to help you," was all I could think to say.

"Do you really think she isn't coming back?" Andy asked.

"I don't know," I answered. "She's scared right now, but she loves you and Emory. She may change her mind after a while, when she realizes nothing is going to happen to her." Even as I said it, I knew I was lying. Evie's devotion had probably been all about keeping her family quiet about their shared secrets.

"Yeah," he said. "I hope so."

"I'm glad you came down to see me," I said. "I was really worried about you."

"I'm feeling a little better," he said. "I don't like being here, though. I can't have my TV, so there isn't much to do. And I can't make any phone calls until I'm back on Grade A, either."

"You want me to come again in a couple of weeks and see how you're doing?"

"Okay."

"I'll do that. I'm going to Australia next month for a couple of weeks to visit my son. I'll send you some postcards, okay?"

"Okay," he said, the medicated flatness back in his voice. He yawned, and, catching the contagion, I did, too.

"Sorry," I said, "not enough coffee this morning."

He gave me a wan smile. "I'll bet you're going to have a big ol' cup of coffee when you get out of here."

"Probably," I replied.

I told him there wasn't anything new happening with his case, that we were still waiting for the attorney general to file their response to his habeas petition. As he always did, he nodded politely, and said, "Okay," in a manner that made it clear he wasn't that interested in thinking about it. After he yawned a couple more times, I suggested that perhaps he really needed to go back to his cell and get some sleep, and he agreed. He knocked on the door behind him to signal to the guards, and we waited several minutes, making awkward conversation until they came.

"Take good care of yourself," I said, as we heard the

keys in the door, "and don't get into trouble. I'll buy you a hamburger and an ice-cream sandwich when you're back in Grade A."

"Okay," he said.

4 8

I stayed the night in San Francisco because I was arguing an appeal there the next morning. My client, Corey Thomas, had been convicted of killing an attendant in a gas-station robbery. Not much distinguished Mr. Thomas's case from those of three or four men I knew on the Row except that the district attorney's office hadn't sought the death penalty against him, so he had been sentenced to life in prison without possibility of parole. The evidence against him was strong, and his trial had been pretty fair, leaving not much to write about on appeal. In short, it wasn't a winning case, and tomorrow's argument wasn't likely to change Mr. Thomas's life for the better.

A winter storm strafed the streets with sheets of cold rain, and I stayed in my motel room, rereading briefs and cases and making notes for the argument, until hunger drove me out onto Lombard Street. I ate a lonely supper at a diner a couple of blocks away, among a scatter of other out-of-towners.

The argument went as I'd expected—fifteen minutes

expounding on an arcane issue about the felony-murder rule before a politely uninterested panel of judges—and after some shopping afterward for coffee and other essentials, I left for home. I was already sick of city traffic, and missing Charlie and my redwood trees.

Along the coast highway, a half-hour from Corbin's Landing, a helicopter, bright orange and white, was hovering over a spot where the road dropped off steeply into a canyon. A minute later I rounded a curve and saw a pullout crowded with a couple of police cars, a fire truck, and an ambulance. A couple of onlookers had pulled their cars onto the narrow shoulder next to the cliff on the other side of the road. I stopped my car ahead of the first of them, got out, and asked a man standing next to his car what was going on.

"Car over the edge, apparently," he said. "Don't know any more than that." The wind from the ocean was spitting cold rain into my face, and I didn't feel like waiting around to learn more. Cars going off the cliff were common enough. Some were accidents, people driving drunk and miscalculating a turn. A surprising number were suicides; one or two people a year decided to end their lives by hurling themselves and their cars onto the rocks at the ocean's edge.

Before moving on I called Ed, who was dog-sitting Charlie. He was home. "Job cancelled for the day because of the weather," he told me. I drove to his place before heading to mine. Ed's door wasn't locked, and as I walked into his living room Pogo half knocked me over while Charlie stood just behind him barking. Ed emerged from his kitchen, shouting at the dogs to be quiet, and I handed him my thank-you gifts, a roasted chicken and a pound of coffee.

"You missed some excitement," he said, "or what passes for it up here."

"So did you," I said. "There's a car off the road in the canyon north of Jenner."

"Ugh," he said. "Guess we'll read about it in the paper tomorrow."

"So what happened here?" I asked.

"There was this woman over at your place this morning."

"Really? What was she doing there?"

"Nothing, really. Sitting in a minivan. I went over there walking the dogs, and I saw her and asked if she was waiting for you. She said she was, so I told her you weren't home and I didn't know when you'd be back. When we came back a half-hour later or so, she was gone."

"That's strange. No one from around here, then?"

"Nope. Didn't recognize her or the van."

"Do you think she was up to something?"

"I doubt it. She was an older woman. Not the burglar type unless she was casing the place for her grandson."

I was starting not to like this. "What color was the van?" I asked.

"Blue—a Toyota."

"Shit."

"So you know who it was?" Ed asked.

"Yeah. I'd better get home."

"Want me to come with you?"

I was feeling unnerved, and I accepted his offer. We piled into my car, with both dogs in the back, and started out.

The house was locked, and I didn't see any sign that anyone had tried to get in. Ed and I went inside together and walked from room to room. "Everything looks fine," I said finally. "Can I make you some coffee for your trouble?"

"Okay," he said. "I'll get a fire going; it's cold in here." He went out to get wood while I changed out of my court suit and into jeans and a sweater, started a kettle of water heating and ground coffee beans.

As I was pouring water through the coffee filter, Ed walked into the kitchen. "Got the stove lit," he said. "And I found this on your deck rail." He handed me a small box, wrapped in brown paper.

I took it from him. The wrapping was wet from the rain, but I could read my name and address, hand-printed in ballpoint pen. "Think that lady left it for you?" Ed asked.

"Maybe." I was turning the little box in my hand, trying to figure out what might be in it. I didn't want to open it, but I felt stupid for being afraid. I sat at the kitchen table and carefully undid the brown paper, thinking, even as I laughed at myself for doing so, that I might want to preserve it as evidence. Under the paper was a plain white cardboard box that might have held a piece of jewelry or a figurine. I opened it. Inside, lying on a bed of white padding, was a small heap of pieces of clear blown glass.

It took me a moment to see that they were—or had been—several small glass animal figures. It was a family of crystal cats, a mother and three kittens. They had been broken, all of them, but left in recognizable pieces—heads, little legs, tails, torsos—jumbled like a tiny, sparkling boneyard on the snowy cushion. I couldn't stop looking at them, seeing the tiny kitten faces with their green glass dot eyes, an ear intact here, another broken there. After a long moment I pushed the box gently to one side. I felt sick and hollow. "Oh, God," I heard myself say softly, and I leaned forward, elbows on the table, and rested my forehead in my hands.

I heard Ed ask, "Are you okay?" And I looked up, trying to compose myself, embarrassed to have lost control.

"Yeah," I said. "Yes. I'm fine."

Ed glanced at the little box and its contents. "God, she must have dropped it. Wasted a trip, I guess. Did they matter to you?"

"No. They were hers."

He looked curiously at the box and at me, but let the subject drop. "You don't look so good," he said. "Want something to drink? Do you have some beer in the fridge?"

Suddenly that seemed like a very good idea.

49

The Press Democrat that showed up in my mailbox the next day had a story on page 3 about the car that had gone off the cliff on Highway One. There had been no witnesses, but a daytripper who had stopped at the pullout had seen the tire tracks and the glint of blue metal below and called the police on his cellphone. When I read that the car was a blue Toyota minivan, my heart sank. The article didn't name the registered owner because the police were holding that information while they looked for the next of kin. But the van was empty when it was found, and the police had searched the area around it for whoever had been in the car and had found no one.

I read the paper obsessively over the next few days, hoping to find out more. There was one other article, naming Eva Hardy as the owner of the van and mentioning that the police had searched the area around the crash site again with cadaver dogs and had found nothing. Then, with something like an institutional shrug, the story disappeared from view.

I told Jim and Dave about Evie's visit to Corbin's Landing, the box of broken crystal animals, and the finding of her van. "I think you were lucky you weren't home," Jim said.

"I don't know," I said. "Maybe she just wanted to talk—maybe pass one last message along to Andy."

"Why the glass animals?" Jim asked.

"I think that was part of the message—what she felt we did to her family."

Dave agreed with me about Evie's meaning in leaving me the broken figurines. "She loved those boys," he said, "even though she messed everything up for them."

"She killed for them," I said. "Jesus."

"Yeah. And they loved her. And covered for her all these years. When you revealed the secret they were all sharing and drove her away, you destroyed all that. No more visits, no more little outlaw band. Funny her body wasn't found," he went on. "That accident seems almost too pat. Maybe I watch too much TV, but I almost wonder if she faked it, rolled the van down the cliff so she could disappear."

I laughed, but the thought had crossed my mind. I didn't tell Dave or Jim that I'd been sleeping with my Browning 9mm on the floor next to my bed.

As busy as I was, getting ready to leave for Australia, the job fell on me to see Andy, to tell him the news. He'd heard it already from his counselor at the prison, and he was taking it much better than I thought he would; in fact, he didn't seem much moved. When I asked him if he would be okay, he said, "I think so. I knew she wasn't coming back anyway." He hesitated for a couple of seconds before adding, "I don't think she's passed away. I just don't feel like she's gone. I think I'd know if it really happened." It was probably better for him that way, I thought.

On my way home, as I passed the pullout where the van still lay a hundred feet below, I opened a window, wondering whether, through some ancient sixth sense, I might be able to feel the presence of Evie's ghost if it were down there, but nothing brushed against me except the cold air.

50

Brenda Collinson, the deputy attorney general, filed a response to Andy's habeas petition at the end of November. "I'll say the woman's efficient," Corey commented when he emailed it to me. I read it through quickly, just to make sure it contained no surprises, and emailed Jim that I would be paying no more attention to it until I got back from Australia.

The response was short—less than half as long as the petition—and dismissive. She presented no exhibits in response to ours, but contented herself with a series of snippy arguments that our petition was filed too late and we'd failed to make a case for overturning the death judgment because we didn't provide enough new evidence or include a declaration from the late Mr. Dobson confirming or denying our claims that he had acted ineffectively in representing Andy at trial. She argued that Andy shouldn't get a hearing on his claim that he was intellectually disabled, either, because the facts of the crime—the planned kidnappings, imprisonment, and murders, and the concealment of the bodies—"exhibited a criminal sophistication entirely inconsistent with petitioner's claim to be mentally retarded." She suggested that he had faked his IQ scores and that Dr. Moss was either too gullible to detect the fraud or complicit in concealing it. It was an answer typical of the attorney general's office, and nothing we hadn't anticipated.

As we'd expected, too, she argued that Carla's second declaration was a vicious fabrication by an alienated daughter; that the discovery of Len's remains—assuming they were his—didn't prove that he'd been killed as Carla claimed; that any value her story might have as mitigating evidence for Andy was minimal because it didn't say anything positive about Andy himself; and that no reasonable juror would have voted against giving Andy the death penalty on the strength of it, given the gruesome crimes he had committed. Since Carla was dead and wouldn't be able to testify at any hearing that might be held, Collinson argued, the court should disregard not just Carla's second declaration, but her first, as well, as inadmissible hearsay. The contradiction between this and her argument that the petition couldn't be won without a declaration from Andy's dead trial attorney seemed to have escaped her notice.

It would probably be years before the court made a decision, either to dismiss the petition outright or award us a hearing on Andy's claims. Death-penalty cases lurch through the system at about the speed of glaciers. Given the strength of the evidence of Andy's mental retardation and how little Collinson had found to say against it, I was sure that the court would order an evidentiary hearing on at least that issue. It might be a long time in the future, but I had a feeling that we had saved his life—that the evidence we had of his retardation and the untold history of his childhood and his father's murder would not be disregarded.

Jim would have to visit Andy and explain the attorney general's response to him. I was too busy getting ready to leave, a painful week of anxiety and overwork at the end of which I wondered whether taking a vacation was ever worth the trouble. I didn't begin to calm down until the shuttle bus from the long-term parking lot dropped me at the international terminal of San Francisco airport. After my passport had been accepted and my luggage checked, and I'd found the gate from which the plane was leaving, I sat for an hour, lightheaded with relief and exhaustion, in the departure area and tried with no success at all to read a magazine, before joining the shuffling queue of passengers boarding the enormous plane.

In the life out of time of a long plane flight, I made the obligatory brief polite conversation with my seat mates that preceded a tacit agreement to ignore each other. After that I drank vodka and grapefruit juice, read idly from a travel book about Australia and a book of P.G. Wodehouse stories, ate the food the flight attendants periodically passed to us, and eventually slept. I dreamed at one point that Terry and Gavin and I were in a compartment on a train. Outside the window, I could see snowy mountains peach-tinted with alpenglow, but I couldn't remember where we were going or why, only that we had left our old house in Berkeley and weren't planning to go back. Terry and Gavin were talking and smiling, but I was filled with sadness and loss.

But then, finally, it was early morning, and the flight attendants, cheery in anticipation of landing, fed us breakfast. We watched, three hundred people, with our various thoughts and emotions, the long approach and the landing in the bright horizontal sunrise. It was six o'clock, or something like that, in Sydney, as I waited, bleary and stiff-legged, at the carousel for my suitcase and then stood in the long warm creeping line to the counters at immigration and customs, my skin prickling from clothes worn too long, my backpack heavy on my shoulders because I was too tired to think of taking it off.

I emerged through double doors into the crowded airport, looking for Gavin among the indistinct faces of strangers, and then I spotted his dark-haired head, familiar in the crowd, and saw him wave and a tall, pretty auburn-haired young woman next to him waving also. Pushing toward each other and finally meeting, Gavin (who looked so much like Terry with his fair skin and dark hair and eyes) hugged me and took my suitcase. And threading our way through the crowds, Gavin and Rita looked back in turn to make sure I was still following, through a confusion of echoing hallways and elevators and to the little blue car parked among many others in the gray, dim garage. And then through the pay gate and out into the bright flashing concrete din of airport traffic, blue sky and clouds and car rental offices, freeway median landscaping, flashing glass cubes of office buildings, stands of gum trees in the middle distance, and unknown birds wheeling overhead, and cool morning air scented with jet fuel and deep-fryer fat and coffee. Stopped at a red light, Gavin looked back at me to ask how I was doing, and his smile warmed me like the spreading sunlight. For a little while I had the remnants of my little family back together, and nothing to do but be happy while it lasted. In a land across the earth, in a city I had never seen, I was home. And it was summer, glorious summer.

AUTHOR'S NOTE

After I began this book, a legal procedure used in Andy Hardy's case, the simultaneous filing of state and federal habeas corpus petitions, changed because a court decision made it no longer necessary in California. I opted to retain the framework I started with, for a couple of reasons. First, it simplified the legal process in the case and made the timeline of the investigation more suitable to a novel. And second, procedures in capital litigation change so frequently in response to court rulings and the passage of new laws that it would be difficult to write a book involving them that wouldn't be out of date by the time it was finished.

ABOUT THE AUTHOR

L.F. Robertson is a practicing defense attorney who for the last two decades has handled only death-penalty appeals. Until recently she worked for the California Appellate Project, which oversees almost all the individual attorneys assigned to capital cases in California. She has written articles for the CACJ (California Attorneys For Criminal Justice) FORUM, as well as op-ed pieces and feature articles for the *San Francisco Chronicle* and other papers. Linda is the co-author of *The Complete Idiot's Guide to Unsolved Mysteries*, and a contributor to the forensic handbooks *How to Try a Murder*, and *Irrefutable Evidence*, and has had short stories published in the anthologies *My Sherlock Holmes, Sherlock Holmes: The Hidden Years* and *Sherlock Holmes: The American Years. Two Lost Boys* is her first novel.